BRODERICK

A SABINE VALLEY NOVEL

KATEE ROBERT

TRINKETS AND TALES LLC

Theirs for the Night
Forever Theirs
Theirs Ever After
His Forbidden Desire
Her Rival's Touch
His Tormented Heart
Her Vengeful Embrace

The Kings Series
The Last King
The Fearless King

The Hidden Sins Series
The Devil's Daughter
The Hunting Grounds
The Surviving Girls

The Make Me Series
Make Me Want
Make Me Crave
Make Me Yours
Make Me Need

The O'Malley Series
The Marriage Contract
The Wedding Pact
An Indecent Proposal
Forbidden Promises
Undercover Attraction
The Bastard's Bargain

CHAPTER 1

BRODERICK

I always knew it would come to this. Handfasted, not to the woman I want, but to the heir to the Amazon faction. Linked to the enemy for a year in the most intimate way possible, all for the sake of revenge.

Monroe Rhodius stands next to me, her silence doing nothing to detract from the danger rolling off her in waves. She's gorgeous, of course; all the ruling Amazon family is. Long blond hair; pretty, green eyes; and a mouth painted blood red. She only comes up to my shoulder, which is the most surprising thing about her.

Given her reputation, I thought she'd be bigger.

She's also not dressed in any kind of formal wear like so many of the others here to celebrate Lammas. Instead she's wearing a pair of cutoff shorts and a cropped white shirt that shows off a toned stomach and equally toned arms. Judging from the scrapes and bruising on her knuckles, she fought tonight. Whoever her opponent was didn't get in a single shot at her face.

All around us, the arena seethes with rage. We've just accomplished the impossible—a mostly bloodless coup of the

Raider territory, a claiming of Brides across all three of Sabine Valley's factions. The first step in a revenge seven years in the making.

It feels like the handfasting ceremony occurs between one blink and the next. The Herald says the appropriate words and then wraps a length of pretty silk around my and Monroe's forearms, binding us together.

There's no going back now.

My older brother, Abel, leads our group through the crowd to the waiting trucks. Seven Paine brothers, our seven Brides—eight Brides, now that Abel has had his way. My brother has plenty of faith that no one will break the code of the feasts and sink a dagger between our shoulder blades, but he's never let faith get in the way of reality. Now that we're actually here, I'm glad for his plan to leave immediately. Raider, Amazon, and Mystic alike brim with fury and violence as they watch us whisk away the heirs to their respective thrones, as well as the favored among them.

Feast days in Sabine Valley are supposed to be sacred and free of non-sanctioned violence. A way for the three factions to iron out any wrinkles and keep war from the city. It's a pretty fantasy. The reality is that all the codes and rules and traditions don't mean shit.

They sure as hell didn't save *us* when all three factions came together in an attempt to stamp the Paines out of existence.

It's only when we've piled into the back of one of the trucks that Monroe breaks her silence. She gives me a slow smile that feels more like a threat than an expression of joy. "Bold move, Broderick Paine. You're going to live just long enough to regret claiming me as your Bride."

I already regret it.

Not the theatrics. They *were* necessary. Arriving back in Sabine Valley during the feast of Lammas, one of the four times when the city's three factions come together in a ritual designed to maintain peace.

Abel stepping into the ring and issuing his challenge— seven fights, a Bride the reward for each victory.

Each of us taking Brides from all three factions, and forging a forced peace as a result. The tradition of Brides is just as old as the tradition of feast days. A long time ago, it used to be the way people forged alliances and navigated tricky moments in Sabine Valley history. A handfasting between one party and a Bride ensures peace for a year. No one connected to either party may move against each other without bringing the entire city down on their heads in retribution.

By taking Brides from all three of the ruling families, we've ensured no one can touch us for the next year. Technically, we can't move against them, either, but it's more than enough time to get our roots in deep and prepare for the coming confrontation.

If we survive this year.

The problem with taking Brides from the enemy factions? It means we're essentially married to that enemy, that we've invited them into our beds and our lives.

The peace between factions only holds as long as the handfasting does. If one of us fucks it up, we'll bring war down upon the Raider territory before we're ready for it to happen. Which means we have to get along with our Brides, no matter how much Monroe looks like she wants to take a literal bite out of me.

I stare at my new Bride. I'm not as hard as some of my brothers, nowhere near as cold as others, but I've survived eight years of exile and put scars on my soul that will be there until the day I die. She might be dangerous, but the sad truth is I'm plenty dangerous on my own. "Cross me, and I won't be the one who regrets it."

Monroe gives a throaty laugh, a sound so full of the promise of sin that it sends a bolt of desire straight to my cock. Damn it, I don't want to react to her. It doesn't matter that she's mine for the year or that she's beautiful. None of that changes the truth.

She's not the one I want.

Not the one I love.

Monroe lets the jostle of the truck bounce her nearly into my lap. She leans against me, her breasts pressing to my upper arm. "I'm a Bride. That means this handfasting isn't official until it's consummated."

I clench my jaw and stare at the buildings we pass. We cross the bridge into Raider territory—territory that used to be ours, at least until we were betrayed and exiled. It doesn't look like home. I don't know if I'll ever consider it home again, not when being back in the city has me expecting a bullet between my eyes at any moment. "I'm aware."

She drags her finger down the center of my chest and over my stomach. I catch her wrist before she reaches the band of my jeans. "No."

Monroe gives another of those throaty laughs. "I was going to do my duty—I'm no oathbreaker, after all—but this is going to be *fun.*"

"What?" I finally drag my gaze to her face. She's got features too perfect to be real. It almost hurts to look at her.

She tugs her wrist out of my grip. "You have to do your duty, too, Broderick." She draws out my name as if tasting it for weakness. "Even if you hate every moment of it."

"I'm aware of my duty." My voice is too hard, giving away how much I don't want to do this. Damn it, I have to get myself in line. She's been in my presence less than thirty minutes, and she's already digging around beneath my skin.

"Like I said: fun."

We pull into the warehouse we've been secretly staying in

while we got everything lined up for the feast. It's as secure as we could make it, which means it *should* be secure enough to consummate with our respective Brides and ensure the next year of peace.

We climb out of the trucks, piling into the open space around the trucks. I look around, checking to make sure everyone is here and everything is as it should be. Once I clock each of my brothers, I catch sight of Maddox standing near the door. He was left in charge of the warehouse while we were gone. He meets my gaze and gives a short nod.

Everything is as it should be.

I exhale slowly and turn back to Abel and his two Brides. Harlow, we planned on—an extra little revenge against the faction that used to be ours. But Abel's second Bride? I study Eli Walsh, the man who was almost a seventh brother to me. The man who stood by while our father and people were killed in a coup eight years ago. *He's* running the Raiders now, which more than speaks for itself about his involvement in what went down that night.

I hope Abel knows what he's doing.

My brother looks at each of us in turn, his expression hard. "Consummate the handfasting tonight. No exceptions. Get it done."

There's nothing to do but exactly what he said: get it done. I turn and head for the bedroom I've been using, and I'm relieved when Monroe keeps pace with me. I don't want to have to drag her behind me. No matter what we want, this has to be done tonight or the handfasting won't hold. It's not necessary for normal handfasting, but Brides are different. The forced peace only works if the rules are followed to the letter.

We're nearly to the door when the person I dreaded seeing appears. Shiloh. She's flushed as if she's been running, her dark hair pulled back in a ponytail. Her gaze skates over

Monroe and lands on me, and the relief on her face has guilt worming through me.

I try for a smile. "Shiloh."

My best friend.

The woman I've been in love with for years.

"You're okay." She doesn't touch me, doesn't close the last bit of distance between us, but she gives me a trembling smile. "I was worried."

"No need to be. Abel took care of everything." *I* was the worried one. For as secure as we've tried to make this warehouse, it's an imperfect safety. Anything could have happened to the people we left here. Just like anything could have happened to my brothers in the moment we stepped onto the sand of the arena. If the Herald hadn't agreed to let Abel fight, they could have descended on us and finished what they started eight years ago.

"Yeah, Abel's good at that." Her smile goes a little strained and her gaze flicks to Monroe again. "I, uh, I guess I'll see you tomorrow."

"Yeah. Sure." I don't look at Monroe, but I *feel* her watching us. She's gone still, a predator scenting weakness. I clear my throat, hating how awkward things have suddenly gotten between us. "Tomorrow."

Shiloh searches my face, gives me one last faint smile, and then she's gone, weaving her way through the trucks and disappearing from sight. I turn toward the door, but Monroe is there, pressing herself to my chest and staring up into my eyes with a devious smile on her red, red lips. "Broderick Paine, you've been holding out on me. Who was *that* delicate little creature? She looks tasty."

Alarm blares, and it's everything I can do to keep it out of my tone. "She's no one." Better that Monroe believe that than literally anything else. *Especially* the actual truth.

Her smile widens, and her green eyes light up. She's never

looked more beautiful than she does in this moment. She's never looked more dangerous, either. "We both know that's not the truth. It looks to me like she's *everyone* to you." She presses her nails to my chest, a cat toying with its prey. "This is going to be even more fun than I expected."

Gods alone know what Monroe considers *fun*.

I'm suddenly sure that I'm going to find out...and that Shiloh is going to bear the cost.

CHAPTER 2

MONROE

I'm so furious, I can barely think straight. The feast was going well enough, if a little boring, until the Paine brothers showed up and sent everyone into a tailspin. The sheer fucking audacity of their picks for Brides might make me admire them if I wasn't among the number.

Not just me.

I turn away from Broderick and survey the warehouse the Paines brought us to. A giant room with doors lining the walls on either side of the massive one we drove through to get here. People have scattered like rats fleeing a sinking ship since we climbed out of the trucks, and I can't find my sister or uncle among them. Winry. Damn it, I should have been thinking of her this whole time instead of needling Broderick Paine.

Winry isn't like me. No amount of training and browbeating by our mother could hammer out the softness she carries. She'll never be ruthless or cold or willing to cut down her enemies first and ask questions later. Why in the name of the gods did they pair her with *Cohen* Paine? Even a glimpse of him is enough to label him a stone-cold killer, just like me.

Better that she end up with someone like the man standing behind me, radiating impatience. Broderick might be the second-born Paine, but he doesn't have the same cold ruthlessness that comes off some of his brothers in waves. "If your brother hurts my sister, I'll skin him alive."

Broderick stops short, looking at me like I'm a poisonous snake that just opened my mouth and spoke. "No one is going to be hurt. No one is going to be forced."

"You say that, and yet your scary big brother just said to consummate the handfasting, *no exceptions.*"

"For fuck's sake, Monroe." He seems legitimately insulted. "There are half a dozen ways to consummate without having sex, and they have all night to figure out a way that won't harm anyone. Give us some credit."

"Yeah, I don't think I will." Will Winry do the smart thing and submit to get it over with? I think she will, but sometimes when she gets scared, she acts against her best interest. My chest gets tight at the thought, but I have too much control to let my worry show on my face. I smile up at Broderick, and his flinch makes me feel the tiniest bit better. "I don't bluff. If Cohen harms Winry or scares her or makes her cry, I'm going to fucking gut him." I doubt I can take the burly redhead in a fair fight, but I've never been in a fair fight in my life—at least outside of feast days.

"No one is going to hurt your sister." Broderick narrows his pretty, blue eyes. Really, all of him is pretty. Most of the Paine brothers have a brutal edge to them, but he's traditionally handsome with a strong jaw, sensual lips, and nice, high cheekbones. He's kept his hair at a length just longer than a buzz cut, and it leaves his features in stark relief. Paired with his broad shoulders and strong body, it creates quite the image.

Sleeping with him is going to be no hardship.

Especially since he's already shown he's so easy to provoke.

"You're not worried about your uncle?"

I almost laugh. As if my uncle isn't one of the best warriors our faction has to offer. It doesn't matter what his history with Ezekiel Paine is; he'll handle himself tonight. "Jasper will be fine." I tilt my head to the side, smiling widely and enjoying the way Broderick's jaw clenches in response. I can do nothing to help my sister right now. Best to get this over with and find her in the morning. "Are you stalling, dear husband? If someone weren't paying attention, they might think you're scared of little old me."

"I'm not stalling." He spins on his heels and resumes his march toward the door that's obviously our destination. It looks identical to the other doors on the side walls of the warehouse—plain and gray.

I cast one last look at the space behind me and force myself to put aside my worry about Winry. She'll be okay. She might be soft, but she's still an Amazon. Someone soft in our faction is still someone a thousand times more capable than anyone else.

The room Broderick leads me to isn't anything to write home about. It's spartan in decorations, containing only a bed, a wardrobe, and nothing else. There *is* a door to what appears to be a private bathroom, which is something, at least.

I turn as Broderick shuts the door. He seems to make himself look at me, and I don't imagine the heat in his eyes. He wants me. He doesn't *want* to want me, but the desire is there all the same. Silly man. Between that and the way he was making heart eyes at the pretty brunette, he's all but handed me the keys to the kingdom, along with a map to navigate his pressure points.

He motions at the bed. "Let's make this quick. We don't have to have sex—"

"Yeah, no. I don't care how you've played this out in your head, but you won yourself a Bride, and you're going to do this properly." It's necessary to ensure the Bridal peace holds…so when I go back to my people at the end of this year, I'll have all the information I need to crush the Raider faction once and for all.

In the years since Broderick and his brothers were driven out of Sabine Valley, the Raider faction has become the weakest of the three. No matter how brilliant Eli Walsh is at leadership, he never reclaimed what the Paine family had previously accomplished. Eight years is a long time. It means Abel and the others are an unknown quantity. The fact they were able to infiltrate the city long enough to stage that show at Lammas means they're a threat in a big way.

I'm the Amazon heir. It's my job to step between my people and whatever threats arise. If that means I need to crawl into bed and ride Broderick's cock until he passes out to ensure we have a year of peace, then I'll do it. I would do it anyways, because I want to. But a year? It's a long time to gather information on the Paine brothers while they can't move against us. I'd be a fool to let that opportunity go by unexploited.

I am no fool.

I start for the bathroom door. "Give me two seconds to shower the blood off, husband."

"Don't call me that."

I don't bother to hide my smile as I glance over my shoulder, and his flinch in response is more than reward enough. "How on earth did you survive this long with skin that thin?"

Broderick opens his mouth, seems to reconsider whatever he was about to say, and huffs out a breath. "I don't have thin skin."

"All evidence points to the contrary." I step into the bathroom and almost laugh. It's just as spartan as the bedroom itself; it's entirely white tile with only a sink, toilet, and showerhead. It's also positioned in such a way that if I leave the door open, anyone in the bedroom will be able to see the entire bathroom. Good for security and ensuring a captive doesn't get into trouble. Bad for Broderick's blood pressure.

I turn on the shower and pull off my clothing slowly. I can *feel* his eyes on me. I know what I look like. Beauty is just another weapon in my arsenal, and Broderick might hate me, but he's affected. Maybe he hates me *because* he's affected. Even knowing him all of one evening is enough to make me suspect that's the truth.

When I'm naked, I step beneath the spray and tilt my head back. The earlier fight in the arena wasn't a particularly long or brutal one, but my knuckles sting and my thigh is a little sore where that bitch got in a few good kicks. Juniper of the Mystics isn't heir, and every time I deal with her, I have cause to be grateful for that fact. She's a blunt instrument waiting for a hand to wield her. She's got a temper, and she's remarkably easy to bait. If I'd been fighting her older sister, Fallon, the fight wouldn't have been nearly as simple.

I slick my hair back. Fallon is a Bride, too. I wonder how *she's* taking the consummation. That woman has ice in her veins, and she's as feral as a wolf when it comes to... Well, literally anything. Poor little Gabriel Paine. He's bitten off more than he can chew, too.

I feel Broderick standing in the doorway before he speaks. "That's enough. Let's get this over with." His voice has gone hoarse.

I turn slowly to face him and open my eyes. Gods, the way he looks at me. Like he wants to fight and fuck and then run as far and fast from me as he can. He's got a shit poker face; another fact I file away. Those blue eyes are practically an inferno as his gaze follows the path of the water down my body, tracing over my lips, my breasts, my stomach, my pussy, my legs.

"See something you like?"

He shakes his head slowly, but he can't seem to raise his gaze from my breasts. The sheer intensity on his face has goose bumps rising over my skin. I don't know what changed in the last few minutes, but any hesitation is gone. He flicks his fingers at me. "Get over here."

I wring out my hair slowly, letting the tension between us become thicker and thicker. It feels like the moment before a storm breaks, the air thick and heavy with promised violence. I lick my lips. "Make me."

"Monroe."

Gods, the way he says my name. A warning I have no intention of heeding. When's the last time I danced on the edge of true danger? I can't remember. No matter how brutal life can be in Sabine Valley, I'm at the top of the hierarchy. Aside from clashes with the other factions from time to time, no one fucks with me. No one even dares to try.

I suddenly very much want Broderick to do more than try.

I flick my hair over my shoulder. "Make me," I repeat. His eyes flare in response, but he doesn't move. That's okay. I have more than enough ammunition to provoke him at this point. Still, Broderick seems to have an honorable streak—to his eventual detriment—so I throw him the smallest of bones. "Play with me, Broderick Paine. If you want to be the conquering warlord, you can't just ride in on your big brother's coattails and let him do all the work. You want the Amazon heir?" I motion to my body, my nipples going tight when he follows the movement. "Earn it."

He tenses, obviously fighting himself. "I have no desire to hurt you by accident."

13

He really is too easy. I laugh. "Please. As if you could." I weave my wet hair into a quick braid to keep it out of my face. "Do you know what I think?"

"I'm sure you're about to tell me."

"I think you're weak." I tilt my head to the side, pretending to think. "Or is it because of the pretty little girl-next-door brunette that we met on the way in here? What was her name..." I snap my fingers. "Shiloh."

"Keep her name out of your mouth." He takes a step forward.

I weigh the distance between us. Close but not close enough. He just needs one last little push to send him hurtling over the edge. I lower my voice and lean forward a bit. "You can call me by her name if you want. Since you're obviously too much a coward to have closed the deal with her."

"*Monroe.*" On his tongue, my name sounds like a curse. I kind of like it.

"Actually, I have a better idea." I give him a slow, predatory smile. "Maybe *I'll* say her name instead. I bet her pussy tastes as sweet and innocent as she looks."

Broderick moves, faster than I would have given him credit for. If I weren't waiting for it, he would have caught me flat-footed. As it is, I sucker punch him and slip past. He careens into the wall with a muffled curse, but he's recovered by the time I reach the bathroom door. *Tough bastard.*

"You *bitch.*"

"Don't think you'll turn my head with pretty compliments." I twist around and back toward the bed.

Broderick looks like he wants to wring my neck. He rushes me, and even though I try to dodge, he hooks an arm around my waist and takes us both to the bed. I'm fighting as soon as my back hits the mattress, but he's ready for me this time. He grabs my wrists and forces them over my head, dodges my attempt to knee him in the balls, and wedges himself between my thighs. All in the span of three seconds.

Impressive.

He growls. "It didn't have to be like this."

"On the contrary." I shiver, my desire making me forget myself for a moment. Broderick really is a worthy opponent, though I'd cut out my own tongue before I admitted as much. "It most definitely had to be like this."

He looks like he wants to argue, but I stop the words by arching up and kissing him. He tenses against me. For a moment, I think he might keep fighting this, but he makes a low sound against my mouth, and then he's kissing me back. It's just as much a battle as everything has been up to this point. We fight for dominance even as he shifts my wrists to one hand and reaches between our bodies to shove two fingers into me.

Broderick lifts his head and glares. "I fucking *loathe* you."

CHAPTER 3

BRODERICK

I had meant to go about this a different way. To keep things as distant as possible when it comes to consummating the handfast. To not do anything to further the enmity between me and my new Bride. To…

It doesn't matter now.

Monroe nips my jaw as I fuck her with my fingers. She's so fucking wet; obviously the manhandling gets her off, even if I don't know how the hell I feel about it.

No, that's not true. I know exactly how I feel about it. My cock is so hard, I'm about to come in my pants, and it started the second she met my gaze and whispered those poisoned words with a smile on her lips. *Make me.* She fucking *sucker punched* me. "I don't do this," I mutter.

Monroe digs her heels into the mattress and lifts her hips as much as she's able to, trying to take my fingers deeper. "Sounds like…a bore."

Even now, she's taunting me. It makes me want to tie her down. It makes me want to fuck her all the more. I pull back, kneeling between her thighs. She tries to kick me, but the position doesn't allow for it. I press my weight onto her wrists. "Spread your legs wider."

I already know exactly what she'll say a moment before the words leave her lips. "Make me, Broderick Paine. You know you want to."

The worst part?

She's right.

I've never, not once, been this rough with a partner. I might not be as big as some of my brothers, but I'm achingly aware of how much stronger I am than someone like Shiloh.

No, I can't think about her right now. It feels wrong, and not just because I currently have three fingers buried in Monroe's pussy. I would never, ever treat Shiloh like this. I would never overpower her or hold her down or fuck her rough. She deserves to be cherished, and you don't treat something you cherish like it's the enemy.

Monroe *is* the enemy.

More, she wants this.

Still…

I move quickly, flipping her onto her stomach and using my weight to pin her again before she has a chance to fight. I catch her wrists and press them to the mattress on either side of her head. My stomach still aches from that sucker punch. I might admire it if she were a different woman and I were a different man. I press my lips to her ear, ignoring the way she arches her hips back in invitation. "You say I want it like this."

"You do."

I ignore that, too. "Sounds to me like no one's been fucking you properly, Monroe." I bite the back of her neck. I don't even know what possesses me to do it, other than I need to feel her skin against my teeth, just a little. The moan she makes has what little blood is left in my body surging to my cock. She likes that just as much as I do. "Tell me you want my cock. Ask nicely, and I might even give it to you."

She surges up, trying to lift me off her, but I'm not going anywhere, and we both know it. Monroe lets out a hoarse laugh. "Give me your cock, Broderick. You've won me, fair and square."

I let go of one of her wrists to undo my pants, but she's not fighting me anymore. I wrap my fist around my cock and notch myself at her entrance. She's so wet, it's achingly easy to slide into her. Some small part of me is trying to sound a warning, but it feels too good to stop. I feed her my cock, inch by inch, driven on by her moans.

It's not enough, not even when I'm sheathed completely. She clenches around me, and it's everything I can do not to come on the spot. If I do that, she wins in truth, and that's something I won't allow. Not tonight. Not ever.

I wedge my hand between her body and the mattress until I cup her pussy. Monroe jolts and then goes liquid in my arms. "Little circles, Broderick." I do as she instructs and circle her clit as I start fucking her. Gods, she feels good. It shouldn't be this pleasurable to fuck someone I hate, but I'm past thinking about it. She drags her braid off her neck. "Bite me again. Harder."

I bite her. She lets out a cry that vibrates through her entire body, and then she's coming, pulsing around my cock so strongly, I'm helpless to do anything but follow her over the edge. I pound into her in rough strokes, chasing my own orgasm, and come hard enough that I'm shaking by the end of it.

It's only as I'm easing out of her that I realize the thing I should have remembered.

I didn't use a condom. I just came inside Monroe bare.

I scramble off her. "Fuck."

Monroe gives that throaty laugh of hers and rolls onto

her back. A fine sheen of sweat covers her skin, and even with panic blaring through my head, part of me wants to taste her. To do more than taste her. To leave bite marks all over that flawless body. To make her come enough times that she can no longer mouth off. To fuck her until I forget all the reasons coming back to Sabine Valley has messed with my head.

I shake my head. "We didn't use a condom."

"Oh. That." She gingerly touches the back of her neck and shivers in a way that can't be interpreted as anything other than pleasure. "I'm on birth control, and I'm tested regularly. I also don't make a habit of having sex without protection."

I want to believe her, if only because the potential consequences of this slip-up have me reeling. "I was tested before we came back to the city," I finally manage. We were all tested, and at the time I thought it bullshit because no way would I be having unprotected sex with the enemy. I can't believe I forgot myself enough to be this reckless. "I have to go."

"Broderick." She sits up, her brows drawing together as she watches me rush to get my pants back in place. For a second, I almost believe that I've hurt her, but that's impossible. The way she shrugs and flops back onto bed seems to support that it's all in my imagination. "Suit yourself."

I don't run out of the bedroom, but it's a near thing. I just need some fucking space, to *think*. The worst danger has passed if she's telling the truth. She won't get pregnant. I don't have to worry about the potential of tying myself to Monroe for life, rather than a single year.

The dark, feral part of me whispers that, with that taken care of, there's no reason to stop fucking her. We only needed to do it once to consummate the handfasting, but that doesn't mean it only *has* to be once.

I shake my head sharply. No. She managed to unravel my

control inside of an hour. Having sex with her again only provides her more opportunity to mess with me. That's out of the question.

"Broderick?"

Shame nearly takes all the strength from my body. I close my eyes, but I hear the familiar footsteps that I know as well as my own. Shiloh. I can't avoid this conversation. Doing so will only hurt her feelings, and that's the last thing I want. I try for a smile, but it feels wrong on my face, so I let it drop. "Hey."

She's wearing her usual jeans, boots, and black tank top. In all the years she's been running with our group, I've never seen her in shorts, even in the height of summer in the South. I know it has something to do with her past, but we've never touched on it beyond broad strokes and I have enough skeletons rattling around in my closet to respect her not wanting to drag hers into the light.

I shouldn't be thinking about Shiloh or her past right now. I should be... Fuck, I don't even know. "Can't sleep?" I finally manage.

"I'm on watch."

Right. Of course. I should have realized that. Monroe has me so rattled, I don't know which way is up. Except, I can't blame it entirely on Monroe. Ever since we crossed the boundary line back into Sabine Valley, things have been different. I knew it would be hard coming back here, but so many of my brothers don't seem affected and I don't understand. How can they be here without being tormented by the phantom scent of smoke? Without constantly looking over their shoulder for enemies. Without being hounded by the past.

"Are you...okay?"

"What?" At first, I think she's intuited that I was sinking into the past, the way we've both learned to do with each other during the course of our friendship. But then I follow Shiloh's gaze down to my forearms, where there are long scratches. I don't even remember Monroe giving them to me.

I flush. "Uh. Yeah." What am I supposed to say? Shiloh is my friend, yes, but I've never let her know how I truly feel. To her, I'm just her best friend, her safe harbor in the midst of all the fuckery the world likes to throw at us. I *am* all that for her, the same way she's that for me.

With all that said, our friendship has never had to navigate something like *this* before. If Shiloh is intimate with people, she's been subtle enough that I've never known about it. As for me, I haven't touched another person once I realized I was in love with her about six months after she joined us. I should have moved on once I realized this is only friendship for her, should have at least tried to create a romantic relationship with someone else, but it never felt right so it just...never happened.

Which means we have no framework for how to deal with the fact we both know I just fucked Monroe.

Shiloh saves us from standing here indefinitely in silence by leaning around me to glance at the door I just came out of. "So that's Monroe, huh?"

"Yeah." Gods, this is awkward, and I don't know what to say to make it less so. "The Amazon heir."

She gives me a small tentative smile. "I guess there are worse Brides you could have to spend time with over the next year. She's gorgeous."

Maybe I'll call her name instead.

I try to shove Monroe's sultry voice from my head, but it's no use. I can't help following that memory to its inevitable conclusion. *I bet her pussy tastes just as sweet and innocent as she looks.* "Stay away from her," the words come out too harsh, too dominant, but it's too late to take them back.

Shiloh raises her brows. "That's not going to be possible. Cohen has me on guard duty for her, at least while we get the new living situation figured out."

That fucking *asshole*. I don't know if my brother did it on purpose to needle me or if Cohen honestly has no idea how I feel about Shiloh. With him, it's difficult to tell, but I explicitly told him to keep Shiloh away from Monroe when we were discussing our plans. Apparently he decided to ignore that request.

Sabine Valley isn't safe for anyone. Not my brothers. Sure as hell not Shiloh. I can't change that, but I already made the mistake of putting Shiloh right in the middle of Monroe's crosshairs. I'll be damned before I put her within Monroe's grasp, too. "I'll talk to him."

"No, Broderick. You can't do that." She shakes her head. "You know our deal. No special treatment just because we're friends."

"It's not special treatment. Monroe is dangerous."

She shrugs. "So is every other Bride chosen tonight. So is being in Sabine Valley. So is every other city we've stayed in since I joined up with you. I appreciate you wanting to look out for me, but I'm here and I'll do my part." Shiloh smiles, though it doesn't quite reach her eyes. "Monroe's just one woman. It'll be fine."

That's the problem, though. I'm not sure it will be fine at all. It took Monroe all of two minutes to figure out that Shiloh is a glaring weak spot for me. She's too ruthless to do anything but exploit it. Shiloh's capable as hell, but can she really hold her own against Monroe?

I want to think so.

I'm afraid I'm wrong, though.

I don't know what the fuck I would do if something happened to Shiloh. I can't think about it. Just like I can't think about how us being back in this cursed city means there will be far too many people gunning for us. Now that Abel's orchestrated us retaking the Raider faction, they know right where to find us, too.

The Bridal peace will hold. It has to.

I try for a smile, but it doesn't quite work out. "Just...be careful." The words feel awkward on my tongue. Everything about this feels awkward and strange. Things changed with me and Shiloh when Abel announced it was time to return to Sabine Valley. She put distance between us that I don't know how to navigate. Or maybe I was the one who unintentionally put distance between us because my head is so messy with the thought of coming back to the place where so many fucked up things happened to the people I care most about.

"It'll be fine, Broderick."

I wish I could believe that. "Just promise me you'll be careful. Please."

Her smile warms up a bit. "You know you don't have to worry about me. I have things under control." She nudges my shoulder with her fingertips. "If you're finished..."

"I am." I sling my arm over her shoulders, loving and hating how good it feels to have her pressed against my side. Being this close to Shiloh is pure agony because it makes me want things I can't have, but I wouldn't give up this casual intimacy for anything. No matter how much it hurts sometimes. "If you want, I'll keep you company for the rest of your watch."

"Of course. I have a deck of cards around here somewhere. We can play for a bit."

"Deal." And maybe by the time the sun rises, I'll have figured out what the hell I'm going to do about Monroe.

CHAPTER 4

SHILOH

 hree Weeks Later

COMING BACK to Sabine Valley was a mistake. No one else seems to agree with me, so I've kept my opinion to myself, but there's no shaking the dread that dogs my steps every waking moment since we breached the city limits. Three weeks of jumping at shadows, startling at every loud sound, and looking over my shoulder for an attack that never comes. It's frazzled my nerves and makes me wonder what the hell I was thinking returning to a city that shares such a complicated history with me.

Sabine Valley.

It's unlike anywhere else. I'm honestly not sure if that's a good thing or a bad thing. I stare out the window of the office Monroe and I have traveled to every day for the past two weeks. It's the tallest building in the Amazon faction, and Monroe's office presents a stellar view to the south, showcasing the river that branches around the island where the three factions hold their feast day rituals. At the island, it splits to the south and east, creating a natural barrier between the factions. Amazons to the north. Raiders to the west. Mystics to the east.

They all look identical from up here.

Really, for all their superficial differences, the factions aren't that different from each other. One ruler, a family that surrounds and supports them. Each nursing a superiority complex that might be funny if they didn't hold so many lives in their hands.

Both Ciar of the Mystics and Aisling Rhodius of the Amazons are ruthless to a fault. I've never had reason to deal directly with Ciar, but the rumors that abound about the Mystics say he holds them in a tight grasp of superstition and fear. Aisling uses cold logic to make her leadership decisions and the Amazons might appear to love her, but she's not above sacrificing a few for the greater good. She won't lose sleep over it, either.

At least I know Abel cares about the people within the compound. I'm honestly not sure about the rest of the Raider faction. Some days, it seems like the only time he has compassion for them is when Harlow is insisting on it.

And Monroe, heir to the Amazon faction?

Three weeks of being glued to her side, and I still don't have a good read on the woman. She's gorgeous and infuriating and strides through life as if nothing can touch her. She also flirts as easily as she breathes and has no concept of personal space. There's a savvy mind behind that pretty face, but she does a damn good job of concealing it.

At least, she does when we're not in this office.

I glance at Monroe's desk, where she and her mother, the Amazon queen, currently have their heads bowed together and are speaking in low voices. They look nearly identical, though Aisling's beauty is icier and Monroe's is far too earthy for my state of mind. When I first started acting as Monroe's babysitter during these forays into Amazon territory, they banished me into the hallway when they had their little meetings.

They don't bother any longer.

I kind of wish they still did. Being in the same room as Aisling is hell on my control. It's far too tempting to grab the nearest item that can be used as a weapon and throw it at her gorgeous face. It won't do much but get me killed, but it might drown out the memories that lurk at the edges of my mind whenever I'm in Amazon territory.

"Profits are trending up this quarter despite the fiasco at Lammas." Aisling's cool voice cuts through my thoughts as she points at a spot on her tablet. Being in the same room as this woman has me clenching my fists and striving to keep my rage off my face. "In particular, the trade agreements with Carver City are doing well."

"Of course they are. Aunt Malone is overseeing them on her end." For once, Monroe doesn't have a mocking expression on her gorgeous face. She's utterly concentrated on the report in front of her. "Still, there's room for improvement."

"There's always room for improvement."

Spending so much time in corporate headquarters for the Amazon faction has only driven home how much I prefer the Paine brothers' way of doing things. The top tier Amazons are all CEOs and COOs and CFOs. They have hierarchies within hierarchies, and the constant dancing around each other exhausts even me, who's outside it. As heir, Monroe is as close to the top as she can be without holding the throne, but that doesn't stop others from challenging her in ways I barely understand. It's a giant fucking headache. In the Raider faction, people seem to say what they mean and follow through on it, for better or worse. There are a lot less thinly veiled insults and undermining a person at every turn.

The Amazons like to pretend they're so much better than everyone else in Sabine Valley. Superior in every way.

They're all a bunch of fucking hypocrites.

"Monroe, can you take this report down in person? I don't trust Rachel to understand our shorthand without having to double-check with me, so talking through it with her will cut down on my headache later."

"Of course, Mother." Monroe doesn't hesitate to gather up the paperwork and start for the door. She might be the baddest bitch when it comes to dealing with everyone else, but when her mother issues commands, she doesn't push back.

As soon as the door closes, Aisling steps between me and the door. "Shiloh, was it?"

I fight not to tense, to strike out, to scream in this woman's face. "Please move out of the way. I'm her security —I'm going with her."

She waves that away. "Monroe will be back in a moment." Aisling might look like a fragile blond woman, but she's got a steel backbone and a heartless streak. She eyes me. "You know, I've been doing some digging on the people who accompanied the Paine boys back to Sabine Valley."

Alarm bells toll through my head, getting louder with each second that passes. She can't know. She *can't*. "And?"

"Every other person has an origin story." She laughs a little. "Abel really went out and decided to build himself an island of misfit toys, didn't he? I suppose one must work with what one has."

It takes everything I have to maintain my relaxed pose. Aisling is across the room from me. While she might have a gun stashed in that smart pantsuit of hers, I highly doubt I'm in physical danger at the moment. She's too smart to play things that way.

But if she recognizes me…

The only other time I saw this woman was twenty years ago. She's barely aged in that time, but I look much different than the malnourished child who caught sight of her through a cracked door during an unexpected visit to my parents' house. There's no way someone looking at me can connect me to that child. No way at all.

"Yes, everyone has an origin story," she continues breezily, as if we're just two friends having a chat. "Except you."

"I'm nobody." I say it slowly, fighting not to snap back and sound defensive. I have worked *hard* to be nobody, to put my past behind me. I always knew being back in Sabine Valley would rattle the skeletons in my closet, but it's a small price to pay in order to be part of Abel Paine's plan to bring the city to its knees.

"Nobody," Aisling repeats. She props her hip against the desk. "I think you're somebody, Shiloh. I'd look into your past even if my daughter weren't fond of you. And Monroe *is* fond of you." She narrows green eyes so like her daughter's. "I'll do anything to protect my daughters."

Apparently that protection only extends to your *daughters, not anyone else's.*

I shut the thought down before it can show on my face. "I'll keep that in mind."

"See that you do." She straightens and heads for the door, opening it just as Monroe slips back into the office. "See you tomorrow, darling."

"Sure." Monroe flips her hair over her shoulder. "See you tomorrow."

Aisling doesn't know. She *can't* know. If she had a clue who I really am, where I really come from, she'd have me removed on the spot, and to hell with the consequences. I'm a blight on the Amazon claim to perfection—or rather, my parents were. Then again, maybe I'm overstating my own importance. I'm just a single woman with a troubled past. Ultimately, I am a cog in the machine. Hardly worth getting worked up over, even if Monroe is *fond* of me.

"Shiloh."

I give myself a mental shake. "What can I help you with, Monroe?"

She smiles. Impossible not to notice how perfect her lips are, especially when she's painted them a bright apple red. Everything about Monroe is perfect. She's gorgeous, has a body that's built deceptively strong, and she practically *breathes* seduction.

I want to hate her.

I really do.

She's the enemy, and I'll never forget that, but she's also… I give myself another mental shake. No use thinking about that, either.

She stands and stretches her arms over her head. Today, she's wearing high-waisted pants almost loose enough to look like a skirt and a cropped form-fitting top that I mistook for lingerie on the first glance. There is a blazer that matches the pants, but it's currently draped over the back of her chair.

I wish she'd put it on. That slice of toned stomach showing between her pants and her top is almost as distracting as the curves of her breasts offered up by the structure of the top. It's not transparent, but that doesn't stop me from having to fight the urge to search the lace for her nipples.

Yeah, Monroe is dangerous in ways I never could have predicted.

She finishes her stretch and leans a hip against her desk. "You don't like me."

"I don't have an opinion about you one way or another." Not true. Not true at all. But admitting that I can't stop picturing her and Broderick having sex, tormenting myself with the images over and over again, is the equivalent of diving into chummed water and hoping the circling shark doesn't eat me. My odds aren't good in either scenario.

She smiles like I said something clever. "Jealousy is so exhausting, Shiloh. Why don't you set it aside for a while?"

"I'm not jealous." I am 100 percent jealous. It doesn't matter if I have no right to it. It wouldn't even matter if I'd ever gotten the courage to admit my feelings to Broderick. Finnegan and Iris are dating, and that didn't stop Abel from assigning him Matteo of the Mystics as Bride. They were expected to put their relationship on hold, at least long enough for the handfasting to be consummated.

It doesn't matter what I might have done if I were braver; Broderick and Monroe would still be handfasted, they still would have consummated it the night of Lammas, and things would still be unbearably awkward between me and Broderick. The carefully balanced throuple might have worked with Abel and his two Brides, but Broderick loathes Monroe, and so my being attracted to her would further complicate an already complicated situation.

And that's the *best* case scenario.

The worst case being Broderick gently, but firmly, sits me down and explains that while he cares about me, it's only in a friendly kind of way, without a shred of the attraction that I feel for him. I'm beyond certain our friendship couldn't survive that step, and I'll do anything to preserve it.

Even deny myself the one man I want.

"Liar. You are the very definition of jealous." She says it so casually, I can almost convince myself I misheard her. Monroe stalks toward me, all smooth, predatory movements. "Broderick might be as dense as the brick wall that surrounds the Paine compound, but I like to think I'm not a complete fool."

Only someone with no sense of self-preservation would ever call Monroe a fool. As she approaches, it feels like the room gets smaller with each step. I hold my ground through sheer force of will. I've dealt with scarier people than this woman, but I can't think of any off the top of my head, not with her so close.

She stops just short of us touching. It's strange to notice that she's several inches shorter than me. She feels larger than life, but she can't be more than five-three. She reaches up with a perfectly manicured finger and winds it through a strand of my hair. "Shiloh."

It's everything I can do not to shiver at the dark promise in her voice. I clear my throat. "Is there something you need?"

"There are many things I need." She tugs on my hair. This time, I lose my battle with the shiver. I have no business being attracted to this woman, but I might as well resent the sun for shining. It feels that inevitable when she's like this. She might be the enemy, but in my heart of hearts, I can admit I want her. She leans forward a little and lowers her voice. "The first is for you to stop planting listening devices in my office."

"I don't know what you're talking about."

"I'm sure you don't." She gives my hair another tug, her expression contemplative. "We've been working hard. What do you say we go have some fun?"

I'm already shaking my head, which only makes her hold on my hair more apparent. "That's not sanctioned."

"Fuck sanctioned." She releases my hair and stalks to her desk, sweeping up her blazer and heading for the door. "I need a drink. You need one, too." I open my mouth to argue, but she never gives me the chance to interrupt. "Don't bother to lie and say you don't drink. I saw you and that fearsome brunette with beer the other night."

I'd like to say Iris isn't fearsome, but there's a reason she's one of Maddox and Cohen's top picks when they put together small teams for dangerous tasks. I sigh and follow Monroe out of the office, waiting while she locks up behind her. I didn't plant another listening device today. I don't have the full details about Abel's plans, but he was very clear on the schedule for hiding bugs in Monroe's office. I suspect it's so, eventually, she'll become complacent and stop scanning the space.

I'm not sure Monroe and *complacent* have ever been used in the same sentence, but Abel seems to know what he's doing. Especially since he's got his two Brides in line and they're all working together. It's made a huge difference in our welcome in the Raider faction.

All good things.

None of it helps make Monroe easier to deal with.

She strides down the hallway, forcing me to rush to keep up with her. It doesn't seem to matter that my legs are longer than hers. The woman is a menace.

We take the elevators down to the main floor and head out to the street. I keep waiting for it to be easier to move through the Amazon faction, but even though my childhood home was far from the city center, there's something about the people here that are innately familiar. It doesn't matter their gender, their race, their age; they all feel like *Amazons* to me. I hate that familiarity. I wish I could scrub it from my brain, could divorce myself from that identity with the same violence I divorced myself from this city the first time.

It won't happen. If it was that easy to purge the secret demons from myself, I would have done it long ago.

The Raider truck is waiting for us at the curb, just like it is every day. I ignore the little stab of disappointment when I see Maddox behind the wheel instead of Broderick. Of course, it wouldn't be Broderick. He hasn't been our driver even once in the last two weeks. He'd rather cut off his arm than spend thirty minutes in an enclosed space with his Bride.

Even if I'm there, too.

At least Maddox is one of the few people Monroe doesn't mess with. It's fascinating, because she has no problem poking at *Cohen*, who's easily the scariest motherfucker in the entire compound, but Maddox, his best-friend-some-times-lover is where she draws the line. The big blond man is handsome and charming, and I don't understand what he did to accomplish putting her on her best behavior when he's around.

I'd love to be able to replicate it.

She climbs up into the truck and slides to the center of the bench seat, leaving me to follow. I yank the door shut and nod at Maddox. "Any trouble?"

"No." He puts the truck into gear and pulls smoothly from the curb.

Monroe slouches against the seat and lays her head on my shoulder. Her shampoo teases my senses. It took me days to identify the scent, to diagnose the maddening combination of apple, vanilla, cedar, and chrysanthemum. I should push her away, but giving her a reaction will only encourage her.

And… Maybe part of me likes the weight of her body against mine. A very, very small part.

She's playing with my hair again, braiding several strands together in an absentminded kind of way. "Maddox, would you agree that Shiloh does a good job?"

He doesn't look over. "I want no part of whatever you're trying to get at, Amazon."

"Yes, yes, I'm the very worst. We can all agree on that." She finishes the braid and starts on another. "But it's been three weeks since Lammas, and Shiloh has been at my side nearly every moment of it. I want to take her out for a drink to say thank you."

Maddox glances at me, his gaze lingering on Monroe's fingers in my hair. His handsome features look chiseled in stone in the fading light of day. "That's not a good idea."

"Please. If I wanted to cause trouble, I would stage an ambush on one of the trips across the river." She smiles sweetly. "Not that I would, of course."

"Of course not," I murmur. "Not when your sister and uncle are still in the compound." Quite the brilliant little hostage situation the Paine brothers have put together. We're still sitting on a ticking time bomb with all the powerful, dangerous people living under the same roof, but they've managed to ensure mostly good behavior up to this point.

"Exactly." She tilts her head to look at me. It's only then that I realize how close we really are. It would take no effort at all to lean down and kiss her, to see if she tastes as sharp as the words she deals. Monroe's gaze drops to my mouth. "We'll just have a few drinks in Old Town. You can come along and ensure our good behavior. Or assign another babysitter if you don't think Shiloh can handle it on her own."

Oh, that was clever. From the way Maddox's hands tighten on the steering wheel, he realizes exactly how clever. If he insists on staying, he's effectively undermining me and saying he doesn't believe I'm capable of doing the job they assigned me after Lammas. It wouldn't even hurt my feelings; I'm the first to admit that Monroe really needs two handlers —or half a dozen. But Maddox is too good at balancing our people to ever pull a stunt like that. "You get an hour."

"You're a peach." She snuggles closer to me, her breasts pressing against my arm.

I honestly can't tell if Monroe is just this touchy of a person or if she uses physical contact to set people on edge. It could be both, honestly. All I know is that she's *always* touching me. "Drop us at the Goat, please."

"Will do."

We cross the bridge back into Raider territory, and a little of the tension bleeds out of my body. No matter what Sabine Valley says about handfasting and Brides, I can't quite believe the tentative peace is anything but an opportunity for someone ruthless and ambitious enough to break the rules. Three weeks isn't nearly enough time to weed out potential issues in the Raider faction, but at least we're making progress there.

In the Amazon faction?

Enemy territory doesn't begin to cover it. Every single person I encounter is aware of what we took from them. Their heir, their spare, their queen's beloved younger brother. They would like nothing more than to stick a knife between my ribs and leave me bleeding out on the sidewalk. They'd even do it, if not for the carefully balanced juggling act that Abel and the rest of the Paines have put into place. I don't have to know every detail to know their entire plan rests on the assumption that Monroe and Fallon are more loyal to their family than they are to their faction. That they don't believe in acceptable losses.

At least, *acceptable losses* that include their family members.

But will it continue to be so?

I have no idea.

And that keeps me up at night.

CHAPTER 5

MONROE

I fall in love with the Goat the moment we walk through the door. It's a tiny bar with sticky floors, one dirty window, and a bartender who looks approximately five hundred years old. I had expected something else, with it being only one block off Old Town. That little neighborhood within the Raider faction is polished to a shine, ruled with an iron fist by the three families who own the majority of businesses contained in that three-by-seven block area. They arguably hold as much power as the Paine brothers, though they don't bother with ruling overtly.

That shit would never fly in the Amazon faction.

But this place? It's something else entirely. I allow Shiloh to lead the way to the bar and slide onto a stool. She looks as deliciously understated as always, wearing what I've come to recognize as her custom clothing and hairstyle. It's a little plain, but I can appreciate a woman who knows what she likes and sticks to it.

I scoot my stool closer to hers just to see her narrow those pretty, hazel eyes. "Since we only have an hour, we're going to make this count."

"Monroe."

I like the disapproving way she says my name. I've come to crave it more than I likely should during our time together. When I decided to seduce her to irritate Broderick, I never expected to enjoy her company so much. She's not the little church mouse I first assumed. The woman has a spine of steel, and I haven't managed to bend it even once since she became my glorified babysitter.

Ah well, I have a little over eleven months left. More than enough time. I catch Shiloh staring at my breasts when she thinks I'm not paying attention; she wants me. She doesn't want to want me any more than Broderick does, but the desire is there all the same.

I glare at the scratched bar for a moment. *Broderick.* That damned coward has been avoiding me since Lammas. I've allowed it for the time being, but I'm over it now. Three weeks is more than long enough for everyone to settle into this new rhythm of life.

Now I'm going to blow this fragile peace all to hell.

I smile at the elderly bartender. She's a tiny Black woman who's mostly bald, except for a tuff of gray hair hovering around her head like a stormy cloud. She glares at me. "Well? What do you want?"

"I like her already," I whisper to Shiloh.

"I'm old, but I hear just fine." She snaps gnarled fingers at me. "Order or get out."

"Three shots of tequila. Each."

"*Monroe.*"

The old woman cackles. "Guess you're not so worthless, after all." She grabs a bottle of tequila and pours six messy shots while Shiloh looks on in horror.

"You drink," I remind her.

"A beer is not three shots of tequila."

"Aw, love." I bump my shoulder against hers. "This is just

the appetizer. I said we're going to make it count, and we will."

She looks like she wants to argue but finally sighs. "Either Maddox or someone will be here to pick us up in exactly an hour. Don't get any funny ideas."

"I'm full of funny ideas." I nudge three of the shot glasses in her direction and pick up my first one. "Here's to the heat. Not the heat that brings down barns and shanties, but the heat that brings down bras and panties." I down my shot to the sound of the bartender laughing.

Shiloh takes her shot without so much as a wince. I knew I liked this woman. She shakes her head. "That's a terrible toast."

"Do me one better."

"I will." She licks her lips and picks up the second shot. "May you work like you don't need the money, love like you've never been hurt, dance like no one is watching, screw like it's being filmed, and drink like a true Irishman."

I snort and take my shot. The tequila burns all the way down. There was a time I could hold my own with any fraternity boy, but I stopped drinking foolishly years ago. Being the heir to the Amazon faction means putting aside anything resembling weakness, and too much alcohol is exactly that. A weakness. Not that it matters now. I might still be the heir, but I'm also a glorified prisoner.

I clear my throat, not liking the direction of my thoughts. "That was poetic, love. Are you Irish? They always get poetic when they drink."

"No." She shrugs. "It's a toast Iris gives when she's feeling nostalgic." Shiloh makes a face at the third shot. "My parents would hate toasts like this, even if we were Irish. Far too crass for them."

It's the tiniest nugget of information, the smallest of cracks I fully intend to worm through. I run the tip of my finger along my shot glass, biting back a smile when Shiloh follows the movement. "Uptight, were they?"

"Fanatically religious, I'm afraid." Her generous mouth turns down, her gaze going somewhere dark.

Can't have that. Her lips were made for smiling, not frowning. Impossible to seduce a pretty woman when she's thinking sad thoughts. I pause. Well, shit. I only get like this when I'm feeling tipsy. "It's entirely possible that I'm a little drunk." Whoops.

Shiloh giggles. *Giggles.* "It's entirely possible that I am, too." She grins at me, firmly back in the present. "Well, go on. Can you beat that toast?"

"Of course I can." I lift my glass and hold her gaze. "To the kisses we've snatched, and vice versa."

We take the shots, and Shiloh sets hers down with a clink. "Monroe, you've got a positively wicked mouth."

"I know." I grin at her. "I'd love to show it to you sometime."

Pink steals across Shiloh's face. "You're Broderick's Bride."

"That's not a no." I reach up and brush my thumb over her skin, alcohol and lust making me even bolder than normal. The pink beneath her skin gets more intense. "I bet you blush all over your body, don't you?"

"Monroe," she says it like she's pleading with me, but she leans in a little, pressing her cheek into the palm of my hand. "*Bride.*"

"You know as well as I do that this handfasting doesn't mean a damn thing beyond politics." I try to keep the bitterness out of my tone, but alcohol loosens my tongue too thoroughly.

"Still…"

I can't stop staring at her mouth. I hadn't meant to actually get tipsy—or even to get her tipsy. I simply thought a change of pace would be enough to get things rolling. Apparently I underestimated tequila. Too late to go back now. "I would really like to kiss you."

"We shouldn't." She licks her lips. "But, uh, I'd really like you to kiss me. Just this once."

Just this once? Over my dead body.

"Hey, Grandmother." I speak without looking away from Shiloh's pretty face. "You have somewhere around here where we can have a private conversation?"

The old woman snorts. "Don't try to butter me up now, blondie."

I dig out my wallet and throw far too much cash onto the bar, alcohol and desire making my hands clumsy. "How about now?"

She eyes the cash and jerks her thumb toward a tiny door in the back corner. "Employee bathroom. Key is on a hook next to the door. Do *not* fuck up my space."

"Yes, ma'am." I grab Shiloh's hand. "Just this once," I lie.

"Just this once." She lets me tow her around the bar and back to the narrow door. I find the key and unlock it, and then we're through. The room is tiny, barely large enough for a toilet, a sink, and a mirror. It's perfect.

Shiloh pulls the door shut behind her. She blinks those big eyes at me. "This changes nothing."

"Of course." Another lie. I know myself well enough to recognize that one taste of this woman won't be nearly enough. Knowing that touching her will drive Broderick out of his fucking mind is only part of the attraction. The truth is that she's grown on me, and I want to find out if I was right that first night, if she tastes as sweet as she looks.

Shiloh doesn't hesitate. She sinks her fingers into my hair and kisses me. She tastes like tequila and goes to my head twice as fast. I grab her hips and push her back against the door. It's supposed to be a smooth move, but I stagger a little, and she ends up straddling my thigh.

Well, this works even better.

I nip her bottom lip, loving the way she shivers as she starts rocking against my leg. There are too many layers between us. I start to go to my knees, but she tightens her grip on my hair. "No."

"No?" My voice is on the far side of raspy.

"The pants stay on." She drags in a shuddering breath. "They stay buttoned."

"Okay, love. They stay on and buttoned." I drag my hands down her back, enjoying the way her lean muscles flex in response, and grab her ass. She's smaller through the breasts and hips than I am, but not by much. I haven't seen Shiloh fight, but from the way she moves and how deceptively muscular she is, I bet she's a scrapper. "Do you really think I need to touch your skin to make you come?"

"No?"

I pause. "Is that an answer to my question, or are you telling me to stop?"

"Don't stop." Shiloh gives a breathless laugh. "What I'm saying is... Prove it."

I grin against her lips. "With pleasure." I grip her ass and pull her closer, guiding her hips in a slow, grinding motion. She catches her breath, and her head bumps the door, her eyes sliding shut. I take the opportunity to kiss up the length of her throat. Her skin is so fucking *soft*, it drives me out of my damned mind. I want to kiss her everywhere, to taste her, to...

I can't focus. This is less seduction than it is a frenzy. Shiloh's exhales shudder out, and then her hands are back in my hair, tugging my mouth up to meet hers. She rolls her body against mine, fucking my leg in a sexy writhing motion. I might be guiding her hips, but she's the one who angles my face for a deeper kiss. She bites my bottom lip hard enough to sting. "Don't stop."

"Never." I release one hip and skate my hand up her side to cup her breast. It's so, so tempting to delve beneath the soft fabric of her tank top, but I manage to resist. Barely. Instead, I pluck lightly at her nipple, teasing it to a hard peak through her thin bra and shirt.

She bucks a little. "Harder."

The pretty little thing likes a dose pain with her pleasure. Of course she does. I'm quickly coming to the realization that Shiloh is a delight in every way. When I finally get her naked and in my bed, I have no doubt she'll delight and surprise me there, too. I pinch her nipple, hard, and kiss her to muffle her moan.

She grinds down harder on my thigh, rocking frantically. Our kiss goes messy, and then she's coming with the sweetest little whimper I've ever heard. I nearly orgasm myself just from that sound alone.

Shiloh slumps back against the door and blinks those big eyes at me. "Whoa."

"Told you so." I press a quick kiss to her lips, but I can read the doubt clouding her face well enough to know not to press the situation now. I smooth my thumb over her skin, but my lipstick is everywhere. "Let's get you cleaned up."

"But—" She closes her eyes and exhales slowly. "Right. You're right. Our ride will be here soon."

I grab some paper towels and stick them beneath the faucet. Shiloh starts to reach for them, but I shake my head. "Let me." Though I expect her to argue, she holds perfectly still as I clean up the worst of it. Without some soap or makeup remover, I can't fully get rid of the red staining her mouth and neck, but I'm good with that. I *like* seeing my mark on her, even one so temporary as this. My mouth is just as much a loss cause. No one looking at us will have any doubt about what we've been up to.

Good.

Except it doesn't really feel like a plot coming together as we stare at each other. I wasn't thinking about anything but making her come...and now I want to do it again as soon as humanly possible.

Patience. I can exhibit some patience. In theory.

So, instead, of kissing Shiloh again, I reach around her body and pull the door open. "Let's go."

I wasn't thinking beyond getting into her pants after that second shot. I really wasn't. But when we walk out of the bathroom, the first thing I see is Broderick fucking Paine standing at the bar. His gaze swings to us, jumping from my mouth to Shiloh's and then to her neck. The control in his expression flickers, and the true fury he directs my way makes my pussy clench.

"Oh fuck," Shiloh whispers.

CHAPTER 6

BRODERICK

I'm going to kill her.

I still can barely believe my eyes, but the signs don't lie. That's Monroe's lipstick on Shiloh's mouth, hastily cleaned up. And her neck. Their clothes might not be out of place, but from their tangled hair and flushed skin, they were just fucking in the bathroom.

Jealousy, hot and scalding, nearly takes me out. Easier to focus on the anger. Easier to let rage flow through me than to examine the fact that I'm not entirely jealous of just Monroe. Did Shiloh take off Monroe's ridiculous pants and eat her pussy? Did Monroe slip her hand into Shiloh's jeans and finger her clit?

No. Damn it. *No.*

This is all Monroe. She's pissed I've been avoiding her, so she decided to get my attention. To mess with *Shiloh* to get to me. I *know* Shiloh is capable and independent, but obviously Monroe's pulled some particularly shady moves because they were *obviously* up close and personal just now. I will not go down this rabbit hole. Except, it's too late, I'm already there and nothing makes sense, and I barely understand my own reactions to it.

Shiloh won't look at me as they head in my direction, but Monroe puts a swing in her step. "Hello, husband."

"I'm not your husband."

"Well, I'm your Bride, so calling you Groom is a little *stiff*." She flicks a glance at the front of my pants, where the fit is feeling a little tight right now. "Since when do you play chauffeur?"

"Since it was you two who needed the ride." I tried to avoid it, but Maddox overrode my excuses. I glance at Shiloh. "Are you okay?" She seems okay, but if I misread this and Monroe held her down and smeared her lipstick all over Shiloh's skin…

Fuck, I really don't want to think about my reaction to *that*, either.

That gets her to look at me, but it takes me several long beats to recognize her expression. She's…angry. She pulls her hair tie out and drags her hand through her hair. "Contrary to what *some* people think, I'm more than capable of taking care of myself—and making my own decisions." She strides out of the bar without looking back.

Monroe's throaty laugh has been haunting my dreams. Even so, the memory doesn't come close to living up to reality. "Wow. You managed to stick your foot in your mouth within thirty seconds without any help from me. Impressive."

"I just want her safe. That's not a bad thing." I don't mean to say it, but of course she capitalizes on it the second I do.

She laughs again. "You really are a fool when it comes to her. It would be irritating if it weren't so useful."

I spin on her, backing her against the bar and planting my hands on either side of her body. As much as I hate to admit it, she looks good. The overwhelming desire to shred her clothes with my bare hands and bend her over the bar nearly takes my breath away. What the fuck is *wrong* with me? This woman is a poison in my blood, and now she's expanding that to my friendship with Shiloh, too. We were already on rocky ground without Monroe swinging in on a wrecking ball to shatter us irreparably.

Except...maybe this isn't Monroe at all. Nothing's been the same since coming back to Sabine Valley. Monroe might drive me up the wall, but I've been on edge since we put this plan into motion. She's just savvy enough to identify my fault lines and drive a semi-truck right through it.

None of that means I'm going to let her run roughshod over one of the people I care about most in this world. "Stay away from her."

"Mmm." She trails a single finger down the center of my chest. "Even if I were inclined to do that—and I'm not —who's going to tell *Shiloh* to stay away from *me?*" She hooks that wandering finger in the band of my pants and tugs. The tiniest of sensations, but I'm instantly hard as a rock. "Want to go a round, Broderick Paine? Your girl is sexy as hell when she comes, but she's a selfish little thing."

The fondness in her voice makes my blood pressure rise. It's an act. It has to be. She's just doing this to punish me. She's willing to *hurt* Shiloh to fuck with me. "I'll get her taken off your guard duty."

Monroe smiles, slow and sure. "Might want to ask her what she thinks before you charge in all high-handed to save her."

"I'm not going to let you fuck around with Shiloh in some misguided attempt to hurt me." Shiloh's only in Sabine Valley —in danger—because of her association with me and my family. It's all too easy to draw the parallels between Shiloh and the people who died the night we were exiled. Just like that, the scent of smoke scorches my nose. So many fucking people *died* and their only crime was being associated with the Paine family.

Just like Shiloh is.

"I will not let you hurt her," I repeat.

"*Hurt* her?" She raises her brows. "Silly man. Who said this had anything to do with you? I'm a woman with needs, and right now those needs include getting Shiloh naked and coming on my tongue. You don't enter into the equation. Neither does *hurting* her—unless she's into that sort of thing."

"Liar."

"You think so little of her that you really believe she's not attractive enough to pull me? I can't decide if that's a compliment or an insult." She tilts her head to the side. "I think it's both—to both of us."

"Listen to me, Monroe, because I will only say this once." My voice is so low and rough, I hardly sound like myself. No, I sound like my brother Cohen right before he does something violent. The thought nearly shocks me back to myself. Or it would if Monroe weren't so damned *close*. She's still tugging on the band of my pants, and I wouldn't put it past her to undo them right here.

I can picture it as clearly as I pictured fucking her over the bar earlier. Digging my hand into that mass of blond hair and driving her to her knees. Of finding the single way to keep her silent—by fucking that wicked mouth.

Damn it.

I'm out of control.

How does she do this? No one gets under my skin so thoroughly, let alone in seconds. "Stay the fuck away from Shiloh," I repeat.

"You don't get to make that decision." The voice comes from behind me, light and clear and angry enough to singe.

The victorious smile on Monroe's face is a perfect match to the sinking in my chest. *Shit*. I release the bar and take one long step from her, disengaging her hand from my pants. My cock is hard, but there's not a lot I can do about it. Just another way I've lost control in the last few minutes. I turn to find Shiloh standing in the doorway. She looks angrier than I've ever seen her.

Gods, I don't know if I've *ever* seen her angry.

Normally she's so easy to be around. Chill and constantly rolling with the punches that came from our group never being able to settle in one place. Her parents were nightmares, and she's ended up on the exact opposite end of that spectrum, choosing never to make waves.

I can't remember a single time we've actually fought. I hold up my hands, trying to think past the swirling of sex and smoke and loss in my thoughts.

"Shiloh—"

"No." She shakes her head. "You do *not* get to say my name in that tone of voice like I'm the one out of line. Are you and your Bride in a monogamous relationship?"

I clench my jaw. "That's not the point. I'm only trying—"

"I asked you a question, Broderick Paine," she snaps. "Are you and your Bride in a monogamous relationship?"

I take a step forward. Surely she, of all people, understands how dangerous this dance is? Monroe isn't a normal woman. Yes, I'd feel jealous to see Shiloh starting something with someone else, but ultimately that's not my call to make. We're friends. But Monroe isn't just someone else. She's the *enemy*. She will use Shiloh and discard her the moment Monroe's finished with her. I wouldn't be a good friend if I just stood back and let it happen. Especially since the danger is *my* Bride. "Can't you see that you're falling right into her trap? This is her way of getting back at me."

Shiloh's tone goes absolutely frigid. "Because that's the only way someone could want me. As a path to get to you."

Too late, I realize my mistake. "That's not what I meant."

"That's what you said," Monroe supplies from behind me.

"Stay out of it, witch."

"You sweet talker, you."

Shiloh closes the distance between us and pokes my chest. "Answer the damned question. Now."

"No," I bite out. "We're not monogamous."

"Have you had any negotiations about having a say in each other's love lives?"

"No," I repeat.

"Yeah, I didn't think so." She glares up at me. "And, as you are my friend and nothing more, you certainly don't get a say on who *I* let into my bed. Fuck off, Broderick." She spins on her heels, flips me the bird, and is gone.

The sound of slow clapping fills the room.

I turn to find Monroe practically giddy with amusement. "Wow. You really fucked that up all on your own. I barely had to help."

"You are *such* a bitch."

"Takes one to know one." She starts for the door.

It's as if my brain skips. One moment, I'm ready to tear into her for pulling such an underhanded move. The next, I'm watching my hand reach out and snag her wrist. All thought and reason take a back seat as I drag her behind me to the door she and Shiloh emerged from. One blink and we're inside. Another and I have Monroe pressed against the closed door. "Did you have her just like this?" I wedge my thigh between her legs.

She lifts her brows, completely unbothered by the manhandling. But then, of course she is. She got off on it last time, too. "Yes, actually."

"Such a smart mouth on you, Monroe. I ought to shove my cock in it and shut you up."

"Not interested." She laughs. "I already played the saint and kept my hands off your little girlfriend's pussy." She arches against me. "Make me come, Broderick. You want to use your cock to punish me? I'm ready and willing."

"Ready and willing," I repeat.

"Mmm." She runs her hands up my chest and leans forward until her lips brush my ear. "Getting Shiloh off got me so fucking wet. She's so pretty when she orgasms, husband. I'll have to show you sometime."

"Stop calling me that," I grind out.

I can hear her smile. "Make me."

Those two little words snap the last bit of leash holding me back. I pull away from her and yank her to bend over the sink. I undo her pants and shove them to the floor. I don't care if they get dirty. I don't give a damn about anything but fucking her until I expel some of the frustration turning me into a goddamned monster. "I ought to have bent you over the bar and fucked you right there."

"Better have charged for it, then."

"Always a snappy comeback." I grip the front of her shirt and jerk it down, baring her breasts. With only the little top thing around her hips, she looks like a sex goddess. It doesn't matter if we're in a dingy bar bathroom. Monroe owns this space just like she owns every space she occupies. I can't blame Shiloh for being drawn to her. I'm right here, in the exact same spot, acting outside of my best interests because of this woman, too.

I grab the back of her neck and bend her forward. She spreads her legs even wider. I can *see* how wet she is, her pussy pink and glistening. Gods, it's like she was built to tempt me. It doesn't matter what I think of this woman. It doesn't matter that she's the enemy and I resent this hand-fasting binding us together

All that matters is that I need to get inside her right this fucking second or I might die.

I wrap a fist around my cock but manage to stop myself. "I don't have a condom."

"You're cute when you're trying to put your leash back on." She laughs. "I told you already—I've been tested, and I have an IUD. You can do anything you want to me, Broderick Paine. No brakes. No consequences." She presses against my hold so she can meet my gaze in the mirror. "That scares you shitless, doesn't it? Nothing holding you to that honorable mask you wear. You can be just as feral as the rest of us."

"Shut up."

"Prove me wrong."

Proving her wrong means crossing half a dozen lines I've drawn for myself. Lines I crossed on Lammas night. I've been avoiding her solely to resist doing what I'm doing right now. I meet Monroe's gaze in the mirror, and the victorious expression on her pretty face feels like a bucket of cold water dumped over my head.

I'm playing right into her hands.

I tighten my grip ever so slightly, and she shivers. No matter what else is true, she's as affected as I am by this thing between us. I can use that. I *have* to use that. "It's a shame Shiloh didn't make you come." Saying Shiloh's name nearly trips me up, but I force myself to continue. "Because I'm not going to, either."

The shock on her face is nearly as good as sinking into her tight cunt would be. Or that's what I tell myself as I release her and step back. "Put yourself back together."

Monroe turns around and leans against the sink. She doesn't seem bothered by her nakedness, but why would she be? She's perfect; at least physically. It takes everything I have to keep my attention on her face as she slowly fixes her top and then pulls up her pants. She runs her fingers through her now-messy blond hair. "You've really fucked things up with Shiloh."

I suspect she's right, but I'll never admit as much aloud. "Stay out of it."

"No, I don't think I will." She fixes her hair. Her expression goes predatory. "After all, I'm your Bride. Your business is my business."

"*Monroe.*"

"Yes, husband?" She must see me clenching my jaw hard enough to shatter teeth, because she grins. "Don't worry, Broderick. I'll get really up close and personal with Shiloh and save your friendship."

"By save, you mean destroy."

She shrugs a single shoulder. "It's not my fault you can't get out of your own way."

"Leave her alone."

She pulls the door open, forcing me to move back to avoid touching her. "Fine."

I blink. "Fine?"

"Yes, fine." Monroe stops and looks over her shoulder. "I'll leave your precious best friend alone."

My feet feel like they've grown roots. I was so braced for a fight, I'm not sure how to react to her easy capitulation. "Oh." I clear my throat. "Good."

"That's not the thing you should be focusing on, husband."

I don't want to ask; I already know I won't like the answer. "What should I be focusing on?" I follow her out of the bathroom, pausing to shut the door behind me. She doesn't answer until we're out on the street. Shiloh is nowhere in evidence, and I'd worry about her, but she's more than capable of taking care of herself and getting back to the compound on her own. Monroe and I fall into step through the crowd.

She gives me a sweet smile. "The fact that *Shiloh* is not going to leave *me* alone."

I shake my head. She's baiting me. She must be. "She won't touch you without some meddling on your part." Shiloh's too good, too focused. How could she be drawn to someone like Monroe, with venom in her very blood?

How could I be drawn to Monroe?

I shove the thought away. "It won't happen."

"Would you like to bet on it?"

Sheer rage has me saying, "Of course."

"If I'm correct, and Shiloh comes to me without any manipulations on my part, then you're mine for a week."

I stop short. "What?"

Monroe stops, too. "A week, husband, where you stop pretending you're a good man and do what you really want." She steps closer. Though she doesn't touch me, the phantom memory of her nails skating up my chest has me fighting back a shiver. "Where you *take* what you really want."

I'd be a fool a thousand times over to make a bet with this woman. No matter what she promises, she will cheat, lie, and steal to win. That's just the kind of person Monroe is; she fights dirty. I open my mouth to tell her to fuck off, but that's not what comes out. "You have yourself a deal."

CHAPTER 7

SHILOH

I'm so furious, I can barely see straight. The walk back to the compound takes half the time it should. The entire time, all I can focus on is how unbelievably over-bearing Broderick has become. He's always been over-protective, but never once in the last seven years has he tried to steamroll me. Not about my ability to do my job. Not about my dating life.

Sure, there hasn't been much of a dating life to speak of, but ultimately that changes nothing. The man was making decrees about me as if I'm a child to be controlled.

I am not a child.

I'm a fucking adult, and he can choke on his decrees for all I care.

I shove through the front doors of the main house so hard, they bounce off the wall. A small voice inside me warns that I need to give myself time to cool off before doing anything else, but for once in my life I'm too angry to listen. There's no room for caution here, no space to be rational.

Gabriel Paine, the youngest of the Paine brothers, jumps

in surprise at my entrance. "Shiloh?" He narrows his eyes. "Is everything okay?"

"No." I barely sound like myself. My voice is so cold, I'm half surprised it doesn't cloud the air in front of me. "Where is Cohen?" I could try approaching Maddox, but he'll just tell me to deal with it on my own. For all that he's the more approachable of the two, he's the least likely to understand how fucked this situation is. I doubt Maddox has ever been in over his head even once in his life.

Not that Cohen has ever been in over his head, but he has six brothers so surely he can sympathize when one of them gets a stick up his ass and starts making commands that are none of his damn business.

"Upstairs."

I don't hesitate, pushing past him and starting up the stairs. It's only when I reach the second floor, where all the private suites are, that I realize I might still be a little drunk and have lipstick smeared on my face and neck. It would be smart to slow down, to give myself time to gather my wits and figure out a game plan, but it's as if I have too much momentum. I can't stop, no matter how ill-advised this is.

Cohen and Maddox's room is at the far end of the north hall. As best as I can tell, his bride, Winry—Monroe's little sister—has been sharing their room the entire time. Unlike Broderick, who ceded his new space to Monroe and has been sleeping alone gods knew where. Because *that* makes sense. Avoid the problem and hope it goes away.

Just like he's been avoiding me.

How *dare* he think he can tell me what I should or shouldn't be doing? I've seen him a grand total of three times in three weeks, and each time he's all but sprinted from my presence the second he gets an opening.

Not too long ago, I might have listened to him if he told me to stay away from Monroe. Our friendship has spanned nearly a full third of my life. In that time, Broderick has been nothing but steady and stable and taken care of everyone around him. He's not the type to fly off the handle or lose his temper over something ridiculous. He just handles shit.

Until now.

Maybe in a day or two, I'll be able to admit that coming back to Sabine Valley has put him into a tailspin, but I'm too busy doing my own spin out to worry about him. If this was any other time, any other place, we'd lean on each other until the ground steadied beneath our feet. It's what we've always done in the past. I've grown to depend on the belief that no matter how scary things get, I will always feel Broderick steady at my back. Just like I'll always have his back, too.

Except... He *doesn't* have my back right now. I'm left here, standing on my own, for the first time in years. The man only shows up to tell me what I can and can't do before disappearing again to hide from his Bride.

Yeah, fuck that.

I lift my hand to knock on Cohen's door, but it opens before I get the chance, revealing the man himself. He's big and burly, with red hair and a red beard and tattoos over most of his exposed skin. Not that I can see much of them with his long-sleeved Henley and jeans. He also looks...frazzled. I blink. I've never seen Cohen anything less than cold and remote. The relief on his face when he sees me has me taking a step back.

"Is everything okay?" I ask warily.

"No." He pulls the door shut behind him and grabs my arm, steering me away from the room. He's moving at such a quick pace that I have to practically skip to keep up with him. I don't get a chance to ask more questions, because he hauls me up another set of stairs and practically hurls me into a dust-filled room that looks like it might have been a living room at some point.

That's about enough of that.

I grab his wrist, applying pressure points to make him release me. He does with a curse and then seems to come back to himself. "Fuck. Sorry."

The urge to rub my upper arm is there, but I resist it. "It's fine. What's going on?" As angry as I still am, anything that makes *Cohen* lose his cool takes priority.

He opens his mouth, seems to consider what he was about to blurt out, and finally curses. "This is going to sound so fucking ridiculous."

Okay, now I'm really worried. I cross my arms over my chest. "I won't understand until you explain."

"I was trying to be fucking *nice*. Maddox is always telling me I'm too fucking harsh with Winry. She's so damn soft, I make one wrong move and I'm worried I'm going to bruise her." He drags his hand through his hair and winces. "Women like to feel wanted."

Women like to feel wanted? What in the hell is going on? "Cohen," I put a little snap in my voice.

"She's fucking furious." He looks at me, his amber eyes a little wild around the edges. "She threw a lamp at my head."

That doesn't sound like the Winry I've slowly come to know over the past three weeks. The curvy blond is as sweet as Monroe is salty. Cohen's right; she's got a softness that makes even *me* move carefully around her. And not just because I'm 100 percent sure Monroe would slit the throat of anyone who made her beloved little sister cry. "She...threw a lamp...at your head?"

"*Yes.*" He rubs his temple. "She's got wicked aim, too."

I don't even know what to say to that. "What did you *do*?"

"I just said..." He clears his throat. "She's in a certain way, so—"

All the blood rushes out of my head. "She's *pregnant?*"

Forget slitting someone's throat. Monroe is going to skin both Cohen and Maddox alive.

"What? No! That's not what I fucking said." He goes so pale, I am slightly horrified to realize he has freckles. "She's on her fucking period."

I wait for the rest, but apparently that's all it is. "Cohen," I say slowly. "I don't care what common culture says about people on their periods. They do *not* turn from sweet people into lamp-wielding maniacs. You did something."

"No shit, I did something." He drags his hand through his hair again. Winces again when he touches where the lamp apparently made contact. "She was talking shit about how she looked and felt, and I just said I don't care about a little blood when it comes to fucking."

I stare. Of course he did. For someone who is easily the most ruthless Paine brother, I don't know if I'm freaked out or strangely amused to see him so out of sorts. "And that's when she threw the lamp."

"Right at my fucking head!"

The upside of this ridiculous conversation is that my anger has all but drained away. I sigh. "Depending on a number of factors, she's probably feeling anywhere from vaguely uncomfortable to in true pain. The last thing she wants is your cock mucking things up."

"I realize that now," he grits out. "How do I make it right?"

Maybe later I'll wonder at the fact Cohen even cares about the feelings of someone beyond Maddox and his brothers. Maybe. "You could try asking her." He makes a face, and I press on. "Easy options—a snack she likes, some kind of movie or book or something to keep her occupied, maybe a hot bath or heating pad if she feels up to it. *Not* sex. Some people like sex on their periods, but for fuck's sake, Cohen, that shouldn't be your go-to."

"How was I supposed to know?"

He's got me there. It's not as if he's close to any of the people who menstruate in our group. Certainly not close enough to be in a comforting role during that time. "Now you do."

"Yeah." He gets a focused look that is, honestly, slightly terrifying. "I'll figure it out."

"Great."

He gives himself a shake. "You needed something?"

"Not anymore." Now that I have the tiniest sliver of distance, I realize that I can't run to Cohen—or anyone else —with this problem. It has nothing to do with the mission or the safety of the faction. It's personal.

That means it needs to be handled personally. "I have it taken care of."

"Good." He's already turning for the door, but he stops before he reaches it. "Maddox and I need to talk to you about the Amazons tomorrow morning. Seven."

"Okay." I take several deep breaths after the door closes behind him. It smells faintly musty in the room. A few more breaths and I know what I need to do—the exact opposite of what I *want* to do.

Talk to Broderick.

It doesn't matter if he's acting like a stranger right now. He's my best friend. We just need to sit down and hash it out. Sure, we've never really had an argument before, but we've had difficult conversations in the past, have trusted each other with things we don't talk about generally.

I know how worried he gets for his brothers, especially during dangerous missions, despite the fact that you'd never realize just looking at him. A side-effect of what they survived the last time they were in this godsforsaken city.

He knows about my past. Oh, not where I'm from and not the horrific details. But he knows my parents were monsters who committed monstrous acts on the one person they should have protected.

If we can talk about those subjects without flinching, we should be able to talk about Monroe without devolving into a screaming fight.

Right?

Once I decide on a course of action, I don't like to wait, so I head back downstairs. Broderick won't be in the room he's supposed to share with Monroe. He avoids it at all cost; even his clothes are kept somewhere else. I intend to figure out where.

I find Gabriel near where he was when I came in. Now that I think about it, it's weird that he's lingering near the entrance. I narrow my eyes. "What are you up to?" He's only a couple years younger than me, but as both the youngest and the sweetest of the Paine brothers, he's often treated as the baby of group. I don't know why they gave him *Fallon* as a Bride. She's so cold, she's liable to torment him just for the sake of watching him squirm.

He's squirming now and trying to look like he isn't. "Nothing."

"Liar."

He glances away, giving me a view of a jawline that's nearly identical to Broderick's. Not that I need the reminder that they're brothers. The Paines fall into two categories— dark-haired or dark-eyed and ginger. Only Abel, Broderick, and Gabriel are the former. The rest of them have variations of Cohen's red hair. "Gabriel."

"I'm waiting for Finnegan and Iris to get back from patrol so I can leave."

After the conflict with Abel and Eli's people that ended with Eli being shot, Abel has strict rules about the Paines leaving the compound. One of which is that they aren't to do it alone. "Who are you going with?"

Gabriel blushes and looks away again. "Is there some-thing you need?"

After a brief internal debate, I finally say, "Take someone with you. I don't care who. Your brothers will tear this city apart if something happens to you because you're off chasing sex with someone who isn't your Bride." Not that I can blame him, exactly. Fallon is gorgeous, but she's terrifying.

There are a lot of terrifying people in this house these days.

"I'll be safe." Which isn't the same thing as taking someone with him or being careful. "I'm not going far."

I take a deep breath. When it comes down to it, Gabriel is twenty-eight and more than capable of handling himself in a fight. "You'll stay in Raider territory?"

"Yeah. I wasn't planning on crossing either river." He gives me a charming smile. "Though I have to ask—how's that glass house look from where you're standing? Monroe's color looks good on you, Shiloh."

Fuck. I forgot I still had remnants of her lipstick on my face. "Yeah, yeah." I adjust my ponytail. "Did Broderick make it back?"

"Not yet."

I thought he was right behind me when I left the bar, but maybe he and Monroe ended up fighting...or fucking. I poke at the thought, trying to decide how I feel about that. I have no claim on the woman. I don't *want* a claim. I like what we did in the bathroom, but ultimately she's not for me.

And Broderick?

He's not for me, either. He couldn't be clearer that he only sees me as a friend, and I value that friendship too much to ruin it by confessing that I regularly masturbate to the fantasy of him. My skin flushes hot, and I have to put that thought away. It serves no purpose here.

I clear my throat. "Do you know where he's sleeping these days?"

"Oh. That." Gabriel rolls his eyes. "Third floor, south hall. One of the rooms that Abel decided we didn't need to worry about yet. He cleaned it up, and he's been camping up there like Rochester's wife in the attic."

"Nice literary reference," I murmur.

Gabriel blushes harder. "I read."

"I know." I've lost count of the number of times I've found him reading on watch over the years when we were occupying hostile territory in one city or another. I clasp his shoulder. "Be careful, okay?"

"You, too."

I head back to the stairs and climb up to the third floor. As tempting as it is to take a shower and gather my wits about me, the truth is that I don't trust my courage to hold if I don't keep up this momentum.

It doesn't take me long to find Broderick's room. As Gabriel said, Abel decided early on to confine people's rooms to the second floor. The better to keep track of all the Brides. Now that he has Harlow, one of his Brides, wrangling the others, it's made everyone's job a bit easier. Still, with the barracks in the compound to house the rest of our people, there just hasn't been a huge need to mess with the third floor.

At least Broderick's room isn't covered in dust like the one Cohen dragged me to. I resist the urge to poke around and simply perch on the edge of the bed and wait for him. Now that my anger isn't driving me, I'm not sure what the hell I'm doing. I want to tell him off, but... Why? Yes, he was a jerk for trying to tell me who I can and cannot sleep with, especially since *he's* not dating me. Friends don't dictate who their friends sleep with. I might have grown up alone and not know what a healthy relationship looked like if it hit me in the face, but after nearly a decade with the Paine brothers, I'm 100 percent sure of *that*.

What am I doing?

Yelling at him might have made me feel better before I calmed down, but it surely won't now. This is ridiculous. I have better things to do than go a round with Broderick. Especially since it feels like our friendship has been fracturing from the moment we arrived in Sabine Valley. Being here is doing a number on my head, but Broderick has to be feeling something similar. The last time he was in this city, all three factions came together in an attempt to kill him and his brothers. I wish I had more emotional capacity to be there for him right now, but I'm barely treading water as it is. Fighting with him is only going to make it worse. This was a mistake.

I shove to my feet, but it's too late.

The door opens, and the man himself stalks into the room.

CHAPTER 8

BRODERICK

*T*he last thing I expect when I get to my room is to find Shiloh waiting for me. Despite myself, my attention snags on the faint red marks on her mouth and neck from Monroe's lipstick. Even through my rising irritation, heat surges hot enough to have me fighting my body's reaction. Of course, I find the idea of them together attractive. They're both gorgeous. I'm only human. It's nothing more than that.

I clear my throat. I need to apologize. I know I need to apologize. I just have to find the words. "Shiloh. What are you doing here?"

"I don't know." She stands slowly. "I was very, very angry when I left the bar, but I've gotten a bit turned around since then."

"I'm sorry." I am. Truly. I never wanted to make her feel bad for anything, and she's right—I don't have a claim to her since we're only friends. The reminder never used to feel like sandpaper beneath my skin. I respect our friendship. Putting Shiloh in an uncomfortable position because of *my* feelings is

64

out of the question. And yet... I drag my hand over my face. "I might have been a bit out of line."

"A bit?"

Heat flushes my face and neck, and I have the uncomfortable suspicion that I'm blushing. "Monroe makes me lose my cool."

"Monroe," she says the other woman's name slowly, seeming to test it. "Yes, Monroe has a way of provoking people." Except Shiloh doesn't sound like she thinks that's a bad thing.

"She's trouble."

"You're right." Just like that, the softening of Shiloh's expression disappears. She crosses her arms over her chest. "Maybe if you stopped avoiding her and actually dealt with the situation, she would get into less trouble."

I take a step back. Shiloh has a point, but I can't bring myself to admit it. Spending more time around my Bride, trying to corral her, will just pave the way for Monroe to provoke me further. I don't recognize myself when I'm around that woman. "She's poison."

"Is she?" Shiloh glares. "She's an ambitious, terrifying woman. She's an enemy of the Raider faction and your family. But that's it. That doesn't make her poison."

"My brothers and I were almost *killed* because of what the Amazons did." Not just the Amazons, but I'm not handfasted to a Mystic currently. "They would have seen every single member of my family burn."

"I know what the Amazons are capable of." Shiloh goes still. "Do you think I could possibly forget?"

No, of course not. We've talked about it more than once, how that night of betrayal and ash changed the course of my family's life forever. We weren't exactly living the dream life, not under my father's rule, but at least we had stability. After the night of the coup, we were *hunted*.

And every single faction in Sabine Valley was responsible. Amazon. Mystics. Even the Raiders in the form of Eli Walsh's father. It's since come to light that Eli wasn't behind the plans that nearly killed me and my brothers in the house fire, that he wasn't even aware of it, but it's still hard to let go of eight years of bad blood. I'm working on it, because Abel loves that asshole, but I can barely look at Eli without tasting ash on my tongue.

Shiloh knows what it means to never be able to go home again. Her parents made my father look like he should be accepting Parent of the Year awards. Even without the specific details, I know she was abused and that they're religious zealots. I try not to think about her past too much, because doing so is shitty for my blood pressure, and she won't thank me for trying to step in and save the child she used to be.

"I know you didn't forget," I say quietly. "But you have to understand how I felt seeing you two in the bar…" I wave my hand at her. "Seeing it now. It feels like you got into bed with the enemy."

"In bed with the enemy," she repeats. Shiloh narrows her eyes. "Correct me if I'm wrong, but did you not fuck Monroe on Lammas night?"

"That's different."

"Is it?" She stalks toward me. "So different that you've been hiding from her ever since. The only other of your brothers who's avoiding his Bride is Gabriel, and he's a baby."

"He's twenty-eight. He can be forgiven for not knowing what to do with Fallon."

"Then she shouldn't have been his selection. Better that he get Matteo or Winry." She stops and makes a face. "Maybe not Winry." Shiloh shakes her head. "None of this addresses the fact that you don't have a say in who I sleep with, Broderick. And if you're determined to avoid Monroe and pretend

Lammas never happened, then you don't have a say in what she does, either."

The fact that Shiloh *isn't going to leave* me *alone.*

Monroe's words echo through my mind in really unpleasant way. "She's dangerous. She'll poison *you.*"

"That's my decision to make." Shiloh laughs, but not like anything is funny. "As for being dangerous, so is every other person in this house. So am *I.* Or did you forget everything I've done since I joined up with you?"

"I haven't forgotten." We all have blood on our hands. Every single one of us. Fighting hasn't been the first course of action, but most of the time it's inevitable. When we were exiled from Sabine Valley, we lost our claim to anything resembling home territory. No matter where we went, we were always the interlopers, always the one that had to be driven off by whoever owned that space. Often violently.

She searches my face. I don't know what my expression is doing, but whatever she's looking for, she doesn't seem to find. "This is a mess."

Mess is a gigantic understatement. I look down at her, and I suddenly miss her so fucking much, I can barely breathe past it. We haven't exactly been apart, but something's changed between us and we both know it. I feel like she's slipping through my fingers, and no matter how tightly I try to grasp her, to reclaim the easy intimacy of our friendship, I only make things worse. "I'm sorry," I say again.

"I know." Shiloh looks away. "But being sorry isn't enough, Broderick. I know being back here isn't easy on you, but you're not the only one having a hard time."

Is she talking about herself? I reach out hesitantly and clasp her shoulder. "Do you want to talk about it?"

For a second, I think she might, but Shiloh finally shakes her head. "No. It doesn't matter in the grand scheme of things." She covers my hand with her own and gives it a squeeze.

We look at each other and it's the way things used to be. I can almost picture how the rest of the night should go. I'll offer to pull out a movie from Finnegan's endless collection, she'll get the snacks, and we'll hole up in the mini movie theater for the duration. For a few hours, things will be *normal* again.

But then Shiloh steps away and I let my hand drop. She moves past me to the door and opens it. "If you want to keep hiding, that's your choice. But not all of us have that option. Not all of us *want* that option. If this is home now, for better or worse. I'm going to make work."

"With Monroe." The words are out before I can call them back.

She gives me a long look. "She's the enemy, but she's also your Bride for the next eleven months. Have you considered how you could use that to the advantage of the Raider faction?" Shiloh is gone before I can come up with a response. It's just as well. I'm not sure what I'd even say.

Use Monroe to my advantage?

That orgasm must have gone to Shiloh's brain, because the woman I know never would have suggested such a thing. The entire reason we came back to Sabine Valley and Abel stepped into the ring on Lammas, the very purpose of our Brides, is to get revenge. Sending Fallon and Monroe back to their respective positions during the day means we have an in with both Amazons and Mystics. A way to get to the very heart of them and rip it out.

The same way they ripped out our hearts eight years ago.

Shiloh doesn't get it. Even as close as we are, as many times as she's heard the stories, she doesn't fucking get it. How could she? She's not from Sabine Valley. She didn't wake up in the middle of the night to the scent of smoke on the air. She wasn't forced to flee a burning building that left forty of our people dead. It was sheer luck that none of my brothers were among them. She didn't become an orphan that night.

My father was a monster. I was more than old enough at twenty-seven to understand just how fucked he was when it came to running the Raider faction. But he wouldn't have run it forever, and Abel is not the same kind of monster. No matter what pieces of himself he carved away over the last eight years to keep us and our people protected, he has more than proven he's fit to lead the Raider faction in the past three weeks.

Things are working out exactly like they're supposed to. So why the fuck can't I get my head on straight? Why can't I escape the feeling of a sword hanging over our heads, just waiting until the right moment to fall and sever us from the world of the living?

I can barely stand to be inside my own head. Desperate to talk to someone with the slightest bit of sanity, I seek out my brother Ezekiel. *He* won't have softened on our main goal. Not when the betrayal he experienced was so damn personal.

When we were driven out of the city, Ezekiel was one of a trio of friends who represented the hope for the future. A Raider, a Mystic, and an Amazon. I'm still not sure how they met, but they were constantly together through most of our childhood. I think Ezekiel expected them to come for him after the exile. It was the first time they were separated since they were little.

They...didn't.

When we were doing our research and planning for our return, we discovered that Jasper and Beatrix were dating. Not only had they moved on from the loss of Ezekiel, but they moved on *together*. When he found that out, my brother went quiet in a way that worries me. He hasn't been the same since.

He insisted on Jasper as his Bride, and Abel allowed it. I don't think anyone expected Beatrix to show up, too.

I make my way down to the second floor and knock on Ezekiel's door. He doesn't make me wait long, but when he opens it, all I can do is stare. He's shirtless, his lean body covered in scratches. That's not what shocks me. No, it's the fact that he has *both* Beatrix and Jasper handcuffed to his bed, wearing nothing but underwear. Ezekiel leans against the doorjamb as if that is not a huge fucking red flag. "Need something?"

"Zeke?" His childhood nickname pops out of my mouth. "What the hell is happening here?"

"Don't worry about it."

I really wish that were an option. Hell, I wish that the only reason I cared was because of the potential fallout of having the Amazon queen's younger brother and the leader of the Mystic's younger sister cuffed. The truth is that it doesn't matter who they are. This isn't okay.

Ezekiel used to be a nice kid. Sweet, even. The kind of innocent that even Gabriel never quite accomplished. All that changed with the exile. The past eight years, he's gotten colder and colder, until he rivals Cohen for being the most monstrous of us.

This is too far, even for him. This is too far for *anyone*.

I shake my head slowly. "You know I have to worry about it." Abel oversees everything. Cohen runs our soldiers. I'm in charge of the household. "Move out of the way."

Ezekiel lifts a brow and moves back. "By all means, please play the hero for *these two*. Your concern isn't required." He lifts his voice. "Do you want me to release you, Beatrix?"

She glares daggers at the back of his head. "No."

"Jasper?"

Jasper's look isn't filled with violence, but he doesn't look particularly pleased, either. "No. We're fine."

I really wish I could believe them. I move past my brother and take in the rest of the room. There are the remnants of a destroyed chair on the floor, and one of the paintings has fallen off the wall. Or been knocked off, more likely. On the large bed, Beatrix and Jasper are side by side, their wrists cuffed to the headboard with padded bondage gear. It's designed not to damage the skin, though I haven't had reason to use it myself.

They both have a scattering of bruises, and Jasper has a set of scratches to match Ezekiel's. I meet both their gazes in turn. "Leave the room, Ezekiel."

"You're wasting your time." But he does as I ask, slamming the door behind him.

I cross my arms over my chest and stare at the two people on the bed. "Answer honestly—are you consenting to this? If you're not, I'll get you out."

Beatrix snorts. She's attractive in the way the ruling Mystic family seems to be—red hair, pale skin, eerie gray eyes. She's softer than her niece Fallon...though she's not as soft as her nephew Matteo. Being soft doesn't make her less dangerous, though. She looks at me like I'm something she'd like to scrape off the bottom of her shoe. "We're fine. Run along, nursemaid."

"Bea," Jasper murmurs. He's Monroe's uncle, but I see none of her in him. In the Amazon faction, there is always a queen and never a king, but our information on Jasper says he's not particularly ambitious. He does what needs to be done, but he has no designs to change Amazon culture and take the crown for himself. He's also got a reputation for being a soothing force on Beatrix's temper.

He meets my gaze steadily, his hazel eyes giving nothing away. "We're fine. We chose this."

I want to argue, but it's not my business what bedroom games Ezekiel gets up to…as long as everyone is on the same page. "If that changes—"

"It won't." Beatrix stretches out on the bed with a sigh. "Now leave us alone, Broderick Paine. I'm sure you have an Amazon heir to corral."

At that, Jasper's gaze sharpens. "How's Monroe holding up?"

I'm not sure how to answer that. She's so fucking bulletproof, it never occurred to me that she might be having issues. Not that I care. I certainly fucking don't. "She's Monroe. I'm sure she's somewhere starting a riot or setting something on fire."

He snorts. "Yeah. Sure."

It seems that there's nothing else to do here. If they insist they consented to this, then stepping in isn't going to do anything but cause some bullshit for no reason. I straighten. "I guess I'll leave you to it."

"About damn time," Beatrix mutters.

"*Bea.*" Jasper gives me a winning smile that's only slightly dampened by the fact he's wearing black briefs and covered in scratches and bruises. "I would like to see my niece. Soon."

"I'll see what I can do." I turn around and stride out of the room.

Ezekiel is waiting in the hallway, leaning against the wall and glaring. "Well?"

"You know I had to check."

"Did you? Because they're the enemy."

This is the reminder I wanted, the reason I sought him out to begin with, but… "We don't torture people."

"Don't we?" He laughs roughly. "Maybe you don't. When Abel needs someone to get their hands dirty, Cohen and I don't get precious about it."

"Zeke—" I don't know how to fix this, how to fix *him*.

Like me, he's unraveled in his own way since coming back to Sabine Valley. Fuck, I can't even fix my own head; how am I supposed to give my little brother advice? "If you want to talk—"

"I don't." He looks away. "Did you need something else or did you just show up to check on us?"

I bite back my questions. Ultimately, we've all made our own choices about how we're going to go forward and survive. Survival is *all* that matters. It's all that's ever mattered. "Why did you let Beatrix stay? She's not your Bride; Jasper is."

"I picked him to punish them both." He shrugs. "Having her here just makes it easier to deal out that punishment."

I knew the answer before I asked the question, didn't I? "Are they sorry?"

Ezekiel finally looks at me. "Who the fuck cares if they're sorry? An apology doesn't change what happened, Broderick. Forty people drugged by shit acquired by the Mystics, dead in a fire that was helped set by the Amazons. Forty people who depended on us for safety and got killed for their loyalty. Someone saying sorry isn't going to bring any of them back."

I've thought the same thing over and over again. So why am I standing here, fighting with an urge to argue with him? I came here for reassurance, not to tell him he's going too far. Fuck, I really hope he's not going too far. "Neither Jasper nor Beatrix had anything to do with that."

Ezekiel opens the door to his bedroom and pauses. "I know you're used to looking out for us, but I don't need a babysitter, and I sure as fuck don't need some kind of father stand-in. We had a father, Broderick. He was a piece of shit. We're all adults now, so stop worrying about us and mind your own Bride."

Monroe. My Bride. The enemy.

CHAPTER 9

MONROE

*T*here are few things I hate more than aborted orgasms. I might admire Broderick's restraint and cruelty the *smallest* amount, but that doesn't make me less likely to crawl the walls as I stalk around the house. Shiloh hasn't found me yet, and I refuse to worry about her. She's fine. More than fine. It's about damn time her and Broderick stopped being so *nice* to each other. He might lie to everyone else, but I know the truth; he's not a nice man. Not even a little bit.

And Shiloh?

No matter what I thought when I first saw her, she's not *nice* either. She's strong, and irritatingly good at her job, and sexy as fuck. She's also a selfish ass for coming all over my thigh and then walking away as if she has no intention of doing it again.

We'll see about that.

"Monroe."

I paste a cheery smile on my face as I spin on my heel. Harlow Byrne strides down the hall in my direction. She's attractive in an understated kind of way. Strong body with

74

curves that might be tempting if they were attached to anyone else. Hair that's been dyed a subtler red than is found in the Mystic faction. I've seen her fight a few times before she and Eli Walsh started dating; she's a hell of a bitch in the arena. I can take her, but it wouldn't be an easy victory.

She's effectively queen of the Raider faction now. Abel took her as his Bride, but unlike the rest of us, he's made it pretty damn clear that she's at his side as an equal. The little prick I feel when I look at her is irritation, of course. It certainly isn't jealousy. I don't need to be seen as on the same level as Broderick, not when I'm leagues above him. "Harlow. What a lovely surprise."

"Liar," she says it easily, not bothered in the least. I hate to say it, but she's damn good at her job, and she manages all the Brides expertly. She's the reason I'm able to go home during the day to work—and avoid any ambitious Amazons getting funny ideas about who's really heir. She's also the reason I've been on what passes for my best behavior.

With everyone but Broderick, of course.

Harlow falls into step beside me. "What happened today?"

"I'm not sure what you're speaking of."

She shoots me a look. "Does anyone ever actually believe that innocent tone coming from you?"

"There's always a first time." From the stubborn set of her shoulders, she's not going to let this go. I bite back a sigh. "It's personal."

"Between you and Broderick."

"Between me and Shiloh."

She raises her brows but finally nods. "Shiloh's greatly beloved by Abel's people. Watch your step. If you toy with her and make her cry, you're going to have every single one of the Paines and all their followers howling for your blood."

"I'll take that into consideration." The funny thing? I don't plan on making Shiloh cry. Making her orgasm until she passes out? Definitely. But the only person I want to sink a dagger into and twist is Broderick. Even the other Paine brothers pale in comparison for the fury I feel for him. Sure, Abel beating one of our champions is the reason I'm a Bride, but that was a fair fight. I might not like the outcome, but I can respect it.

Broderick? I want him on his knees, crawling and broken. I want it with a strength that surpasses reason. It's not because he's rejected me. It's because he's a fucking liar and hypocrite. I can't stand either. Really, I'm determined to make him suffer on principle. I'm practically obligated to do it.

She looks like she wants to say something else but finally shrugs. "I'll be checking in with the Brides again in a few days. Let me know if you need anything in the meantime."

"I'm good." I've made a few requests to Harlow for various things, and she's filled every single one without question or complaint. It would almost be enough to make me like her if we weren't from rival factions that have hated each other since the dawn of Sabine Valley. She'd make one hell of an Amazon.

"See you in a couple days."

"Harlow." I speak without thinking. "I'd like to see my sister and uncle. Without the other Brides."

Her expression goes careful. "You'll be required to have at least one of our people present."

"*Your* people." I can't help needling her, just a little. "How quickly you cleave to the Paine way of life. Abel must be one hell of a fuck."

"No comment." She doesn't blink. "Agree, or it's off."

"Agreed." It's not as if the Paine brothers and their people aren't already watching my every step.

"Good." Harlow nods. "It's getting late, so it won't be

tonight, but I'll see what I can do about tomorrow. I'll send for you when it's arranged."

No doubt the meeting will include the fancy tea setup she favors. For someone so badass, Harlow sure loves that tea cart and forcing us all to drink that shit. It's actually pretty good, but I'll never admit it. "Works for me."

We parts ways when the hall branches, her heading downstairs and me heading to the room that's become mine. I was never meant for captivity. If it weren't for the daily trips to the Amazon faction and tower, I'd be going out of my mind by now.

I half expect Shiloh to be in the room when I get there, but it's empty. I frown. She better be okay. Abel seems to have a choke hold on the Raider faction, but that doesn't mean that there aren't still loyalists meandering around with itchy trigger fingers, just waiting for one of his people to pass by. No matter how capable she is, she's not bulletproof.

If Broderick weren't such an ass, he wouldn't have let her walk out alone. He doesn't see clearly where she's concerned. Obviously he has a thing for her, but instead of admitting it, he veers too far in the other direction, holding her at a distance even though they're supposedly such good *friends*. I don't know how other people treat their friends, but I don't avoid mine like they have the plague.

Though most of my friends are actually family.

Fuck.

I'm spiraling. This is ridiculous. I march into the closet and pull off my work clothing, switching to a pair of leggings and an oversized white shirt that looks like something that should be on a romance novel cover, complete with deep V down the chest. It's ridiculously dramatic, and normally wearing it cheers me up immediately.

Nothing happens this time.

"I shouldn't have let her walk out of that bar, either," I

mutter. It doesn't matter that the power imbalance seems permanently off when it comes to me and Broderick. I could have kneecapped him and marched out of there on Shiloh's heels. It's not like it would have been hard.

The door to my bedroom opens, and the woman herself walks in. I don't breathe a sigh of relief. I truly don't. It's just a tiny soundless exhale as I survey her, and I'm certainly *not* looking to make sure she's okay and unharmed.

She shoots me a long look. "What's got that expression on your face?"

I shrug. "It's my face. I'm a person who has expressions."

"Whatever." She strides past me, pulling her shirt off in the process.

"What are you doing?" The question comes out too high, too fast, but *what the fuck?*

She doesn't look at me, doesn't stop. "I moved my stuff in here earlier. I've been sleeping in this room anyways, so there's no point in taking up space in the barracks."

"Um."

She stops in the doorway to the bathroom, wearing only a black bra and jeans. It's not even a fancy bra—no lace, and it's a perfectly serviceable style—but my mouth goes dry at the sight. "Do you have a problem with that?"

"No." The word is out before I can think of a reason I should have a problem with it. Surely there's something? Yes, she's with me pretty much twenty-four-seven, but maintaining some level of space is important... Isn't it?

I haven't been this thrown off by a pair of tits since I was fifteen and Casey LaRue showed up at school in a V-neck with a pushup bra on. I was so busy staring, I ran into an open locker like a complete fool. I was dating her less than a week later, but that doesn't change the fact that it's one of the few times in my life when I forgot myself so completely, I acted totally out of character.

Shiloh is about to make me add to the list. Especially when she turns around and her hands go to the front of her jeans. "I need a shower." She glances at me over her shoulder. "That wasn't an invitation, by the way."

"Oh." Surely I can do better than this? I'm still trying to come up with a word that isn't two letters when she kicks the door shut, closing us off from each other. The click of a lock makes it clear that she meant it.

The water turns on.

Right now, she'll be sliding off those jeans. Probably unhooking her bra and shimmying out of her panties.

I press my lips together, but all the thwarted desire comes back tenfold knowing that she's naked in the next room. Before I can talk myself out of it—and really, why would I bother?—I slide off my leggings and drop onto the bed. I waste no time dipping my hand between my thighs and stroking my clit. Fuck, I'm halfway there and all I did was look at her.

I should take my time, but I've never been all that good at doing things I *should* do. I trace my opening and then spread my wetness up to my clit. Light circles, designed to tease me right to the edge. A tiny moan slips free. Will Shiloh masturbate in my shower? I really, really hope she does. That detachable showerhead is a piece of art and should be appreciated fully.

Maybe I'll show her sometime…

The image roots itself in my mind. Both of us naked in the shower. Pressing against the back of her lean body as I maneuver the showerhead to her pussy, to her clit. I already know what she sounds like when she comes. I'm going to hear that cute little whimper in my dreams tonight.

I can't wait to coax another out of her.

I come hard, not bothering to muffle my moans. I'm in my room, after all. It's her damn fault for teasing me.

I've barely brought myself down when the bathroom door opens and Shiloh appears, wrapped in a towel. She stops short, her gaze going from me on the bed to my hand buried between my thighs. "Monroe," she says slowly. "Were you just masturbating to the image of me in the shower?"

"To clarify, I was masturbating to the image of both of us in the shower." I give my clit one last circle, shiver, and withdraw my hand from my panties.

"I see." She moves slowly, crossing to stand next to the bed.

Before I can decide how I want to play this, Shiloh grabs my wrist and lifts my hand up until it's even with her face. The same hand with fingers still wet from my orgasm. She leans down and draws my pointer finger into her mouth. Her tongue, the slight sucking motion...

I shift on the bed. "Tease." My voice is too breathy, too affected.

Shiloh ignores me and gives my next finger the same treatment. Tasting me. Cleaning every bit of evidence from my skin. It doesn't take a large jump to picture her tasting me from the source. I shift again.

She flicks her tongue against my fingertips and releases me. "I'm very angry at you."

"You came in that bathroom. I didn't. If anyone should be angry, it's me."

Shiloh raises a dark brow. "I wasn't aware orgasms were transactional with you."

She has me there. I sigh. "Okay, fine. They're not. I enjoyed making you come for the sake of making you come." I'd like to do it again. And again. And again.

"Thought so." She absently trails a finger over her collarbone. "You're seducing me to hurt Broderick."

There's no reason to lie. She's a smart girl, and she'll see right through it. "That's part of it, yes, but I'd seduce you even if he weren't involved." I wouldn't say I have a particular taste in partners. I don't think attraction can be boiled down to something as mundane as liking a certain hair color or body type or gender. There's too much nuance for that. Yeah, I liked the look of her face when we first met, but what really draws me to Shiloh is her steadiness and the way she cuts through whatever bullshit I throw at her without so much as raising her eyebrows. She feels unshakable...or she did until she was coming.

"How am I supposed to believe that?"

"That's not the right question to be asking."

"Oh yeah?" Shiloh smiles a little. "And what question should I be asking?"

It strikes me that I've never seen her with her hair down. It's longer than I thought, well past her shoulders. I glance at her legs, note the intense scars there, and look back at her face before she can get self-conscious. They're obviously the reason she only wears jeans. They don't look like knife wounds or anything like that. Best guess, they're burns, but they're too regular to be from something like a fire.

Understanding dawns.

Someone burned her legs. On purpose.

Rage surges in me, so strong that it takes my breath away. I forget my intention to ignore her scars. "Who did that?"

She doesn't ask me what I mean. She just shakes her head and moves toward the closet. "It doesn't matter."

"It does to me."

Shiloh pauses, looking at me like she's never seen me before. There's something on her face, something shocked and a little angry. "Why are you upset? It was a long time ago."

A long time ago can mean anything, but I heard Harlow say that Shiloh has been with the Paine brothers since their first year of exile. She can't be more than thirty, if that, and if

81

she's been with the Paines that long, this must have happened when she was a teenager. Maybe younger. "How long ago?"

She sighs. "You're not going to let this go, are you?"

Since she obviously doesn't want to talk about it, I *should* let it go. One does not successfully seduce another person by dredging out their past trauma. That kind of depth isn't required for sex, and judging by the sheer number of scars, neither of us will be in the mood if I know the full story. With that in mind, moving on is the only thing that makes sense for my goals.

Instead, I open my mouth and tell the truth. "No, love, I'm not going to let this go."

CHAPTER 10

SHILOH

J wasn't thinking when I walked into the bathroom without a change of clothes. I can only blame Monroe's presence on my sheer lack of brain cells and planning. I never let anyone see my legs for this very reason. It creates questions that dredge up stuff I'd rather not think about. For the nearly eight years I've been with the Paine brothers, I've learned valuable lessons.

The first being that trauma doesn't make you special. Everyone has some flavor of it. Mine was horrific, but it's nothing compared to what Broderick has experienced, let alone some of the others who joined up over the years.

More, I don't want to be pitied.

I sure as hell don't want to take a walk down memory lane to the first eighteen years of my life. I've worked hard to move past that time, to forget as much as I'm able. I knew coming to Sabine Valley would be difficult for a number of reasons, but I never expected *this*.

An Amazon demanding to know what happened to me.

The irony would make me laugh if I could find breath in my lungs. Monroe's sitting on that bed, looking sexy as hell in that ridiculous shirt, and ready to commit murder. If only she knew the truth.

She crosses her legs and studies me. "Tell me." After the briefest hesitation. "Please, Shiloh."

I've never felt so naked, and this towel covers me from mid-chest to nearly my knees. Monroe can be conniving and manipulative, but I haven't found her to be overly cruel. At least not to me. I don't understand why she's so insistent on this. "Why?"

"So I can kill them, preferably rather slowly, but I'm willing to do it quickly if you'd rather they not suffer overmuch."

I blink. Wait for the punchline. But Monroe is still staring at me with that intent expression, not a single smile in sight. "You're serious."

"Of course. I never joke about murder. People might not take me seriously when I need to threaten them."

But... That doesn't make any sense. As far as she's aware, I'm not one of her people. She has absolutely no reason to go to battle for me. If anything, as a newly minted Raider, she should be happy for whatever harm I experience. I'm the enemy, after all. "I don't understand."

"I'll use small words." She smiles a little as she says it, but her green eyes stay icy. "Someone tortured you when you were a *child*."

"You say that like children aren't harmed every day in this country—in this city, even."

"Not in the Amazon faction."

I roll my eyes. I can't help it. *There* is the Amazon superiority complex I get hints of from her on occasion. The deep belief that Amazons are somehow better than anyone else, that they aren't capable of being just as monstrous as the rest of the world. She doesn't know how wrong she is. "Amazons are no different than other people at their core. That means you have predators just like the rest of the population, and sometimes predators harm children." Sometimes those predators torture their own children for eighteen long years before that child escapes and runs for their life.

Sometimes.

"You're right." She nods slowly. "It's not unheard of. But we value our children highly. As such, the punishment is..." Monroe trails off, her gaze going distant for a moment. She blinks and she's back, and angrier than ever. "Child predators don't stay in our faction for long. Not alive, at least. The punishment isn't worth the risk. My family has made sure of that."

My mouth goes dry. She says it so simply. As if that's really the truth and not some fantasy she's spun because true harm has never come from inside her household. *She's* never hidden and held her breath, hoping her parents don't come looking. "I never thought you'd be that naive."

"It's not naivety. It's fact." She tucks her blond hair behind her ears, staring intently at me. "It does happen from time to time. I won't lie and say it doesn't, but we don't bother with the song and dance of a public trial or jail time when it comes to someone who harms a child. The investigation is handled quietly to avoid the child being ostracized. Once the facts are assured, someone from the royal family handles it."

She's serious. She really *is* naive. No matter what she thinks, Amazons truly *aren't* different from other communities when it comes to monsters in their midst. I'm more than proof of that. And the royal family taking care of it the moment they know? Don't make me laugh. "Child abuse is prevalent, and most victims never come forward."

"In the rest of the world, yes." She shrugs. "I don't blame them. The justice system leaves a lot to be desired. Predators rarely see the consequences they should."

She truly believes that. That it's as simple as a victim

coming forward and removing the predator, as if there aren't people conditioned to silence by the time they learn how to speak. I open my mouth to keep arguing, but I don't have the heart for it right now. More, I can't say anything that won't reveal far too much about me and my past. Finally, I settle on, "I'm not an Amazon, so I don't see why it matters."

"Aren't you?" Before I can react to *that* statement, she continues. "Do you know where we get our name from?"

"The all-women Greek warriors."

"You're a warrior, Shiloh." She grins suddenly. "Even if you're technically a Raider. If you ever feel like flipping sides, we'd take you in a heartbeat."

Been there, done that, never want to go back. "Pass."

She nods. "I figured you'd say that. Now, stop trying to change the subject and tell me."

Better to get it out and be done with it. Monroe is like a cat. If I try to dodge this subject indefinitely, it will activate all her predator instincts, and she'll latch on to it. Better to give her just enough truth to satisfy her. "Give me a minute."

"Take your time." She says it almost gently, as if she recognizes I need more armor than just a towel to have this conversation. To have *any* conversation. I go to the small dresser that I shoved my stuff in earlier before Monroe and Broderick got back and pull on a pair of sweats and a T-shirt. It's late enough that I doubt even Monroe will get up to no good before she passes out.

Back in the bedroom, I find her exactly where I left her, cross-legged on the bed. As tempting as it is to start pacing, I refuse to give even that much energy to the memories weighing me down. I sink onto the edge of the mattress and stare at the door. "My story sucks, but it could be worse. Poor little rich girl with her religious zealot parents who wanted to burn the sin right out of her." Parents who held prestige by proximity to the Amazon throne, by being distantly related to some past Herald. I'm still not sure why they latched on to *sin* as the thing I contained. For all that Sabine Valley harkens back to ancient practices, the only faction that's truly religious is the Mystic.

Most everyone else gives some kind of nod to the various gods but doesn't dive deep. Unfortunately, my parents were the exception. Best I can tell, they picked a god at random and devoted themselves entirely to her. Astrea. Goddess of many things, but among them...purity.

A purity I never had when they looked at me.

I take a deep breath, hating that it shudders a little. "For all that, they didn't have much in the way of creativity, so they used a curling iron." Sometimes, in my nightmares, I can still smell the scent of my skin burning.

They did so much worse than that, but I'm not about to get into *that* now. Or ever.

I can't help glancing at Monroe. She's got her expression locked down, but the fury in her green eyes makes them almost glow. Rage. Not pity. That's something, at least. There is more than one reason I don't like talking about my past, and it's not simply to avoid being pigeonholed by the location I happened to be born into. I don't want anyone's pity. I survived. I've done more than survive.

Monroe finally says, "No one helped you."

That gives me the strength to answer. "No. No one helped me." Not even the Amazon queen who at least had some hint of what I was experiencing. I was hardly the picture of childhood health the one time she laid eyes on me. "I got myself out when I turned eighteen."

"How old are you, Shiloh?"

My throat feels too tight. "Thirty."

"How long have you been with the Paines?"

I can see where she's going with this, but there's no point in trying to detour. "Seven years, give or take."

Monroe narrows her eyes. "Four years between leaving your parents and finding the Paines."

The sensation of choking gets stronger. I swallow hard. Finding the Paine brothers was sheer luck on my part, and them taking me in was even more luck. That situation could have gone so much worse for me.

They had more than their fair share of trauma, too. Even without asking too many questions, I felt a kinship with Broderick and his brothers and the people they'd gathered around them. I...fit. In a way that I had never experienced before in my life.

I didn't want to come back to this city, but these people are the family I chose. I figured it wouldn't be the same, that I could navigate my way through whatever challenges that arose from the ghosts of my past.

I never bargained on Broderick being paired with the Amazon heir. Or on my being assigned as her permanent guard. Or for her to take such a pointed interest in me.

In short, I never bargained on Monroe.

"It was closer to five before I found them." She opens her mouth to continue questioning me, but I cut in before she gets the words out. "I survived. End of story." I wouldn't talk about what I had to do to survive. I had little life experience when I landed in Chicago. I didn't know how to deal with people, didn't know how to control the rage that bubbled up in me after too many years kept locked down. After I smashed a glass over the head of a customer who grabbed my ass at the restaurant where I worked, I realized customer service wasn't going to get me anything but arrested.

"Yes. You did."

"Violence is easy." My voice is barely above a whisper. I want to stop talking, to cut this off before I bare my still-beating heart for this woman, but the only other person I've talked to about this is Broderick. And even then, I filtered so much, even more than I'm doing now. If he pitied me, I might just die. I exhale slowly. "It came naturally to me—it still does." I guess I really am an Amazon down to my core. The thought might make me laugh if I could work up the energy for it. "I ended up as an enforcer for one of the local *groups*. They taught me everything I needed to know."

"And the Paines?"

At that, I smile a little. "I tried to rob Broderick. He kicked my ass a little and then hauled me back to their sad excuse for a base. Within a couple days, I was taking orders from Abel. I haven't looked back since."

"Quick turnaround."

I look at her. "You've been the heir to the Amazon throne your whole life. You don't know what it's like out there. The Paine brothers actually care about their people. They ask a lot of us, yes, but they value our lives and our safety. That kind of thing isn't common."

"I suppose not." She combs her fingers through her hair, expression still contemplative. "Where did you say you were from, again?"

That surprises a laugh out of me. Does she really think she can trick me into telling her? Absolutely not. "You didn't seriously mean it when you said you wanted to kill my parents."

"When did they start burning you?"

Frustration bubbles up inside me, bringing the truth with it. "I was six. I had been playing with one of the neighborhood boys. Those silly kid games. He kissed me."

She narrows her eyes. "Normal childhood stuff."

"My parents didn't think so." I refuse to revisit that memory; their hateful words, my screams and sobbing.

Monroe nods slowly. "Twelve years is a long time, love. Someone has to balance the scales."

"Stop calling me *love*."

"Do you really want me to stop?" she fires back.

I'm speechless for a moment. Of course, I want her to stop. It's... Damn it. "No."

"Again, stop trying to change the subject. I would like the town name."

I stare. "You're serious."

"I already told you I don't bluff."

She had. I just... "But I'm not one of your people." Not anymore. Not ever as far as she knows. "You don't have to play avenging Valkyrie for me."

"You're mixing up your mythologies." She examines her nails. She's painted them a matte beige color that looks professional and sleek. Monroe seems to change her nails a lot. That surprised me the first week, but now I suspect that doing so calms her and gives her some control when she's feeling out of sorts.

She's been feeling out of sorts a lot lately.

Or maybe I'm just projecting and the reason she changes her nails a lot is because she is a fickle woman who likes pretty things.

"Shiloh."

"But *why?*"

She focuses entirely on me. After a pause where I find myself holding my breath, she crawls across the bed to kneel at my side and take my hand. "Because all children deserve to be protected. I can't go back and save the child you were, but I can rain down hellfire and damnation on those responsible." She gets a faraway look in her eyes. "Though, truly, there's no way at least some people in that town didn't know. They might have lied to themselves about the warning signs or looked away because it's easier than fighting on behalf of someone being victimized, but they at least suspected."

She's right, of course. Someone did know. Her mother. Oh, I can't be sure Aisling was aware of the extent of the abuse, but when she caught sight of me that single time, I was a borderline malnourished child. *Obviously* something was wrong, and she turned away instead of enacting that famous Amazonian justice.

What would Monroe think if she knew that?

It might drive a wedge between her and her mother. Or she might call *me* a liar and that would be the end of us, right here and now.

"Maybe I should burn the whole fucking town down," she muses. "That would certainly send a message."

I don't mean to take her face in my hands. I really don't. But my body moves without permission, and her skin is so fucking soft, completely at odds with the fierce violence in her voice. "Monroe," I say, soft and slow. "You cannot burn down a town for me." *You cannot start a conflict with your own mother for me.*

"I most certainly can." She refocuses on me. "Whether or not I do it is still up for debate. My mother wouldn't like it, but she wouldn't stand in my way."

Saying her mother wouldn't like it is a giant understatement. Monroe takes my breath away. Rationally, I know she's the enemy. No matter what I yelled at Broderick earlier, I recognize that Monroe would feed us all to literal wolves if it meant keeping her people safe. Her people that I don't number among, haven't for well over ten years. That is admirable from where I'm sitting, but since we're on opposite sides of the line, it means she's a threat.

But not even Broderick reacted this strongly to my story.

I don't want my parents dead…I don't think. I won't lie and say that revenge fantasies didn't get me through my teens and early twenties. But things changed when I joined the Paine brothers. For the first time in my life, I was able to focus on the future instead of the past.

Still…

It's a heady thing to have all of Monroe's not-insignificant fury and violence focused on people who hurt me. Focused on them *because* they hurt me. It's enough to make me wonder what would have happened if she was the queen who noticed the child being harmed by someone in her inner circle. Maybe it's naïve to think she would have placed that child's safety above the petty politics that are demanded of the one who holds the throne.

Maybe… But I can't shake the feeling that she would have reigned down the same fire and brimstone that she's threatening to right now.

I don't have a good response for her. I don't even know what I want. "I won't tell you."

"That's okay." I barely have a chance to relax when she says, "I'll ask Broderick instead."

That's a dead end. Broderick doesn't know where I'm from, either. I never told him, and he respected me enough not to ask. Funny how he understood how to respect boundaries for so long, only to lose that skill the second we arrived back in Sabine Valley. I sigh. "You are something else."

"You're not the first one to say it. Though most of the time when people do, it sounds less like a compliment."

I kiss her. Another mistake, but not one I'll take back. I can count on one hand how many people I've told that story to, and while everyone was sympathetic to my experiences, the sheer ferocity of Monroe's leaves me breathless.

What would it be like to be loved by this woman?

Never boring, that's for sure.

She goes still for one long moment, and then she's kissing me back with all the energy she put into plotting my parents' demise. Like she has a thousand things to tell me that she knows I don't want to hear, so she'll convey them with her tongue and lips and teeth instead.

I prefer it this way.

There's no time to worry about this being a mistake or what happens next. I can't even blame tequila or anger. There's just me and Monroe and this kiss.

She laughs against my mouth and pulls away a little bit. "I should offer to kill people on your behalf more often if this is the response I get."

"Monroe?"

"Yes?"

"Shut up." I dig my hands into her hair and kiss her again, toppling her back to the bed. She goes willingly. We land in a tangle of limbs, and I've never regretted putting on clothing so much. I want to be skin to skin. There's nothing to hide any longer. She's seen the scars, she's heard the story, and she still desires me. I don't have to worry about making sure the lights are off before we go farther because there's nothing to hide.

The realization leaves me giddy and a bit drunk off the knowledge.

I sit back on my heels between her spread thighs and look at her. She's rumpled, and her oversized shirt is bunched up around her waist, leaving her lacy white panties on display. They're sexy, but I suspect Monroe could be wearing a paper bag and covered in a weeks' worth of dirt and still be sexy. It's just *her*.

I slide my hands up her toned thighs and hook the sides of her panties. "I'm taking these off."

"Please do."

The urge to rush nearly overwhelms me, but I force myself to go slow, tugging the fabric down an inch at a time, easing it over her hips. She has to move her legs for me to get them down farther, and she does without hesitation, pressing them together. I take advantage, pushing her legs up toward her chest. I leave her panties midway up her thighs, my attention on her bared pussy. She's perfect here, too. Of course she is. She's Monroe.

"Shiloh." She sounds out of breath. "Let me take them off."

"In a moment." I wrap my fist around the fabric, forcing her legs tighter together and using the hold to press them up until she's basically bent in half. Then I drag a single finger down her slit. She's soaked, but then I knew she would be. She just came while I was in the shower, after all.

I ease a single finger into her and then two, enjoying the way her breath hisses out and she clamps around me. For the first time since we met, she's letting me take the lead. It's not submission, not really; more that she's letting me set the pace. I appreciate it. It's been a long time for me, and never like this. Never with all the lights on.

I intend to enjoy every moment of it.

Monroe lets out a breathless laugh. "Gods, you really are a gift, love. You little sadist."

"Hush, I'm enjoying myself." I spread her pussy a little and rub her clit with my thumb. "I'm going to taste you now."

She moans a little. "Do it."

I'm in the process of leaning down to do just that when the door slams open...and Broderick stalks into the room.

CHAPTER 11

BRODERICK

*S*hock steals my breath. Desire follows on its heels, nearly taking me off my feet. I stagger back against the door I just barged through, completely speechless. I expected to find Monroe here, to have another go-round with her before I inform her about the meeting I agreed to with her family.

I didn't expect to find Shiloh kneeling on the bed, two fingers in Monroe's pussy. There's no way to misinterpret this scene. She's not holding Shiloh down. She's bent in fucking half and simply taking what Shiloh gives. "Well, fuck."

Shiloh narrows her eyes, but she doesn't do anything I expect. She doesn't scramble to explain herself or shove away from Monroe. She just pumps slowly into Monroe's pussy. "You should really learn to knock."

I've fucked this up rather spectacularly. There's no other conclusion to come to. That I'm standing here, watching the woman I love with the woman I both hate and desire... "What's going on here?"

Monroe gives a breathless laugh that turns into a little

moan when Shiloh does something with her fingers. "I'd think that's readily apparent."

"Broderick." Shiloh's hazel eyes are merciless. "Turn around. Walk out the door. Come back in the morning."

"The morning?" Monroe shivers. "Someone's ambitious."

"Hush." Shiloh pins me with a look. "Unless you have something vital to share that needs to be discussed right this moment, it can wait until morning."

"Okay," I finally manage. I move slowly, my body obeying even as my mind rebels. This isn't how it's supposed to be. None of this is how it's supposed to be. I open the door and step back into the hall. The second it closes behind me, the strength goes out of my body, and I slump back against it.

I can...hear them.

Monroe's throaty laugh. Shiloh's low murmur.

And then Monroe starts moaning.

I wish I could say she's just putting on a show for me, but she made that exact same sound when I was inside her. It's not fake. It's not for my benefit. It's because Shiloh is doing something to her that is driving her out of her mind.

I should walk away and come back in the morning. Standing here and listening to them is an exquisite form of torture. Jealousy sinks its barbs into me and digs deep. That *Monroe* has caught Shiloh's interest boggles my mind. That Shiloh seems to soften some of Monroe's edges... I don't know what to think about that, either. It's as if my brain simply cannot compute it. Both women have clear roles in my life, for better or worse, and they're acting against those expectations.

"Broderick?"

I open my eyes to find my older brother standing there. Being back in Sabine Valley agrees with Abel. He's lost a little of the tightness in his shoulders that I thought a permanent fixture. Sure enough, I can see Eli over his shoulder. The man is typing away at something on his phone, his handsome face lit with the screen, but his proximity has my brother softening even if his attention is obviously on something else. There's no other explanation for it.

Abel's...happy.

I should be happy for him. He deserves happiness after everything he's sacrificed to keep us alive and together. If it were just Harlow, it wouldn't be a problem. She's fierce, and she obviously cares a great deal about this faction and the people in it. I suspect she's just as ruthless as Abel, but she still provides a bit of a counterweight to some of his ideas and plans.

But it's not just Harlow.

He's not part of a contented couple. He's in a throuple, and the third person is Eli fucking Walsh. Even standing in the same space as Eli right now has me remembering how smoke coated my throat as we ran for our lives. I realize Eli wasn't directly responsible, but damn if I can let it go. No matter what else is true, it's been almost too easy to slip right back into our roles in the Raider faction.

As if nothing has changed, when the truth is that *everything* has changed.

Look at Abel, hardened to someone I barely recognize some days. And Ezekiel, who's more monster than the sweet brother I once knew. Even Gabriel and Donovan have changed, and they're the most easy-going of the seven of us.

I've changed too.

I stare at my brother, not sure what the fuck I'm supposed to say. He knows it, too. Abel is many things, but he's not a fool. His dark gaze flicks to the door at my back as a particularly loud moan sounds. "Monroe and...Shiloh?"

"Yes."

He raises his eyebrows a fraction of an inch. "Interesting. Not surprising, but interesting."

That overrides my desire to be literally anywhere else. "What are you talking about? Shiloh's a good girl. It's surprising as fuck."

Abel snorts. "You've always had tunnel vision when it comes to that woman. She's not an innocent, and Monroe might be a gigantic pain in the ass, but she's magnetic."

"Monroe's also happy to stick it to you however she can." Eli doesn't look up from his phone. "No wonder she's set her eyes on Shiloh."

"No one fucking asked *you*."

Abel gives me a long look as if weighing the venom in my voice. I know I should tone it down, should just let shit go, but I don't know how to. I don't even know where to begin. "He's right."

"I'm aware of that," I grit out.

"Then stop fucking around and handle your business." He glances down the hall and then back at me. "Everyone knows you're sleeping in one of the spare bedrooms because you're scared of your Bride."

"I'm not—"

"It makes us look weak."

I welcome the surge of anger and push off the door. "Who the fuck are we looking weak to, Abel? It's no one's business where I sleep."

"Wrong." He slides his hands into his pockets, every inch the arrogant prick. "All of our brothers are doing their duty —except you. You don't think Monroe's running to tell her mother how weak the Paine brothers are when the man she's handfasted to avoids her? When he can't fucking handle her?" Abel shakes his head slowly. "You know better."

He's right. I hate that he's right. "Mind your own goddamned business."

"This is my business. I didn't fight and win so you could

get cold feet now. Handle your shit, Broderick. Or I'll do it for you."

My verbal brakes disappear. "Won't your happy little relationship go up in smoke if you fuck Monroe? That'd be a shame."

Abel moves so fast, I never see it coming. He grabs the front of my shirt and swings me around to slam into the wall opposite the door I was just leaning on. The impact rattles me, and it rattles me worse when he jerks me forward and slams me back again. His face has gone cold. "I don't need my cock to handle the Monroe problem, Broderick. This is a big house. Lot of stairs. Be a fucking shame if she fell down them and snapped that pretty neck of hers."

I stare at him. We're the same height, but he's got more than a few pounds of muscle on me. That's not the only difference between us. Abel is ruthless in a way I'll never be able to match. He's not bluffing. I swallow hard. "You'd risk breaking the treaty by killing her."

"Fuck no." He barely lets me get a breath out before he continues, "But accidents happen, and we can't be liable. It's a known fact that she likes to slip her handler so she can get into trouble. It'll be a pain in the ass to deal with the fallout, but better that than have her making one of us the laughing-stock of Sabine Valley. Our position is too precarious to allow it, and you'd realize that if you pulled your head out of your ass long enough to look around and take stock of the situation."

"What the *fuck*, Abel?"

"Abel." Eli is there, taking my brother's shoulders and pulling him off me. Or at least trying to. "That's enough."

My brother gives me one last shake and releases me, stepping away and sliding his hands back into his pockets. He shrugs off Eli's hands, but gives the man a look so sexually charged, it makes me mildly uncomfortable. When Abel speaks again, he sounds cold and perfectly composed. "No need to get so emotional, Broderick. If you're not willing to solve the problem, then I will. I'll do what I always do when it comes to our people—clean up their messes. *Your* mess this time. You're welcome, by the way." He turns and strides down the hallway, Eli easily falling into step beside him.

Trust Abel to cut to the heart of the situation without a shred of mercy.

Figure this shit out, or Monroe dies.

I should be grateful. She's the enemy. Not to mention the whole seducing-Shiloh thing.

Except…

Shiloh's right. Monroe was only nineteen when that shit went down eight years ago. She was heir, yes, but she's not the one who made the call to ally with Eli's father in his attempt to wipe our family off the face of the earth. I doubt she was part of the raiding party, either.

She might be a pain in the ass and an Amazon, but neither of those things should be a death sentence. And as much as the thought of her and Shiloh together makes me feel twisted up and fucked in the head, *that* isn't a death sentence, either.

Damn my brother for backing me into a corner. I can't in good conscience sit back and let Abel take care of things in that particular *Abel* way.

Which means I have to do as he said and get my house in order.

That starts now.

I glance at the door. Or, rather, it starts in the morning.

* * *

I DON'T SLEEP. Of course I don't. My brain is too busy running a montage of devastating and infuriating images behind my eyes. Shiloh and Monroe. In bed, making each other orgasm until they're too exhausted to continue.

As a result, I'm already frazzled as fuck when I dress and head down to Monroe's room, far too early to be polite. It doesn't matter. I can't find anything worse than what I walked in on last night.

Worse...or better?

I take a deep breath and knock on the door. The barest pause and then Shiloh's voice emerges. "Come in."

I don't actually expect to find them still fucking, but it's jarring to find both women sitting on the bed. Shiloh is wearing her customary jeans and plain top. Monroe has changed into jeans and another oversized top that should dwarf her figure but somehow manages to show it off instead.

I glance at the couch, taking in the blankets and pillow there. They...didn't sleep together? I don't know if that's a relief or not. I don't what to think at all anymore.

I push the thought away. "We need to talk."

"Do we?"

I blink at Shiloh. "Are you going to be pissed at me forever?" The thought hollows out my stomach. I hope to the gods I haven't ruined things between us permanently. Surely there's a way to figure this out and reclaim our friendship. As much as I want to prioritize that, she *really* won't forgive me if my negligence gets Monroe killed.

"I don't know. Are you going to be a raging dickhead forever?"

Monroe laughs and leans against Shiloh. There's a faint flush to her cheeks, and her eyes are heavy-lidded with remembered pleasure. The sight sends a bolt of lust through me, but I muscle it back. "I'm sorry," I grit out. "How many times do I have to say it before it sticks?"

Shiloh looks at me for a long moment. "Until you actually mean it—which you don't right now. But let's move on."

I hate this new distance between us. I hate that I feel like I don't know her anymore. Or that maybe Abel and Monroe are right and maybe I only ever saw a filtered version of her. The realization isn't a comfortable one. I want to ask her what the hell happened, but she won't thank me for the question.

Focus.

"Jasper has requested Monroe's presence." I glance at her. "And Winry's."

Monroe perks up at that. "When?"

"This morning."

Shiloh smooths her hair back. "Convenient timing. I have to update Maddox and Cohen, so you can escort Monroe to the meeting."

It was the plan, but having her dictate it to me in that cold voice sets my teeth on edge. It makes me want to... I muscle the urge down. This isn't Monroe mouthing off. This is *Shiloh*.

Up until the shitshow at Lammas, I wouldn't have even had the urge to put her in her place. It's like having sex with Monroe woke something inside me that had been slumbering my entire life. I don't know how the fuck I'm supposed to deal with it now.

Or maybe it's wasn't Monroe at all. Maybe it was coming back to Sabine Valley that changed things permanently. "Afterward, the three of us are going to have a chat."

"We'll see." Shiloh gets up and walks into the bathroom. She shuts the door with a finality that makes me want to kick it the fuck down.

"Goddamn it."

"Problem?" Monroe stands and stretches. Her clothing isn't suggestive in the least, but I can't get over the image of

Shiloh bending her in half, the flowy white fabric of her shirt bunched up around her ribs, leaving her naked from the waist down. The memory sends a wave of heat through me.

I feel like I'm being torn in two. There was a smart course of action, the logical way to proceed. I know there was. It dissipates through my fingers like smoke. All that's left is what the feral creature inside me wants.

I move before I can think of the thousands of reasons not to and wrap my fist around Monroe's blond hair. She doesn't tense, doesn't fight me. She simply goes fluid and lets me tilt her head back as I step close enough that we're damn near plastered together. "Keep that smart mouth in line, Monroe."

She holds my gaze and licks her lips. "Oh, so we're just going to gloss over the fact that I won that bet fair and square? Interesting that you won't honor your word."

Rage crystalizes inside me. How does she do this? How does she slide beneath my skin "I'll honor my word."

"Good boy."

I tug on her hair, a little too hard. "We'll discuss it later."

"As you wish." Monroe shivers. For all that she's chaos incarnate, she isn't faking her attraction to me. I'd bet my life on it. I don't know if that makes this shit better or worse.

I release her and start for the door. "Let's go."

I half expect her to start some shit, but Monroe follows along obediently and silently... At least until we're in the hall and have shut the door behind us. "You're a giant fool, do you know that?"

Even knowing better than to take the bait, I still chomp down on it with all my strength. "You don't know what you're talking about."

"That's rich coming from you." She manages to match my longer stride with seeming ease, which irritates me beyond all reason. Monroe laughs. "You all but drove Shiloh right into my arms. What did you say to piss her off so thoroughly?"

"That's none of your business."

"If you say so." She shrugs. "I honestly have no motivation to convince you to stop being a pushy neanderthal. It's working out well for me."

I spin on her, but she's already moving. Monroe catches my wrist and shoves it away. "Let's get one thing straight, shall we? I might like some slap and tickle when it comes to fucking, but you will *not* touch me in anger outside of that. Do you understand me?"

It's as if someone else takes control of my body. I stalk her across the hallway, and she lets me, though she narrows her green eyes in suspicion. I don't stop until I plant my hands on the wall on either side of her body. "It's *you* who needs to understand me, *Bride*." I lean down until we're face to face. "Everything we do is in conjunction to fucking. That's all it is. Aside from the alliance this handfasting brought us, you're just a pretty pussy to me and nothing more."

She laughs in my face. "Gods, you're too much. Cute, Broderick, really cute."

Still acting on pure instinct, I spin her around and step forward, pressing my front to her back. She drags in a harsh breath, but I'm not finished yet. I dip my hand beneath her loose shirt and hook the front of her jeans with my thumb. "This fucking enough for you, Monroe?"

"This is hardly foreplay," she snarls.

I don't hesitate. It takes half a second to unbutton her jeans and drag down the zipper. Then my hand is in her pants and, *fuck*, she's so goddamn wet. I know it's not for me. This is the aftermath of what Shiloh did to her last night. The jeans are too tight to do what I want, so I curse and move back enough to shove them down her hips. I don't give a fuck that we're in the middle of the hallway. I don't care who might see. I just need to put this siren of a woman in her place, just one single fucking time.

I shift to the side so I can spear two fingers into her pussy from behind and rub her clit with my free hand. For her part, she hasn't moved her stance, her hands still plastered to the wall where she caught herself. I stroke her, tormenting myself with how fucking good she feels. "Did she lick your pussy, Monroe?" The words feel dragged from me. "Did she fuck you with her tongue?"

"Yes." She arches her hips, trying to take my fingers deeper. Monroe lets her head fall forward as I circle her clit just the way she likes. "She made me come so fucking hard. I can't wait to do it again."

I don't give in to the temptation to increase my pace. I just hold steady as Monroe starts to shake in my arms. For all her shit-talking, she does come sweetly. She whimpers and clamps around my fingers hard enough to make me groan. I lean down and nip her earlobe. "You might have me for a week, Monroe, but make no mistake—I'll be having *you* during that time. Over and over again."

She barely lets me get my hands out of the way before she yanks up her jeans and fastens them. It's only when her clothing is back in place that she finally looks at me. "Can't wait."

For the first time since I met her, I can't shake the feeling that she just lied to me.

CHAPTER 12

MONROE

I have never run from a fight in my life. What just happened with Broderick can hardly be called a fight, and yet I feel like I'm fleeing it all the same as I step into the library with him shadowing my steps. My body still tingles with the aftermath of that orgasm, only made stronger by the few I had last night with Shiloh.

They're using me as a battleground between them.

It was what I intended all along. The moment I realized how deep the emotions ran between those two, how determined they were to avoid stepping on that particular landmine, I planned to dance all over their buttons.

What I didn't intend?

To feel…strange while doing it.

Neither of them really want *me*. They want each other, and I'm the inciting event that will end with them fucking. I'll go down at the footnote in their relationship, assuming they both survive what comes next. Sabine Valley is not a peaceful city, and the forced truce between the Raiders and the other two factions will only hold the year.

If that.

There are no guarantees in this life, especially in this city.

I just... I didn't expect to like Shiloh so much. I meant every word I said to her about being the conductor of justice for the harms committed against her as a child. Even thinking about it has anger simmering inside me. I have few lines—one can't be precious when they're going to be the next queen of the Amazons—but harming children is an unforgivable offense. Shiloh was right; we've had our share of predators in the Amazon faction. But we do not victim-blame, and we do not make excuses for them so they can harm more innocents.

We make fucking examples of them.

Obviously I know the greater world isn't like that. I can't say the rest of Sabine Valley conducts itself in the same way. But knowing that *Shiloh* experienced torture at her parents' hands...

I clench my fists. I want to see them burn.

"Monroe?"

I give myself a mental shake and have my expression under control by the time I turn to face Broderick. "Yes, husband?"

He searches my face. I've never seen a person so conflicted with themself. His identity seems to be so wrapped up in being the calm Paine, the rational brother, that he doesn't seem to realize that he loves being harsh and brutal. No one can fake how he is with me. Especially when he seems to hate it so.

Right now, he's feeling irrational guilt and wondering if he pushed me too far in the hallway. I should leave him hanging, should twist the knife every chance I get and use that guilt to manipulate him. It's what my mother would do, what I'd advise any other Amazon to do in this situation. I am not without weapons, but I'd be a fool to turn away from one so potentially lucrative.

I don't know why I open my mouth and say, "We're good, Broderick."

Instantly, his expression shuts down. "I don't know what you're talking about."

"Oh? You weren't just whipping yourself for being a big, bad villain and forcing yourself on poor, defenseless me?"

He flinches. "That's nothing to joke about."

"You're right. It's not." I can't quite help myself. I close the distance between us and run my hands up his chest. I lower my voice, until he has to lean down to catch my words. "Broderick, if I didn't want what you do to me, I would gut you and leave you to bleed out in the hallway. No one, not any of your brothers, not a single Raider in this faction, not even Shiloh, could stop me."

He doesn't relax. "I'm bigger than you. Stronger."

Gods, this man's respectable streak is tiresome.

Even knowing it will give away my edge, I bend down, dip my hand into the open edge of my boot and draw the long knife I lifted off Shiloh when she wasn't paying attention the other day. "I would have gutted you," I repeat.

Broderick blinks. "You have a knife."

"Yes." Nothing more to say to that. With a sigh, I turn the knife around and offer it to him, hilt first. "I suppose you'll be taking this, since it's a prohibited item for a Bride to have and all that."

He gets a strange look on his face. "Keep it."

"Excuse me?"

"Promise me you won't stab someone without cause, and you can keep it."

Now it's my turn to blink. Surely he's not going to actually let me keep the knife. It's a weapon, and Broderick isn't the kind of fool who hands his enemies weapons without a fight. "Define *cause*."

"Monroe."

I sigh. "Okay, fine. I won't stab someone unless I feel directly threatened. Is that good enough?"

This is where he crushes my fledgling hope, dim though it is, and tells me that no way will he allow me to keep it, promise or no. What good is the word of an Amazon to a Raider, after all? But he simply nods. "Good enough. Now put that away before your uncle and sister get here."

"I don't suppose you'll wait outside while we talk."

He gives me the look that question deserves. "I will give you the relative privacy of reading a book over there while you talk." He points at a short chair tucked back within the bookshelves.

It's far enough away from the couches and chairs in the center of the room that it *should* actually offer privacy, but I've spent more evenings than I care to count in the last three weeks wandering this library. The acoustics are such that any conversation held within this room seems to echo to each corner of it.

As soon as I realized *that*, my fantasy of fucking Shiloh against some bookshelves went up in smoke—at least if we didn't want to get caught.

I slip the knife back into my boot and give Broderick a brilliant smile. "Works for me." I don't actually expect my family to have much in the way of information to impart. They've been trapped in this place, collateral against my good behavior while I travel back and forth from the Amazon faction. Still, there's plenty of gossip to share, and I just *miss* Winry. We've only seen each other a handful of times since Lammas, almost always with the other Brides around.

If Cohen's mistreating her, I'll fucking kill him.

I don't have to wait long for Winry to show. My little sister is practically glowing, her pale cheeks pink and her blond hair looking particularly bouncy. Oh, she has a bitchy look on her face, but she's obviously not suffering through being a Bride or being tortured by Cohen. That's something at least. She's wearing a pair of sweats and a sweatshirt, both of which I'm *certain* aren't hers. They dwarf her curvy body, baggy in a way that can't be intentional. I frown at them. "Are you stealing Cohen's clothing?"

She blushes a bright red. "These are Maddox's, actually."

I stare. "You're wearing the clothing of your husband's best friend."

If anything, she gets redder. "Don't you dare accuse me of causing problems, Monroe. It's not like I'm sneaking around behind Cohen's back."

I didn't think my little sister could shock me. Apparently I was wrong. Obviously, I knew she was sharing the room with both men, but sharing more than that? "I'm going to need you to explain yourself."

"*I'm* going to need you to mind your own damn business." She crosses her arms over her generous chest. "You're in enough trouble as it is."

I'm about to ask her what the fuck she's talking about, but our uncle chooses that moment to walk into the room. Jasper, quite frankly, looks like shit. He's lost weight since I saw him last, and he wasn't a particularly large man to begin with. His beard has also become long and almost unkept. If not for the clean clothes on his body, he might be mistaken for some mountain man wandering into the city by accident. His smile when he sees us, though, is bright enough. "Hey, girls."

"Uncle Jasper." Winry throws herself at him, hugging him for all she's worth. He was a late-in-life baby for our grandmother, so he's only a few years older than me and seven years older than Winry. She's been greeting him exactly like this ever since she could walk.

He keeps an easy arm around her shoulders and walks over to pull me into a hug, too. "How are you holding up?" he murmurs.

"Oh, you know me. Causing chaos and sowing discord."

Jasper gives me a long look and then glances over my shoulder to where I can practically feel Broderick drilling a hole in the back of my head. "Your groom is spiraling."

"Pity. I can't imagine why."

Instead of laughing like I expect him to, he sighs. "I'm not one to tell you how to go about your business, Monroe. Aisling has taught you well, and you're more than ready to take over running the faction."

I raise my brows. "I'm sensing a *but* coming."

"*But*." He lowers his voice. "You can't afford to underestimate the Paines. You were still so damn young when they were run out of town. Don't bite off more than you can chew."

I blink. Of all the people I might have expected to underestimate me, Jasper never numbered among them. He's the perfect Amazon, especially when it comes to supporting the women in the family. "It's not like you were that much older than me, Grandfather Time. You were only twenty-two."

"Old enough to make decisions I regret."

I wonder about that. Best I can tell, he's been pretty damn happy with Beatrix of the Mystics for the last eight years. No one on the outside looking in would begin to guess that he still had unresolved feelings for Ezekiel Paine.

That's personal, though.

"I was briefed on the history," I finally say. For all that I was technically named second-in-command when the coup happened, the truth is more complicated. I spent most of that year being run ragged while learning the ropes of the company my mother is CEO of. It wasn't until later that I was also trained on some of the more brutal aspects of running our faction. I didn't know the assault on the Paine family was going down until after it had already happened.

I never thought to be grateful for that, but I find myself exhaling slowly all the same.

Still, Jasper's lack of faith hurts. "I can take care of myself." I glance from him to Winry. "I'm more worried about you two. Your pairings are both...not ideal."

"I have it under control." They say it together and then share a rueful look.

Jasper clears his throat. "Obviously being Ezekiel's Bride is challenging, but it's fine."

Winry tucks her hair behind her ears. She's blushing again. "Cohen is an asshole, but it's nothing I can't handle."

"An asshole," I repeat. Cohen Paine is a whole lot more than an asshole. He's a fucking *monster*. I don't use that word lightly, but it's the truth. Every faction has people who have to be willing to do the dirty work. I try not to issue any orders that I won't be able to do myself, especially if it involves blood on someone's hands, but some tasks aren't possible for a queen to do herself. Cohen serves that purpose for Abel. "Winry—"

"You need to worry about yourself," Jasper says in a low voice. "I don't care how capable you are, Monroe. You're in over your head. Don't try to break the Bridal peace."

I snort. "Do you know my mother at all?" The topic hasn't come up yet, but it's only been three weeks since Lammas. It will sooner or later. My mother has never been one to sit back and let a situation unfold without her input. She's still furious that Abel Paine pulled one over on us, which means she'll be angling for some kind of revenge before too long. As her heir, I support her in whatever way she sees fit, whether I agree with it or not.

"The handfasting between a victor and their Bride is a tradition that goes back to the beginning of Sabine Valley. Not even Aisling should fuck with that, and you're smart enough to know it."

"Some traditions were made to be broken." I don't believe it, even as I say it.

Jasper holds my gaze. "Not this one. No matter who got their pride stung with what happened Lammas night, the fact remains that the Paine brothers are more than justified in wanting revenge for what happened the night of their exile."

"And yet not a single one among their Brides had anything to do with giving those orders."

Winry snorts. "You know why they did that."

Yeah, I do. What better way to punish the responsible parties than by taking their loved ones? It's rather genius in its cruelty, and I might admire it if my family weren't wrapped up in the mess.

My mother still hasn't told me what the fuck she was thinking all those years ago, throwing her support in with Deacon Walsh, of all people. Everyone knew that the Paine brothers' father, Bauer Paine, was dangerous and unpredictable, but Deacon Walsh was hardly better. If he hadn't died a few years after taking over the Raider faction, if his son Eli weren't a better leader, Sabine Valley would have been in even worse shape than it originally was. My mother is an expert tactician. Why the hell did she make that call?

Now she's got egg on her face, and she wants the responsible parties to pay. Which, of course, I agree that the Paine brothers need to pay—especially Broderick. It's just... I gave my word to Harlow that I wouldn't stab them in the back. Even considering such an option puts my sister and uncle in danger. It doesn't matter that Cohen hasn't traumatized Winry and Jasper seems to be dealing with Ezekiel well enough; neither of them can stand against Abel if he decides to punish me for stepping out line.

The reminder makes my stomach tight. I paste a smile on my face. "Don't worry about it. I have everything under control."

I hope like hell that I'm not lying.

CHAPTER 13

"The Amazons are going to be a problem."

I rub my temples with my fingertips and try to smother my frustration. It's not Maddox or Cohen's fault that I want to wring Broderick's neck, and they won't thank me for being an asshole because of it. It's also not their fault that even mentioning the Amazons as a whole is enough to raise my blood pressure.

Still, Maddox's comment doesn't make sense. "I would hardly say Monroe's been on her best behavior, but the fact remains that she hasn't killed anyone, and, while the Amazons have removed every listening device I've planted in her office, she's going about her workdays like normal." She might be driving *me* to distraction, but that's a personal thing.

Cohen leans forward and crosses his arms over the back of the chair he's straddling. "Aisling Rhodius is a fucking shark, and she's furious that we stole her precious little heir. They're going to be a problem."

Maddox nods. "Aisling's been calling Winry regularly, and while they don't appear to be talking about anything important, Winry is becoming more and more stressed out by those conversations." His gaze goes flinty, but I can't tell if it's because of Winry's distress or Aisling's machinations. Maybe it's both.

"You think it's code."

He shrugs. "I don't know if it's as refined as that, but there are obviously layers that we're missing. It could be the same with Aisling and Monroe."

I think back over all the times Aisling has come into Monroe's office and gone over things or attended meeting after meeting. Could something have slipped into those interactions without my noticing? It's more than likely, especially since I try to avoid Aisling as much as I can.

I frown. "It's possible. Probable even. Monroe has one hell of a poker face." At least when she's not coming all over my hands and face. She didn't bother to hide her delight or desire even once when we were in bed last night.

"Shiloh?"

I realize I'm blushing, but there's no way to combat it. I clear my throat. "I'll keep an ear out for anything that might be out of the ordinary. Do you want me to wear a wire?"

"No." Cohen shakes his head. "We don't have the manpower to listen back through, and even if we did, you're more likely to pick up on stuff than someone is over a recording. You spend most of your time with her and in that building."

It's not an accusation. It's pure fact. They assigned me to keep watch over Monroe, and that's what I'm doing. The only reason for the guilt threatening to choke me is my own conscience. Monroe has gone to my head in a way I never could have anticipated. "Do you think they're planning something? Even with the hostages involved?"

"We can't afford to assume anything." Cohen's expression doesn't change. There's no indication of the rattled man I spoke to earlier. It's comforting, in a way. At least *this* is back to normal.

I'm going to have to face the consequences for the move I pulled last night with Monroe and Broderick. There's no way around it. I still can't quite believe I went there. I'm still so fucking *angry*. It doesn't make sense. Broderick might be acting like a jerk and being high-handed, but he's always been overprotective of me. And, frankly, Monroe just offered to murder an entire town for me. I don't understand why her words, while shocking, didn't fill me with any anger at all. Broderick, on the other hand, makes me want to shove him out a window these days.

It's Sabine Valley. It has to be, because the only other option is that our friendship is ruined beyond repair, and I can't handle the thought of *that* being true.

"Shiloh?" Maddox shifts. "You good? You seem...off."

As much as I want to lie to him, Maddox has known me so long, he'll see right through the deception. I sigh. "It's personal."

He narrows his eyes. The man is too smart by half, and if he seems like the kinder, gentler half of Cohen, it's only surface-deep. He's just as ruthless and just as willing to make the unpopular, hard calls if it serves the mission. "Is it—"

The door opens behind me before he can finish. I tense, half expecting Broderick to come barreling through and start spouting high-handed nonsense again, but it's Ezekiel. He's wearing slacks, a tank top, and suspenders. And...nothing else. On anyone else, that would be a complete outfit. For Ezekiel, with his fondness for three-piece suits, he's practically naked. Even his red hair is mussed, and his full beard looks haggard.

He gives a mocking salute. "You called, Cohen."

Cohen stares. I can practically see him categorizing the little details of his brother's appearance and coming to the same conclusion I am; Ezekiel is unraveling. He finally says, "You're late."

"I didn't want to come." Ezekiel wanders to the empty chair and drops into it. "Let's wrap this up quickly."

Cohen still hasn't moved. He hasn't seemed to breathe at all. The tension in the room spikes, and I want to be anywhere but here. I might not have personal experience with it, but even I know that siblings clash. I don't think normal siblings clash like the Paines do when things get tense—especially when Abel isn't around to knock some sense into them. Normally, Cohen doesn't get involved in the squabbles, but if what happened earlier is any indication, he's off his game right now.

Maddox leans forward. All his attention seems to be on Ezekiel, but he's angled his body slightly toward Cohen. "We need to talk about Jasper."

Ezekiel doesn't blink. "There's nothing to talk about. He's been tied up in my bed for the last three weeks. The first time he's talked with his family is today, and you can take *that* up with Broderick."

Tied up in his bed...

For *three weeks?*

I haven't seen Jasper since the first time the Brides gathered after Lammas, but surely Ezekiel doesn't mean he's literally had the man tied to his bed this entire time?

"And Beatrix?" Cohen's voice is terrifyingly even.

"Tied to my bed, too." Ezekiel snorts. "Did you think I'd let her run around freely?"

It's Maddox who pushes slowly to his feet. "You have an Amazon and a Mystic tied up in your bed, and they've been there for *three fucking weeks?* Are you out of your fucking mind? That constitutes torture, and it will violate the handfasting your brothers worked so hard to put into place."

I glance at the door, but moving right now means

bringing attention to myself. Better to just sit still and wait this out. Selfishly, I'm glad that Ezekiel is getting their full attention—and taking it off me. There was a time in my life when I desperately wanted siblings, but conversations like this remind me that it's not a bad thing to be an only child.

Not to mention, it meant I was the only one who suffered through my parents' abuse.

"Don't worry about it." Ezekiel sounds completely unconcerned. "They're fine."

"No, Zeke. I'm going to fucking worry about it." Cohen's still speaking softly. On anyone else, that would be reassuring. With Cohen, it means he's a breath away from violence. "We cannot let anything jeopardize this peace until we're ready for it to end. You're setting us up to repeat history with both the Amazon and Mystic factions coming for our heads."

Maddox curses. "I knew it was a mistake to give you Jasper as your Bride. You have too much history together."

"Mind your own fucking business." Ezekiel says it mildly, but his hand drifts to his hip.

Best guess, he has some kind of weapon stashed there. If he attacks Maddox, Cohen will beat the shit out of him. If it were any of the other Paine brothers, I'd keep my mouth shut, but Cohen is unpredictable. Especially where Maddox is concerned. I don't believe for a second he'd kill Ezekiel, but I also don't know if he'd stop before his brother is a bloody pulp, and that's a mess I have no interest in cleaning up.

I cross my legs, drawing their attention. "Beatrix came here of her own choice."

Cohen stares. "And?"

She's a fool, but no one in this room will thank me for pointing it out. I can't imagine facing the choice she did, where her partner was taken from her by a man who used to be their best friend. Beatrix and Jasper aren't married, but it wouldn't have mattered if they were. A Bridal handfasting supersedes all previous relationships and completely nullifies them. Theoretically, the Bride could go back to their spouse after the year is over, but it's a tangled situation no matter which way you look at it.

I can't say I'd make a different choice in her situation, but that doesn't change the fact that she made a shitty one. She should have stayed free instead of offering herself up as yet another hostage and effectively putting the safety of the entire Paine faction in Ezekiel's unhinged hands.

He wasn't always like this. I joined up with the Paine brothers in the first year after they were driven out of Sabine Valley. Back then, Ezekiel was sweet. A kind man who went through a traumatic event. But, as the years passed and information from Sabine Valley came in bits and pieces, I watched him cut off those soft parts of himself and offer them up on the altar of vengeance. When he heard that Jasper and Beatrix had made their relationship official?

He went cold, and he's never come back.

Still, even Ezekiel has lines left.

I hope.

I steel my spine and hold his gaze. "Are you torturing them?"

His lips quirk in what, on any other man, might be called a smile. "They're paying penance." When I just stare, he relents. "No permanent harm is being done."

Maddox tenses, and I make a show of rolling my eyes. When facing down a predator, it's vital to never show fear. I keep my voice nice and even. "Did they consent to paying penance, Ezekiel?"

He stares, trying to intimidate me with his cold amber eyes. I regularly deal with Cohen, so I'm used to that thousand-yard stare. I simply wait. Finally, he curses. "Yes."

Immediately, Cohen and Maddox relax. Maddox finally

says, "Keep an eye on Jasper. If he says or does anything that might be useful—"

"His only use is as a hostage." Ezekiel pushes to his feet. "If we're done here?"

"Go," Cohen bites out.

We sit silently for a long moment after the door slams behind him. Maddox grips Cohen's shoulder, the smallest touch, the tiniest reassurance. It speaks to how rattled both of them are that they let even this small moment slip by in the presence of another person. Normally, they keep things strictly business in public.

No reason to feel a strange sort of jealousy witnessing evidence of their relationship. *Their* friendship hasn't been damaged by being in Sabine Valley the way mine and Broderick's has. If anything, they seem stronger than ever. Then again, Broderick and I have never been intimate the way Cohen and Maddox have.

I can't think about *that*, though. No matter my attraction to Broderick, no matter how much he's irritating me right now, the fact remains that he is one of the most important people in my life. Eventually things will settle down and we'll reclaim those soft moments and the easy conversation and everything that's disappeared between us.

We have to.

I attempt a smile, even as my insides twist uncomfortably. "Ezekiel was messing with you. You just weren't asking the right questions."

Cohen releases a long breath. "The right questions, huh? Let's not make that same mistake twice." He holds my gaze. "Are you fucking Monroe, Shiloh?"

Part of me expected the question. It's the one I would have asked in their position, with the information they have at hand. Even after trying to prepare myself, my face goes so hot that I get a little light-headed. There's no point in lying. If they haven't figured it out already, they will soon because Monroe is about as subtle as a brick through a window. I shouldn't like that about her, especially when it's complicating my life right now.

I finally nod. "Yes."

I expect them to be angry—or at least irritated—but Cohen slaps his hand against his thigh and stands. "That will be useful. Stick to that woman. She's making moves, and we need to figure out what they are. I don't care how you find out, whether it's listening in during the day or at night with pillow talk. Just get it done."

"Okay," I say slowly.

For his part, Maddox looks conflicted. "Does Broderick know?"

No use lying about this, either. "Yes."

They exchange a glance. Maddox finally says, "You want to talk to him, or should I?"

"I'll do it." Cohen starts for the door. "Right about the time I break up that little family get-together he arranged."

Maddox waits until he's gone to say, "I hope you know what you're doing. Monroe isn't like our people. She's looking out for the Amazons, and she's not about to let something as soft as emotions get in her way, no matter how fond of you she is."

Just like that, my uncomfortableness is gone, replaced by the anger that's quickly becoming my go-to emotion. I have fought and won and lost and bled with these people, and all it takes is Broderick losing his head for them to start looking at me like I'm a damsel in distress. I'm a fucking warrior. Gods, I used to be an *Amazon*. I know more about what Amazons are capable of than anyone in this compound, Brides excluded.

I am so damn tired of being underestimated.

I hardly recognize myself as I stand and pin him with a

look. "Have I once, in the entire time we've known each other, given you reason to question my conduct?"

Maddox opens his mouth, seems to reconsider what he was about to say, and finally shrugs. "No."

Yeah, I didn't think so. "I understand that you and the others see me as some sort of stand-in little sister, but I am not an innocent. I haven't been one since long before I ever knew the Paine brothers existed. I can handle Monroe." I don't know if the last bit is the truth, but I'm also not about to let my infatuation with the woman undermine my loyalty to the people I've spent the last seven years shoulder to shoulder with.

I *hate* that everyone is questioning that, as if I'm a babe in the woods who will be swept away by the first person showing me a kind word. Though I wouldn't call anything about Monroe *kind*.

Even if she was so fucking sweet on my tongue last night.

"I have it under control," I finally say.

"For all our sakes, I sure as fuck hope you do."

CHAPTER 14

BRODERICK

*W*atching the Rhodius family speak softly to each other makes me so fucking uncomfortable. I have spent so much of my life hating the other factions, a hate that only ramped up after the night that changed everything. From what we've pieced together since, Aisling worked with Ciar of the Mystics and Deacon Walsh to conspire against us. The Mystics provided the drugs that the dinner was dosed with, and the Amazons sent a squad to barricade the exits and light the building on fire. If not for the fact that my brothers and I had skipped dinner because Abel called a surprise meeting, we would have died in that fire.

Aisling is Monroe and Winry's mother, Jasper's older sister. These three might not have been any part of the decision that ended with forty innocent people being killed, but they are part of the ruling family. They'll have made different hard decisions that involved different deaths.

It's easy to hate from a distance, to pinpoint their differences, their sins, and build them up to be larger than life. To be villains. With that kind of hate, it's so easy to build up or tear down people in your head. They stop being people altogether and become the enemy.

In this moment, Monroe, Winry, and Jasper are all too real. I see the blatant love in the way they check in with each other, in the gentle ribbing and sharp words that evolve to them chatting easily. It reminds me of how I interact with my brothers, and isn't that a bitch of a realization?

When it comes right down to it, they think the same things about us that we think about them. That we're monsters. That they have to go to great lengths to protect their people from us.

It's not a comfortable realization.

This is a side of Monroe I've never seen before, one that is tender and protective in turns. I don't know how to fit the puzzle piece into the hellion that I've interacted with up to this point. I don't know why I'm even trying. Who gives a shit if she loves her family?

Even monsters have families.

I jolt as the doors fly open, and Cohen stalks into the room. He gives the trio a long look and jerks his thumb at the door. "All right, kids. Playtime's over. Get back to your rooms."

Jasper puts his hands on Winry's and Monroe's shoulders and smiles at them. "You're doing great. Hang in there."

Monroe covers his hand with hers and glares. "If you look like this next time I see you, I'm going to cut off Ezekiel's cock and shove it down his throat."

I flinch. Even Cohen misses a step at the vehemence in her tone. Jasper just grins and pulls her into a quick hug. He turns and strides from the room. All that said, that's less interesting to me than Winry and Cohen. They circle each other widely, her going so far as to round the couch on her way to the door. She doesn't so much as glance at him. But he watches her like he wants to pounce.

I've never seen my brother look at someone like that before.

It's disconcerting in the extreme.

He barely waits for Winry to shut the door behind her before he turns on me and Monroe. "What the fuck was that about?"

Monroe lifts her brows. "Are you sure you want me here for this? Seems like a family affair."

He gives me a look and turns to her. "I don't give a shit what your plans are or what you're trying to accomplish. You fuck over Shiloh, I'm going to fuck you up."

I expect her to do what anyone else when faced with a threat like that from Cohen would do—back up, flinch, show some kind of fear. I really should know better by now.

Monroe laughs in his face. "You Paine boys. You're so predictable. It's honestly pathetic."

"Monroe," I caution. Abel's warning is still ringing in my ears. The directive to take care of my Monroe problem before someone else does it for me. Provoking Cohen is a really fucked up way to commit suicide. No matter how fierce she is, she can't take my brother.

"Do *not* say my name in that tone of voice." The look she gives me is pure venom. "Have either of you assholes asked Shiloh what she wants? Have you considered that she's an adult who's more than capable of making her own decisions?" She switches her attention to Cohen. "No. You haven't. You're too busy threatening little old me, trying to protect someone who doesn't need your protection."

"You don't know what you're talking about. You haven't seen—"

"The scars on her legs." She says it flatly, for once not seeming to enjoy that she's shocked me. "I've seen them."

Cohen crosses his arms over his chest. "She tell you how she got them?" Like me, my brother knows the basics of what

Shiloh survived as a child. We've taken in all kinds of people over the years, but Cohen vets each one of them to ensure they're not adding to our already plentiful roster of enemies.

"Yes." The word is still too flat. Too…angry.

Surely I'm misinterpreting. I must be. Because only a fool would look at her reaction and actually believe she's feeling protective of Shiloh. It's all an act. It has to be. "Then you know she deserves better than to be fucked with."

Monroe snorts. "Her past doesn't mean she's not capable of making her own decisions. Respect them."

Cohen jerks his thumb toward the door. "Get out."

"Happily."

We both watch her leave. He barely lets me sigh before he's in my face. "What the fuck were you thinking?"

I'm getting really fucking tired of my brothers acting like this. I know I haven't handled this situation as ideally as possible, but that doesn't change the fact that none of *them* would be successful going toe-to-toe with Monroe. "You're going to have to be more specific."

"You let those three sit around and chat for how long?"

I don't react to his rage. "About an hour, all said and done."

"Why the fuck did you think that's a good idea?"

"*I* didn't think it was a good idea, but Harlow set it up, so I handled chaperoning." I clench my fists, but I make no other move. Cohen is wound more tightly than I expected. He's practically emoting, even if it's rage. "She's right, though. They work better as hostages if we allow them to see each other."

"It gives them too much time to plot."

"Are we supposed to keep them prisoners for the entire year? Should we all take a page out of Ezekiel's book and tie our Brides to the bed? You think soft little Winry would survive that without untold mental trauma?"

He flinches. It's the tiniest of movements, but it's there nonetheless. "I didn't say that."

"We had a plan when we came into this. It involves letting Monroe and Fallon travel back and forth between here and their respective factions. Their good behavior is solely dependent on the quality of hostages we have here. Keeping them from their family is counterproductive."

Cohen exhales and looks away. "I'm aware."

"What's the real problem, then?"

"Your Bride."

Now it's my turn to flinch. "Excuse me?"

"I'm sure Abel already talked to you, but if you don't get this situation under control, it's going to get ugly."

All this is true. It also doesn't explain why Cohen is so fucking emotional. He doesn't know Monroe, and even if he did—she's not family. Cohen's priority lines are stark and clear; the few people he cares about and everyone else. "And?"

"And what?"

"Why do you care? She's just some Amazon. Who gives a fuck if she lives or dies?" *I do.* I push the words down, hoping they don't show on my face. "Why is everyone on my shit about this?"

Cohen stares at me for a long moment, the menace coming off him nearly filling the room. He finally says, "If Monroe dies, it will make Winry sad." Without another word, he turns on his heel and stalks out of the room.

I release the breath I was holding. I expected the coldness from Cohen, same as I expected it from Abel. I didn't reckon on the reason. I don't know what to make of that. My brother has been acting strangely, but we've *all* been acting strangely since returning to Sabine Valley, from Abel down to Gabriel. This situation, no matter how much we've planned around it, is a lot more complicated than we expected. These Brides aren't just pawns to be moved about a chessboard at Abel's whim.

They're people.

Sabine Valley isn't just another city for us to linger in until it's time to move on. It was home once. I know at least half of my brothers hope it will be home again. I don't know if that's possible. This place has held some of the happiest and some of the most horrific times of my life. My feelings are too damn complicated, and if I could just scrape the taste of ash from my tongue, maybe I could *think* properly.

If I can't figure this shit out and Monroe dies as a result, more than Winry will be sad, and Cohen will be at my throat. *Shiloh* will be sad. She cares about Monroe enough to get intimate with her, and that's reason enough for me to have a frank conversation with both of them.

Not because *I* care.

I want Monroe, but I don't give a fuck about her. Not one bit.

It takes longer than I want to admit to get my head on straight. By the time I go to the room that's supposed to be mine and Monroe's, it's late. I don't really expect the women to be asleep—or otherwise engaged—but I knock all the same. Just in case.

A few seconds later, Monroe opens the door and leans against it. She's wearing an oversized T-shirt and little else. She grins. "Hey, handsome. Come here often?"

"Don't do that."

"Why? It's so funny to see the way your jaw clenches when I do." She steps back, holding the door open for me. "From the very serious look on your face, I suppose you're not here for fun."

"No. I'm not."

"How unfortunate."

I step into the room and look around. "Where's Shiloh?"

"Not back yet." She shrugs. "I thought she might be with you."

"She wasn't." Despite my best efforts, I can't help staring at the bed, picturing the sight that greeted me last time I was in this room. I clear my throat. "She's not happy with me."

"You think?" Monroe drops onto the bed and stretches her long, bare legs out. I notice the most absurd thing. Her toes are painted purple. She wiggles them at me. "See something you like?"

"No, of course not," I lie. "Just my pain in the ass of a Bride."

Monroe just grins, though the expression fades slowly. "If you stopped seeing Shiloh as some damsel in distress, she'd stop being unhappy with you."

The words seem simple enough, but that doesn't explain why she's offering them. "Aren't you invested in driving the wedge between us deeper? Why try to mend it?" Surely this is some sort of trap, but I can't divine the dimensions of it.

"I don't like seeing Shiloh unhappy any more than you like making her unhappy." She fiddles with the hem of the shirt, lifting it an inch. For the first time since we met, I don't think she's trying to provoke me. "It was fun to prod at your relationship at first, but she's really upset at you and I know her well enough now to recognize that ruining your friendship further will hurt her. That doesn't work for me, no matter how irritating I find you."

I really need to stop staring at that bared inch of her hip. Right now. I swallow hard. "You can't really expect me to believe you care about her."

"I don't really give a shit what you believe." She frowns. "Broderick."

"Yeah?"

"Don't freak out, but I do believe we're having something resembling a civil conversation."

My skin goes hot, and I have to look away. "I won't tell if you won't." I really have been an unforgivable ass to both Monroe and Shiloh. Monroe might delight in provoking me, but she hasn't forced me to do any of the things I feel so fucking tormented about. She just dangled the bait and prodded me, and I went after her like a bull charging a red flag.

I clear my throat. "I don't want to ruin my friendship with Shiloh further, either." I also don't want to lean on *Monroe* in regards to this. She's just as likely to harm me as she is to help me. But I'm starting to believe her when she says she cares about Shiloh.

We have that in common.

What a strange thought; one that puts us on the same side for the first time since I met this woman.

"I have a few ideas if you're willing to listen."

Shiloh chooses that moment to save me from having to come up with an answer. She stops short when she sees me. "What are you doing here?"

I am so damn tired of fighting with this woman and constantly saying the wrong thing. I miss us. I miss spending time with her and the easy banter and knowing we have each other's backs no matter what. I don't know how to reclaim the closeness, how to undo the damage being back in Sabine Valley has caused.

But I know where to start. "I've been an unbelievable ass."

She crosses her arms over her chest. "Go on."

Trust Shiloh not to make this easy on me. We haven't fought often over the years, but she more than holds her own when we do. How had I forgotten that? Or the fact that she holds a grudge better than anyone I've met? Gods, I *miss* her.

I clear my throat. "I'm sorry. I should have trusted that you knew what you were doing. I shouldn't have tried to override your choices or acted like I knew better than you did when it comes to yourself."

"You also should have done your duty instead of dodging it."

"And I should have done my duty instead of dodging it," I admit.

She stares at me for a long moment. There's something lingering in her eyes, something almost like the relief and hope I feel blossoming in my chest. "Is this apology just because you can't stand for me to be mad at you? Or are you actually going to change your behavior going forward?"

"The latter." When she stares, I feel compelled to add. "I'm going to try. Being in this city is fucking up my head more than I expected, and I can't pretend I'm not going to mess up in the future, but I'm going to try. I promise."

"I'll try, too." Shiloh nods. "You're forgiven."

"How entertaining." Monroe claps her hands. "You two are sickeningly sweet. Really, you're giving me cavities. How is that you aren't married with half a dozen babies by now?"

I stare at her, my face heating. Monroe is a human-shaped wrecking ball, and I kind of want to toss her right out the window. She *knows* I want Shiloh, and even if she's not actively trying to fuck with our friendship at the moment, she can't seem to help poking at it and saying things I'd rather kept silent. "Shut up, Monroe."

"We're friends." There's something strange in Shiloh's voice, a note that draws my gaze despite my best intention to look everywhere but at her. She's…blushing?

I blink. "We're friends?" I mean it to come out like a statement, but the words tilt up at the end, morphing it into a question. I know how *I* feel, but Shiloh has never given me the slightest indication that she might feel the same way.

Monroe snorts. "Okay, let's try this a different way. Broderick, do you want to strip Shiloh down and do all sorts of filthy things to her?"

I choke. "What the fuck, Monroe?"

She laughs and lowers her voice. "That's a yes, husband." She focuses on Shiloh. "And you? Do you want to see what kind of heat he's packing in those fitted pants of his? Maybe try out the thing he does with his fingers?"

"*Monroe.*"

"Also a yes." She claps her hands together. "So glad we got this out of the way. Let's get naked."

CHAPTER 15

MONROE

*T*here's a little voice in my head that's trying very valiantly to remind me that keeping Broderick and Shiloh apart is the best way to torment him. To punish him for thinking he can cage the heir to the Amazon throne. That was the plan from day one, after all.

I'm tired of it.

I still don't like Broderick all that much. He's stuffy and too concerned with what he should be doing, rather than what he wants to do. Yes, I like the way he fucks when I push him past the edge. And yes, I actually enjoy the act of shoving him right into recklessness. But I don't *like* him.

Shiloh, on the other hand?

She's a different story altogether. She was just a pretty girl when I first put my plan together, someone I was attracted to but nothing else. The past three hours have changed that. Fuck, the past three *days* have changed that. I like Shiloh. I like her strength, the sense of humor she keeps locked down, how kick-ass she is.

I also like how sweet she tastes.

What I'm not too keen on is how she and Broderick are staring at me like I've sprouted a second head. "What?"

"You can't just say stuff like that," Shiloh finally manages. She's bright red and trying her best not to fidget. It's cute—or it would be if it didn't signal that tonight isn't going to go the way I'd like it to. "I know you like being outrageous but—"

"Shiloh." I wait for her to look at me. "I like you. You like me. You like Broderick. Broderick likes you. I like to fuck Broderick, and he tells himself he just fucks me because he has to. One plus one plus one equals a triad."

"That's not how math works." Her eyes are a little too wide.

Gods, I've traumatized my girl.

I take a breath. It's okay. She'll get over it once we wade through this first step. I turn my attention to Broderick. "What we have isn't working right now."

"That doesn't mean we light the whole fucking thing on fire." He's trying to lock down his reaction, but he wants this just as badly as I do. The man exhausts me with his determination to deny himself the things he desires.

I frown at him. "What's the holdup? Are you afraid you're going to bruise little, innocent Shiloh? She can hold her own."

"Monroe!" Shiloh slashes a hand through the air. "Broderick is my friend, and that means something. Maybe you fuck your friends—"

"Sometimes." I shrug. "Depends on the friend and their preferences."

"Oh gods, you're serious." Broderick drags his hand through his hair. He hasn't managed to get it cut since Lammas, and it's just long enough that it stands on end from the motion. "Not all friendships are like that."

They're both so damn stubborn, we could go around like this all night. It's late, I'm tired and horny, and I need to have my game face back on in time to return to the Amazon faction in the morning. I sit up and cross my legs, barely managing not to roll my eyes when they both zero in on my hips where the T-shirt bunches. For such noble fools, they're both so damn lusty. I really don't understand how they haven't had sex before now.

I sigh. "So, let me get this straight. The tension between you that's so thick, you can cut it with a knife, but instead of fucking your way through it, you'd both rather keep fucking *me*, separately. And driving each other wild with jealousy while you do? How does that sound like a good time for anyone but me?"

"You underestimate yourself," Broderick mutters.

"On that, we can agree," Shiloh says.

I want to shake them. Instead, I just wait. Despite what everyone believes, I *can* be patient on occasion. In theory. Under normal circumstances, at least.

This situation has been stressing me the fuck out. Not just Broderick and Shiloh, but the whole Bride situation. No matter how intensely I try to distract myself, the truth is that even my mother is looking at me differently now that I'm a Bride to a Paine. To a Raider. She's trying very hard not to, but she also hasn't so much as attempted to plan something with me since I struck the deal to be able to return to working. That speaks volumes even more than the reassurances she's given me.

My mother doesn't trust me anymore.

Why am I thinking about this *now*, when I'm faced with two very gorgeous people who have both proven they know how to make me orgasm fast and hard?

I rub my face. I'm tired. That's all it is. This has been an incredibly long day, and it's wearing me down. "Okay, fine. If we're not going to have a sexy triad, can we wrap this up? I need my beauty rest."

Something flickers over Shiloh's face, and if I were a romantic person, I'd accuse her of worrying about me. That's silly, though. I'm bulletproof. Everyone knows it. Knock me down and I come back up swinging without hesitation, ready to do double the damage in half the time.

So why does my chest feel so tight?

I'm a shark. Keep swimming or drown.

Just have to keep moving.

"There's something else." Broderick's tone has the small hairs on the back of my neck standing on end. The fact he won't meet my gaze only has my internal alarms blaring louder. He curses. "We have to figure our shit out, and we have to do it now."

"Why? We're functioning just fine by avoiding each other." Obviously I'm aware of the message that sends to people both inside and outside of the compound, but that's Broderick's problem, not mine.

"If we don't find a happy medium, I don't know if you'll survive the month."

I blink, letting the words roll over me. Letting my brain process. "You're the one who's been avoiding me." But of course, that doesn't matter what the cause is, only the perception of those around us. If I were in Abel's position, I wouldn't have let it go on this long. Broderick avoiding his Bride sends a clear message about the power dynamics between us—that they aren't in his favor. The stunt Abel pulled on Lammas means all of Sabine Valley has its gaze turned in our direction. They can't afford to falter now, to show the least bit of weakness, or the rest of the city will fall on them like rabid dogs.

My chest goes tight, but I muscle past the physical response and paste a smile on my face. "So Abel's going to clean up your mess." My laugh sounds a little hysterical, but I can't help that. "Will it be poison, or will he shove me out a window? I'm assuming violence is out, because my mother would raze this fucking faction to the ground if she could prove you'd murdered me."

Which means Winry would take over as heir.

The thought makes me sick. My little sister is brilliant and kind and loving, but she would wither away as the Amazon queen, having to sacrifice piece after piece of herself until she became just as cold and ruthless as our mother and I are. I don't want that for her. *She* doesn't want the role, either.

Shiloh spins to stare at Broderick. "He wouldn't."

"You know better. Abel only cares about establishing us here as securely as possible and the safety of our people. Monroe isn't one of ours."

"I can hear you." I mean for it to come out jokingly, but the words fall flatly between us.

Shiloh clenches her fists. "No. Absolutely not. We might kill when we have to, but we don't just *murder* people." She narrows her eyes. "Especially when *you're* choosing to avoid her. It's not like she's barricaded the door against you."

"Still sitting right here," I say.

Shiloh advances on Broderick, and I have to give him credit for holding his ground. I might even take a step back if she came at me with *that* look on her face. She pokes his chest. "Fix this right fucking now, Broderick."

"That's what I'm trying to do." He exhales roughly. "It's why I'm here. Why we're having this conversation right now."

Do either of them notice how close they are right now? His gaze drops to her mouth before he forcibly jerks it back to her eyes. Their determination to ignore the chemistry flaring hotly between them would make me laugh if I didn't feel so sick to my stomach over the topic of this conversation.

Broderick looks at me. "Starting tonight, I'll be staying here. That's the first step, probably the most important. We'll figure out the rest tomorrow."

"One problem with that brilliant plan of yours." I hold up a finger. "Shiloh also sleeps here." She hadn't been sharing a bed with me, preferring to sleep on the horribly uncomfortable-looking couch tucked up against the wall, but I was hoping tonight that would change. "You aren't planning to kick her out just because you made an executive decision without speaking with either of us, were you?"

He opens his mouth, looks at me and then at Shiloh, and hesitates. Finally, Broderick says stiffly, "Do you have an alternate option?"

Yeah, that all three of us sleep in that massive bed together. I start to suggest exactly that, but Shiloh speaks first. "If you're here, I don't have to be. I'll sleep in the barracks and circle back in the morning." She starts for the door.

Yeah, I don't think so.

"Shiloh." I put enough snap in my tone to stop her in her tracks. She slowly turns to face me, and the redness spreading from her face down her neck is all the confirmation I need. She was just about to run from me. From us. I hold her gaze. "That is not a good solution, and you know it. All your stuff is here. It's late, and mid-shift at that. Are you going to take someone away from their job to help you haul your shit to the barracks just because you're scared of a little conversation between *friends?*"

She glares. "That's not it."

"Then stay the night, and we'll discuss options in the morning at a reasonable hour." A plan starts to come to life in the back of my mind, a wonderful, devious plan that will get all three of us exactly what we want.

For a moment, I think she'll argue, but she finally nods. "Only for one night."

Fuck that. I want them both, but if I have to choose right now, I choose her. "The couch is only big enough for one, so one of you will have to be in the bed with me." I tug on the hem of my shirt as I consider options. For once, I'm not sure the best way to play this. If my ultimate goal is to seduce both of them into being a throuple, would it be better if Shiloh or Broderick shared the bed with me tonight? Since I don't know, I can't help poking them a little. "I could take the couch, of course. Since you're so friendly, you shouldn't have a problem sleeping together."

"I'll take the couch." Broderick offers it without hesitation, barely letting me finish before he's throwing himself on the first sword available on Shiloh's behalf.

From the look on her face, she isn't pleased with either of us. "*I* will take the couch. If you really want to prove you're ready to start treating Monroe like a Bride, this is a good place to start."

He hesitates but finally nods. "I'm going to get a few of my things. I'll be right back."

Shiloh's shoulders slump a little as he leaves the room. They're so fucking transparent, it irritates me. I flip my hair off my shoulder. No time like the present to put my plan into motion. "So, you and Broderick are just friends."

"Yes." She sounds so wary, I almost smile. She's smart enough to sense a trap, but I'm not going to give her a chance to avoid it.

"Are you sure?" I give her a concerned look. "He's really sexy. You haven't even thought about it? Felt a spark? Anything?"

"No," she says firmly. Too firmly to be anything but a lie.

Gotcha. I finally allow myself to smile. "In that case, you won't mind if I fuck him tonight. Since I'm his Bride and all." I lean forward and lick my lips. "I promise to make it up to you in the morning. I've been dying for another taste of your pretty pussy."

Shiloh won't look at me, but she's turned a darling shade of red. When she finally manages to speak, her voice is too high. "Of course I don't care if you fuck him. You're his Bride, and we might be intimate, but we're not exclusive. Do what you want."

I want to drag her down onto the bed and kiss that lying mouth. "It won't make you uncomfortable? You know I'm not quiet."

She's blushing so hard, she's practically purple. "Why would it make me uncomfortable? I don't see Broderick like that."

Yes, she does. She really, really does. "You see *me* like that."

Shiloh clears her throat. "Yeah, I guess I do."

I grab her hand and tug her closer to the bed. She comes without hesitation, and I waste no time leaning forward and nuzzling her breasts. "Shiloh?"

"Yes?"

"Promise me something."

"What?" She looks like she's staring down a tiger, but she digs her hands into my hair and arches her back a little, guiding my mouth to one nipple. Her bra is so thin, it's nothing at all to nip and suck her until first one nipple and then the other are hard points against the fabric.

I palm her pussy through her jeans. "Promise me that if you feel even the *tiniest* bit turned on, you'll take care of your pretty pussy the way I would. Properly. Until you come enough times that you're sated."

She's breathing hard and rocking her hips against my

palm, ever so slightly. "That won't be a problem. I'm not going to be turned on if you have sex with Broderick while I'm in the room."

Liar. "Then you should have no issue promising me."

Another hesitation, longer this time. "I promise."

I pull her down to straddle me and speak the next words against her lips. "I take my promises very seriously, love. You can lie as much as you like about other things, but not about this. Got it?"

"Yes." And then she's kissing me, bearing me down to the bed and taking my mouth as if she'll find her next breath on the other side. I could pretend this lust is all for me, but I know better. There's nothing that burns as hot as thwarted desire, and both Shiloh and Broderick have that in spades. As much as I want to roll her over and play with her until she comes half a dozen times, I don't want her the least bit sated before we turn off the lights and do things in the dark.

Better to focus on getting both Broderick and Shiloh into my bed than the alternative.

I'll have to deal with all of it soon—Abel's threat, my mother's distance, the future that used to feel so concrete but has somehow gone liquid in the last few weeks. But not tonight.

Tonight, I'm going to start the next stage of my seduction.

CHAPTER 16

SHILOH

*M*aking that promise to Monroe seemed like the simplest thing in the world. Of course I don't desire Broderick. That would be ridiculous...

I'm a fucking liar.

He's my friend. My *best* friend. Nothing is worth endangering that relationship, not even my own lust. Especially now that it looks like we might be on the path to mending what we've spent breaking since arriving in Sabine Valley. It doesn't matter that what's between us could be more than lust. I wasn't willing to risk making a move even before he took Monroe as his Bride. Now? Now, things are infinitely more complicated.

But, as I lay on the uncomfortable couch and listen to them shift on the bed, I have to admit that I've made a gross miscalculation. Especially when Monroe gives that throaty laugh, the one I like so much.

Despite my best efforts, I can't help turning onto my side to face the bed. The moonlight from the narrow window seems designed specifically to highlight the mattress...the people on the mattress. Monroe murmurs something, too low for me to hear, and Broderick responds at the same volume. What are they talking about? He doesn't sound happy, but his curse turns into a groan as the sheets shift, and I catch sight of a distinctive motion. She's...jacking him. Another murmured exchange and Monroe slips beneath the sheets. I watch her form move, watch her settle between his thighs.

Holy shit, she wasn't kidding about that promise.

Still, I don't know if it's desire I'm feeling right now. It's too hot, too painful. It's a whole lot like jealousy. I don't even know *who* I'm jealous of. Monroe, currently sucking Broderick's cock and making his body tense as he tries to keep quiet? Broderick, for having Monroe's clever mouth bringing him pleasure?

Both.

The answer is both.

Fuck.

I shift. My leggings and shirt feel too tight on my body, for all that they were both more than comfortable a few minutes ago. I should turn away, should put my pillow over my head, should do anything but watch avidly as Monroe seduces Broderick.

She emerges from the sheets, climbing up his body to take his mouth. If Broderick was simply allowing her to do her worst before, he's actively encouraging her now. He sinks his big hands into her hair, and he kisses her hard and furious.

My breath catches as he drags his hands down her back to her hips, jerking her forward a few inches. The slightest hesitation, and I know without a shadow of a doubt that he's working his cock into her pussy.

Desire hits me hard enough to make my head spin. The feeling only gets worse as Monroe sits up, sending the sheet pooling around her hips. She's so fucking beautiful, it makes me shake. Her body is lean, her breasts high and perfect. Her ass is so goddamned bitable. Especially when she rolls her hips like that.

I don't stop to think. I hold my breath as I lift my hips and slide off my leggings and panties. I have a promise to keep. That's all. That's the only reason I'm practically panting with need as I delve my hand between my thighs and stroke my pussy. I'm soaked, but that's no surprise. I might be able to lie with my words, but not with my body.

With every roll of Monroe's hips, the sheet slides a little farther down, revealing the full curve of her ass, the tops of Broderick's tense thighs. I can almost *almost* see his cock enter her in the shadows between them. There's not enough light, and I curse that fact even as I'm grateful for the privacy those same shadows provide me.

I press one finger and then two into me. It feels good, but not as good as someone else's would. Not as good as her tongue. As his cock.

Monroe plants her hands on his chest and slows down. Teasing him. Teasing me. I could curse her if I had the breath for it. All I have is need, though. I spread my wetness up to my clit, matching her strokes. It feels so fucking good. An exquisite torment I both love and hate.

This is one hell of a seduction.

Broderick curses and grabs her waist. One moment Monroe is riding his cock, and the next he rolls them. He arches back and loops her legs over his arms, spreading her legs wide as he drives into her. The angle is wrong to see her the way I want to, leaving me to focus on how the muscles in his back and ass flex with each thrust.

How *rough* the thrusts are.

He's fucking her like he's mad at her, like he knows exactly how much she can take and he's going to push her to that line.

He's never touched me with anything but gentleness.

It's all too easy to insert myself in her place in my mind. To put myself between them. My exhale comes out almost as a moan, and I pick up my pace, once again matching their fucking. Broderick's forgotten I'm here. I'm certain of it. Whatever Monroe whispered to him at the start of this drove him to distraction. There's no way he'd do this if he remembered I was watching...

Unless he's lying? Unless he sees me as more than a friend, too.

Monroe comes with a cry, arching up to take Broderick's mouth as he keeps fucking her. He slows down the slightest bit, grinding into her in a way I can almost feel. Pleasure spirals through me, tighter and tighter. With it, unforgivable thoughts surge forth from the careful corral I've kept them in until now.

I want him to fuck me like that.

I want her riding my face the way she rode his cock.

I want it at the same time.

My orgasm takes me by surprise. I don't mean to cry out. I really don't. The sound just slips free as my body goes tight and hot.

I don't realize there's silence in the room until a few moments later. I open my eyes to find Broderick has shifted to the side. He brought Monroe with him, is still settled between her spread thighs. Is still...fucking her slowly.

But he's watching *me* as he does.

I keep stroking myself, coaxing my pleasure back to a boil. Monroe locks her legs around Broderick's hips and laughs. "Let us see, Shiloh. Turnabout is fair play, and we just gave you a show."

Without thinking, I obey. I kick down the blankets. My shirt is bunched around my waist. But the moonlight doesn't reach me the same way it does them.

"Come here." This from Broderick. He hardly sounds like

himself. He pulls out of Monroe and flips her onto her stomach, moving her roughly like he would a doll. She seems to love it, immediately lifting her hips so he can enter her from behind.

"You heard him." She reaches out an impatient hand and slaps the mattress next to her head. "Come here, love."

It feels like my body moves on its own, answering her siren call even as my mind is trying to catch up with this turn of events. If I think too hard, I'll stop this, so I...don't. I don't want to stop. Not yet. Not with Broderick still fucking Monroe while he watches me. I can feel his gaze even if I can't see his eyes properly in the darkness.

It's the darkness that makes me bold. Makes me feel like another person entirely, one who can be wild and reckless without consequences. One who hooks the bottom of her shirt and tows it over her head to stand before these two people naked.

Monroe moans. "Good girl. Now get up here."

I carefully climb onto the mattress, but I'm not sure where I'm supposed to go from here. Monroe decides for me. She hooks my thighs and drags me until my hips are even with her face. "Much better." She laughs again. "She's so wet, husband. She likes watching us fuck. I bet she'll like joining us even more."

Broderick reaches down and sinks his hand into Monroe's hair, guiding her face to my pussy. "Make her come again, Bride."

"Gladly," she murmurs against my heated flesh. She presses my thighs wide, and then she's dragging her tongue up my center. She flicks my clit and moans. "Just as sweet as I thought." Monroe dips back down, and then her tongue is inside me, thrusting deep. I can't keep my whimper inside. I don't even try.

She lifts her head just as Broderick shifts his grip to her

throat and pulls her up. He takes her mouth, and I freeze as understanding dawns. He's tasting my pussy on her lips, her tongue. He lifts his head. "More."

"It's better directly from the source," she murmurs. Her features are cast in shadow, but I can clearly see the sinful curve of her lips. "Don't you want a taste, husband?" She wraps her fingers around the wrist of his free hand, and he allows her to guide his hand down...

Holy shit.

She presses two of his fingers into me. Two of *Broderick's* fingers are inside me. I whimper, and he curses. But even if he's letting Monroe do this, letting her guide us, letting her take the choice away, he still moves inside me, curling up to stroke his fingertips against my G-spot.

"*Fuck.*"

"Clever boy. You found it so quickly." She leans down, and then her mouth is on my clit, licking and sucking as Broderick keeps up that devastating stroking inside me. As he keeps fucking her in short, slow thrusts as if he has all night and won't be coming anytime soon.

I don't mean to wrap my fists around Monroe's hair, but I haven't meant to do anything that's happened tonight. My fingers lace with Broderick's, both of us holding Monroe to my pussy. "Make me come," I whisper. "Please."

"We will, love. Just lie there, and let us make you feel good." Her words are pure temptation, her tongue following through on it eagerly. Even as a voice inside me whispers that I'll regret this, my body doesn't care. It feels too good to stop.

Broderick wedges a third finger into me, the fit tight, but he's showing no mercy. That's fine. I don't want any. I drag in a breath and then I'm coming, clamping down on his fingers hard enough to make him curse. He lets me ride his hand, Monroe's mouth, for a several long beats before he slowly withdraws. He holds my gaze as he slides his fingers into his mouth, tasting me again. The fingers laced with mine in Monroe's hair spasm. "Keep eating her out. Don't stop until I do."

"Wouldn't dream of it." And then Monroe's tongue is inside me again, as if she wants to lick away every bit of my orgasm.

This feels like a fever dream. Surely I've fallen asleep on the couch and my mind has conjured up this sexy fantasy. Surely my best friend isn't fucking his Bride as she goes down on me. Surely our fingers aren't linked in her hair, guiding her where we want her.

The shadows give permission that I never would have taken otherwise. To lift my hips and rub myself against Monroe's mouth. To simply *feel* instead of thinking so damn hard all the time.

I'll regret this in the morning. But right now, beneath the light of the waning moon, the sun and reality have no hold. There is only the three of us in this bed and nothing else.

Broderick picks up his pace, fucking Monroe so hard that her face moves against me in time with his thrusts. Another orgasm surges inside me, driven by jealousy once again. I can feel his eyes on me, strong enough that it's almost a touch, but it's not *me* he's fucking.

I can't let it be me that he's fucking.

Some things, you can't take back.

I come with a cry. Monroe coaxes me through wave after wave, until each breath escapes on a sob and my body goes limp. Broderick doesn't untangle his fingers from mine as he slides his free hand around Monroe's hip. I don't need to see the path clearly to know his destination. It's there in how she jolts and then goes liquid. He's stroking her clit.

He keeps up that punishing pace as she moans and starts shaking, doesn't so much as miss a stroke until she comes with a cry that vibrates through my body. Only then does he release us both to grab Monroe's hips and chase his own pleasure. I don't know if I'm relieved or disappointed that he pulls out of her at the last moment and comes across her back in great spurts.

It's only when we're all lying there, breathing hard, that reality finally tears through the fantasy with vicious teeth and claws.

I have to get out of here.

CHAPTER 17

I see Shiloh tense, and I know her so fucking well, I know exactly what she intends to do. To run. To get as far from us as possible. "Do *not* move." I speak without having any intention of doing it.

She freezes. "I was just going to…"

"No." I never talk to Shiloh this way. *Never.* Fuck, I never talk to anyone but Monroe this way. That doesn't change the fact that I don't want her to leave, to break this strange spell that we created here in this bed.

I can't believe it happened.

I can't believe I let myself get swept up in Monroe's wicked taunting, that it spawned *this* outcome. I can still hear her low voice in my ear before things spiraled out of control. *You gave your word, husband. You're mine for a week, and I want this cock right now*. Truth be told, I barely resisted. I refuse to look at my motivations too closely, not when I can still taste Shiloh on my tongue.

If I let Shiloh leave right now, this will never happen again. The next time I see her, she'll have her barriers firmly in place, will have edged us back into the safety of friends. If I were smart, I'd let her do it. I value her friendship above all else, and moving forward with this puts that friendship in danger.

Monroe stretches. "Go get a towel and clean up the mess you made." She flicks her fingers at my come all over her ass and back.

As much as I want to argue, to stay and ensure Shiloh doesn't leave, I do as Monroe asks. I owe her, after all. Maybe later, I'll think about how seamlessly we worked as a unit when we had the same goal in mind. There was no jockeying for position, no undermining. Yeah, it was sex, but Monroe and I don't stop the power plays for sex. If anything, we ramp them up. It's part of the reason I've been avoiding her. I hardly know myself when I get my hands on her.

I didn't expect that to bleed over to Shiloh in any way, shape, or form, but now that it has, I'm not willing to let it go without at least having a conversation.

Two minutes later, I have a warm damp cloth in my hands as I walk back into the room. The women are exactly where I left them, Monroe draped over Shiloh's lower body; if I didn't know better, I'd say Monroe was pinning her to the mattress.

Monroe jolts a little as I lean over the bed and clean up my mess. Did she think I'd just toss the cloth at her and make her do it herself?

You would have even a day ago.

The knowledge shames me. I really have been an unbelievable ass when it comes to both of these women. In different ways, yes, but the fact remains. I want to turn on the lights, to see their faces, but something tells me if I try, it will end this all the sooner. The shadows conceal all manner of things, and maybe each of us need to hide a little for this conversation to happen. "I'm sorry."

Monroe lifts her head off Shiloh's stomach. "Don't you

dare apologize for what we just did." Her voice is so sharp, it sounds almost brittle. Almost vulnerable.

"No, not for that." I shake my head. "I'm sorry for the past three weeks. I've mishandled things."

Shiloh lets out a harsh laugh. "This is the third time you've apologized. You should know by now that quality matters more than quantity, Broderick."

"Hush." Monroe lets her head drop and gives Shiloh's thigh a light smack. "Not everyone is as practical as we are. You have to learn to appreciate the moments when someone particularly stubborn comes around. This is two of those moments in one."

"Who else—" Shiloh curses. "You're talking about me, aren't you?"

"Yes, love, I'm talking about you." She plants a kiss on the center of Shiloh's stomach and sits up.

The casual sexual intimacy sends a shard of jealousy through me, but it feels faint and unfocused. What if we got out of our own way and tried this? I've loved Shiloh for years, first as a friend, and then as something more, but she never showed the slightest indication that we were anything but friends. She matters too much to me for me to lose her completely because I want more, so I kept my feelings to myself.

But she didn't come to this bed solely for Monroe.

I'd stake my life on it.

I'm about to stake so much more. Nerves make my voice harsh. "You said you only saw me as a friend."

"I do." Shiloh grabs Monroe's wrist before she can smack her again. "Stop that."

"Stop lying." Monroe reverses their grip easily and brings Shiloh's hand to her mouth to press a kiss to her wrist. "You didn't lose control until he flipped me. Were you imaging it was *you* beneath Broderick?" She gives Shiloh's hand a little shake. "Don't lie."

The silence stretches out long enough for it to become uncomfortable. My stomach drops, and my head goes light and fuzzy. We miscalculated. Holy fuck, we miscalculated, and now I'm going to lose everything. "Monroe—"

"Yes," Shiloh says softly. She jerks her wrist out of Monroe's grip. "Are you happy now? Yes, I was jealous that you got to experience that and I didn't."

Again, I start to shut this whole thing down, but Monroe laughs. "That's not the only thing you were jealous of, was it?"

Shiloh looks away. "No."

"Give us the rest, love." When she still hesitates, Monroe lowers her voice to a sexy murmur. "Communication is hard and scary, but the rewards are more than worth the challenge. I would think your *three* orgasms prove that."

"One of those was at my own hand."

Monroe laughs again. "Fine, then call it two if you want to get picky. Didn't Broderick's big fingers feel good inside you?" My body goes hot at her words, and Shiloh inhales sharply, but Monroe doesn't give either of us a chance to say anything. "You don't have to answer. I already know it feels phenomenal when he strokes your G-spot. He's rather good at finding it and quickly. Just like I know that *my* oral skills are unsurpassed." She shoots me a look that I can't quite define because of the lack of light in the room. "Then again, I bet he's just as good with his mouth as I am. Maybe we can have a competition sometime."

My cock goes rock hard at the thought. Of her coaxing Shiloh to orgasm and then shifting aside and giving me a turn. Over and over again until we've had our fill or Shiloh's body gives out. It's intoxicating to be unified in purpose with Monroe. It feels like riding a giant wave, moving faster than should be possible with so much force behind you. It's exhilarating. "Do you ever get tired of playing the devil on my shoulder, Monroe?" The question comes out almost playful.

She snorts. "Why would I? It's so damn *fun*."

I finally clear my throat. I don't want to rush into this, but rushing feels the most natural thing in the world. Still… "Do I get a say in this?"

Monroe tilts her head to the side. "That depends. Are you going to admit that you're practically coming in your pants at the idea of getting Shiloh naked and under you—or over you, or in front of you?"

"*Monroe.*"

She ignores Shiloh, focusing all that formative willpower on me. "Because Shiloh isn't the only one who's played it safe when it comes to your relationship. If I hadn't forced the issue, you two would live to a ripe old age and never have a difficult conversation about the fact that she wants to sit on your cock and you're dying to eat her pussy until she damn near passes out."

"The only one I want to pass out right now is *you* with your fucking mouth." The words feel vaguely sharp, but nowhere near the vehemence I've dredged up in the past. Because she's right. It's terrifying how right she is.

Monroe leans back against the headboard and waves her hand at her lower body. "Well, I'm not going to argue with oral sex. Go ahead then."

I snort. "That's not what I meant, and you know it."

"Do I? You're so terrible with words, Broderick. I have to prod and prod and prod until you charge me, and then it's all fucking and no communication. Can you blame me for provoking you?"

Not when she puts it like that. "You have a point. Get to it."

"My *point* is that what we just did was fun. It was damn

near seamless, and that kind of thing is worth its weight in gold when you're having group sex. You both enjoyed yourselves. I enjoyed myself. There is no reason we shouldn't do it again, preferably repeatedly for the next eleven months."

Until she's no longer my Bride.

Before, the thought filled me with nothing but relief and impatience. A year isn't a long time in the grand scheme of things, but every moment with Monroe frays my patience to dangerous levels of loss of control. Now…

No, it's not complicated. I can't let it be complicated.

It doesn't matter if what happened in this bed with Shiloh felt so fucking right, I can barely put it into words. It doesn't matter that having Monroe in my corner and aligned in my purpose was practically magic. At the end of this handfasting, I will still be glad to send her back to her faction for good.

Shiloh crosses her arms over her chest, which is doing a number on my ability to pretend we're not all sitting here naked. "Maybe I came to this bed for *you*. And Broderick was fucking *you*. One could argue that we're only attracted to you, not each other."

"There you go with that lying mouth again." Monroe sighs, but it's almost mock exasperation in her tone. "I ought to wrap it around Broderick's cock and see who's attracted to who at that point."

The air in the room gains a thickness and heat that makes me achingly aware of each inhale. "You can't say shit like that."

"And yet I just did." She shakes her head. "Fine. Have it your way, you stubborn asses. You can both fuck me, sometimes together, and keep it at that. Are you happy?"

No. Of course not. I want Shiloh in every way, but I can recognize it for the selfish desire it is. If I use this situation to take advantage of things, I'll be worse than a fucking monster. It takes everything I have to lock down my emotions and keep them out of my voice. "If that's what Shiloh wants."

"It's the *smart* thing to do." She slides off the bed, and I watch helplessly as she bends to grab the oversized sleep shirt off the floor.

I would give my right arm for good light to see her properly in this moment. To trace the curves and slopes of her naked body with my gaze in a way I'm not permitted to with my hands. Then again, maybe it's for the best. Wanting Shiloh is one thing when we're very clearly defined as friends. This thing with Monroe smudges those lines by definition. No need to erase them completely.

Shiloh pulls the shirt over her head and hurries to the couch. It a rush of motion, she yanks on her pants and practically dives beneath the covers. "Good night."

"Good night," I respond automatically.

No reason for the yawning feeling akin to loss in my chest. No *good* reason, at least. Of course, Shiloh wants to preserve what little distance she can between us. Of course, she wouldn't want to share a bed with me for something as intimate as sleeping.

Of course.

A light touch to the center of my chest. I look down to find Monroe watching me. Her teeth flash in the low light, and she climbs onto her knees to whisper in my ear, "Have faith, husband."

"I'm not your husband." I've said it so many times, the response is more habit than anything else.

She twines her arms around my neck and presses a quick kiss to my cheek. She's gone before I can decide if I want to welcome the contact or not, moving to her side of the bed and sliding beneath the covers.

Have faith.

In *what?* What is Monroe's motivation for doing all this? That, more than anything, confuses me. I believe her attraction to Shiloh is genuine, and she seems to actually care for my best friend as well. Feelings that are mutual between both women as best I can tell.

But Monroe hates me. She has every reason to. Us colliding sexually a handful of times doesn't change the fact that she's been handfasted to me against her will. No matter what her motivations are now, she initially sought out Shiloh to hurt me.

I can't trust her.

No matter how good the sex. No matter how perfect it felt to have our wills aligned instead of in conflict. No matter how much we both seem to want Shiloh.

Trusting Monroe is playing directly into her hands.

CHAPTER 18

*S*hiloh is gone when I wake up the next morning. That doesn't surprise me. The fact that Broderick is still in the room, however, *does*. He sits on the edge of the bed, his hair wet from the shower, and looks at me. "We have to work together."

"To seduce Shiloh, yes." I answer too quickly, maybe, but I don't know how to deal with this newfound peace between us. It feels strange and fragile and I kind of want to smash it with a hammer so at least I know when to expect it to explode in my face.

He snorts. "Get your mind out of the gutter, Monroe. I meant what I said last night—you're in danger if we can't get our shit ironed out."

Ah. That.

I sit up, letting the sheet fall to my waist, and can't help the shiver of pleasure that goes through me when his attention drops to my breasts...and stays there. It would be the simplest thing in the world to provoke him, to seduce him, to stop this conversation in its tracks.

I am stronger than that weak impulse. I have to be.

I also can't afford to ignore Broderick reaching out a hand, no matter how reluctantly.

With a sigh, I drag the sheet back up to cover myself and am saint enough to ignore the way his skin goes red in response. Still, I can't help poking at him, just a little. "One would think you'd be grateful someone else was willing to get rid of me. It'd take care of your little problem so you don't have to."

"I don't want you dead." The words are so soft, I almost convince myself I imagined them.

"Why not?" Maybe I'm not that smart, after all. This conversation stings in ways I'm not prepared to examine, but I can't stop prodding the wound. "I'm a pain in your ass. When you're around me, you constantly act in ways you claim aren't normal for you, and you hate that. I seduced the woman you're in love with right under your nose and then flaunted it in your face."

He clenches his jaw like he's biting down on a bunch of words that would send us spiraling. Finally, he grinds out. "I don't like you overmuch, but it took two of us to get to this place. I'm not blameless and you don't deserve to die just because you're a pain in my ass."

Of course he doesn't like me. I don't like him *overmuch*, either. No reason for that to worm beneath my skin and eat away at me. I clear my throat. "Okay, I'll bite. What's your plan?"

"We spend some time together." He catches my look. "We don't have to keep sleeping together, but—"

"Broderick."

"Yeah?"

I smother the strange fluttering in my throat. "I like fucking you. I don't think I'm overstating things saying that you like fucking me, too."

He stares at me, hard. "No, you're not overstating things."

"Then there's no reason to stop." I don't mention Shiloh, but the possibility of her is between us all the same. Did he get off even harder last night because we were working together to get *her* off? I'm suddenly afraid to ask, afraid it was all in my head. It felt *so good* to team up with him. So good it scares me a little bit. I've seen this man as an opponent for so long, I don't know how to work with him as a partner. At least outside the bedroom.

Broderick is silent for a long moment. Finally, he says, "No, there's no reason to stop."

I don't breathe a sigh of relief. I have too much control for that. But... I want to. "Okay."

"Okay."

We sit for a long moment, long enough that things begin to feel awkward. I clear my throat. "Now that that's out of the way, I suppose you want us to be seen together in public?"

"Yeah."

I think about my plan last night, how well it worked. How much all three of us enjoyed ourselves. Shiloh might have rabbited out of here the first chance she got, but that doesn't mean we have to backslide. Especially if Broderick and I are on the same page. *That* is such a strange concept, I'm still having a hard time wrapping my head around it. I tap my fingers to my bottom lip. "Can I ask you a question?"

Some of the tension that bled out of his shoulders previously courses back in. "I might not answer. But sure, go ahead and ask."

Oh, I think he will answer. I hold his gaze, searching those pretty, blue eyes. "We both know you want Shiloh."

I can see the exact moment he decides to stop attempting to lie to me about it. He relaxes back against the bed next to me. "I guess there's no point in denying it. You had my number down within an hour of meeting me."

I smile a little. "Only part of it. You're just *so obvious* when you look at her. I'm honestly surprised you don't have literal hearts in your eyes. It's cute."

"Uh huh." He nudges me with his elbow. "And you don't? You go all soft and sugary sweet with her. You're not like that with anyone else."

He's right. I might provoke Shiloh a bit, but she brings out a softer side of me. I grin down at him. It strikes me that we're having yet another civil conversation, but this time I don't point it out. "She's been with you, what, seven years? How have you not gotten drunk and tried to kiss her even once? I don't understand that level of restraint."

Broderick shrugs. "We're friends. I value that more than anything. I might have been fucking things up since we got back to Sabine Valley, but she's too important to me to mess things up with sex." His expression clouds. "It doesn't matter what I want. She's obviously not on the same page. I don't want to make her uncomfortable."

That draws a laugh from me before I can stifle the sound. "Broderick, she was coming all over your fingers a few hours ago. She might pretend that it was *me* causing that, but we both know the truth."

"Do we?"

The vulnerability in his tone is a pressure point I should leap to exploit. Shiloh has always been Broderick's weakness; it's why I zeroed in on her from the beginning. My mother might not have tasked me with destabilizing the Paine brothers in whatever way I can safely manage, but it's the smart thing to do. Broderick is Abel's second-in-command. He's softer than some of his brothers, but that doesn't make him less formidable. If not for Shiloh, I doubt I'd have gotten to him so quickly.

But a selfish part of me wants what we had last night. I want *more* of it. I want the high of us working together and putting both our formidable wills toward one goal.

Not to mention…I'm hesitant to do anything that might hurt Shiloh or put her in harm's way.

Destabilizing the Paine brothers—and the Raider faction, by extension—would potentially hurt Shiloh. Not just if something happens to Broderick. I've seen her fight. If it comes to a conflict, she'll be on the front lines. She might be good, but she's no Amazon. If our factions go to war, she'll be harmed or even killed.

I really am a fool, because I smile at my temporary husband and speak the truth that seals my fate. Seals all our fates together into one braided knot. "She wouldn't be so skittish if she didn't want you. She wouldn't have been fucking herself with her fingers and pretending it was your cock, and she wouldn't have nearly come on the spot when you kissed me after I ate her out. So, yeah, Broderick, it's safe to say she wants you."

He narrows his eyes, but he's not a good enough liar to hide the hope my words bring to life. "You're sure."

Gods, how can this man be so clever in some ways and also so determined to ignore the truth right in front of his face? "I'd bet my life on it."

He weighs that for a long moment. "You have a point."

"In fact, I do." I fling off the blankets and get to my feet. I'm vain enough to love the way he follows me with his gaze as I round the mattress and head for the bathroom. I stop in the doorway, knowing full well that the light frames me from the back, creating one hell of an image. "My *point*, dear husband, is that we're going to seduce our sexy little Shiloh. Together."

He goes perfectly still. "How the fuck are we going to manage that?"

We.

He says it so easily, as if us teaming up isn't strange and borderline unnatural. Did it feel as good, as *right*, for him last night as it did for me? I grin. "Well, to start, you're going to be the one to pick us up after I'm done working. Then we're going to take our girl out for a drink and have a little fun."

"A little fun," he says slowly. "Monroe, has anyone ever told you that you're fucking terrifying?"

"Only every day that ends in a Y." I pause. This should be where I end it, but I can't help the question that bubbles up. "You're really going to trust me in this?"

"Considering it was you who got her into bed with us last night, I do." Now it's his turn to pause. "I know you care about her, so I don't think this has to be said, but I don't want her to do anything she doesn't want to. I don't want to pressure her."

Oh, this sweet man. He makes me want to muddy him right up. "You're right. I do care about her and I'd never pressure her into anything. We're not going to do anything but give her a taste of what it would be like to close this triangle, so to speak."

"Ah."

I walk slowly to him, putting a little sway in my hips. "Would you like to know how I plan to do that?"

"Yes," he says warily.

"You're going to seduce her by proxy." I wave at my body, fully enjoying the way his gaze follows the sweep of my hand. "I'm your proxy."

"Monroe—"

"Walk and talk, husband. I have to get ready." I turn on my heel and head into the bathroom. Broderick, of course, follows me. He's so damn sexy as he leans against the counter and watches me get the shower going. A wave of remembered pleasure goes through me just from being in the same room as him. I'd say it's a shame we don't get along this well normally, but the truth is that conflict adds to the spice.

We were getting along last night.

We're getting along right now.

I step beneath the water before I can follow that thought anywhere. It doesn't matter if it feels good to be aligned in purpose. He's not for me. Fuck, Shiloh isn't for me, either. It's going to be everything I can do to avoid a war at the end of this year. I don't have time for two sexy, high-maintenance partners. Not that either of them are jumping at the idea of being linked to me permanently. They aren't.

The Amazons aren't like the Mystics. Political marriages are rare, especially with other factions. Any outsider who marries into the Amazons has a long road ahead of them. It's not that we ostracize outsiders; more that we simply don't hand over power that isn't earned. Even then, whoever I end up with won't be an equal in the eyes of the faction. I will always be queen, they will always be consort.

Why am I thinking about this now?

I wash my hair and body quickly, keenly aware of Broderick's gaze on me. The sensation only gets stronger when I turn off the water and grab a towel. We're long past any point of modesty, and I'm hardly a shy person on my best day, so I don't bother to try and cover up as I dry off. I also don't put on a show, either.

We don't have time to get into it right now, not if I don't want to be late.

"I'd like more details," he finally says. "If you're willing to share them."

"Sure." I head out of the bathroom and into the walk-in closet, him trailing behind. I managed to get a decent amount of my clothing brought here the first week, so I have plenty to choose from. I flip through the options. "We're going to go get a drink somewhere nice and shadowy, with booths or a private back room. And then you're going to sit across from us and use that stern voice of yours to dictate how I touch Shiloh."

"I don't have a stern voice."

I flick my fingertips in his direction. "You're using it right now."

"Monroe."

I sigh and turn to face him. "Broderick, why are you questioning this so hard? Tell me it's not sexy as fuck to think about sitting there watching me slide my hand down Shiloh's jeans and get her off on your instructions."

He frowns and shifts, trying to subtly adjust the front of his pants. "Yeah, it's hot."

"Then what's the problem?"

"I still don't get why you're doing this."

I finally land on a green dress that does wonders for my eyes. I slide into it and walk to Broderick to present my back. "Zip me up."

He hesitates, and then there's the slightest tug of the zipper. I don't expect him to touch me. Broderick coasts a knuckle up my spine, a slow drag that has my skin breaking out in goose bumps. He fastens the little button at the top but doesn't remove his hand. Instead, he slides it around to bracket my throat and steps forward to press against my back. "Are you playing tricks, Bride?"

"Only sexy ones." I can't quite draw in a full breath. I'm don't have a submissive bone in my body, but I'm still fighting not to shake from this touch alone. There's nothing I love more than a good man gone feral, and Broderick's leash snaps every time he gets his hands on me.

He lowers his voice. "Shiloh likes watching us fuck."

It takes me two tries to find my words. "I would think that's obvious after last night."

"Two birds, one stone," he murmurs. "I can't fucking *wait* to get inside you again. You make me lose myself, but it feels too good to stop." He curses. "I want you right now. Want to shove up this tease of a dress and fill you up with me. Have you walking around Amazon headquarters with a Paine brother dripping down your thighs."

My whole body clenches in response. "Filthy boy."

"You have no fucking idea. I don't recognize myself when I'm with you."

I don't intend to roll my hips, to rub my ass against his erection. It's an involuntary response to the rough promise in his voice. "Maybe that's a good thing."

"Only time will tell." His free hand comes around to press against my mound through my dress. "I have an edit to your plan."

I bite my bottom lip. "I'm open to suggestions."

"When you coax Shiloh's jeans open and slip your hand inside…" He presses the heel of his hand hard against my clit, dragging it up and down in a tortuously good rhythm. "You're going to be riding my cock when you do. Think I can make you come before *you* make *her* come?"

This is rapidly spinning away from me. It was one thing when I was guiding the action, but Broderick has effectively yanked control from my grasp. "Maybe?"

His chuckle is dark and full of promise. "Guess we'll find out." He releases me slowly, and when I wobble, he catches my elbows and keeps me on my feet. That tiny touch undoes me almost as much as the sexual ones did. No reason to look into it. No reason at all.

Once he's certain I'm steady, Broderick releases me. "I'll see you tonight." Then he's gone, striding away and leaving me shaking in the closet.

I finish dressing quickly and circle back to the bathroom to do my hair and makeup. By the time I'm ready to leave, I almost feel like myself again.

Almost.

CHAPTER 19

SHILOH

I'm an unforgivable coward. Instead of having a conversation with Monroe and Broderick like a mature adult, I slipped out of the bedroom while they were still sleeping. I even go so far as to beg Iris to take my shift in the Amazon territory for me today.

She gives me a sympathetic look as she pours herself a cup of coffee in a to-go mug. "Sorry, Shiloh. I have some stuff going on, and I can't move it. Maddox got a little anal with the assignments and shifting them now will cause problems."

She's right. I know she's right. There's a reason I'm on Monroe duty and a reason Maddox has assigned Iris to Matteo, Finnegan's Bride, the son of the Mystic. It might have to do with the fact that Iris and Finnegan are dating and have been for a long time, or it might be because she's deadly with a shotgun and Maddox thinks her skills are needed. If he and Cohen are as concerned about Fallon and the Mystics as they are about Monroe and the Amazons, then it makes sense.

That doesn't stop me from wanting to stomp my foot and

throw a fit like a child. "Okay," I say miserably. "You have a point."

She passes me the mug. "You want to talk about it?"

Yes, but I'm too embarrassed to admit how out of control things got last night. It's expected for Broderick to sleep with Monroe. Not required, not after the consummation, but hardly something to raise eyebrows at. Even me sleeping with Monroe isn't exactly against the rules. There *aren't* any rules about fraternization with this group or this faction. We're a close-knit group, and sometimes that means friendship, but there are plenty of people who have paired off over the years. Iris and Finnegan and Maddox and Cohen are just two examples of it.

But explaining that I got myself off while watching Broderick fuck Monroe, that I joined them in the bed and crossed so many lines? I can't do it. It's too messy. Iris and I are friends, and I won't be able to stand if it she looks at me like I'm as out of line as I feel.

I try for a smile. "Maybe later."

"Offer stands." She shrugs. "We're definitely swimming in the deep end now, aren't we?"

"You can say that again." My phone beeps, a reminder that Monroe and I need to leave now if we're going to make it to Amazon territory on time.

There's no help for it. I have to go get her. With one last smile at Iris, I leave the kitchen. I find Monroe standing at the front door, looking absolutely stunning in a fitted green dress that hits just above her knees. Her blond hair is styled in messy waves that my hands itch to sink into, and she's got her customary bloodred lipstick on. I stare at her mouth for a long moment. Impossible not to be hit with the memory of how good it felt to have her between my thighs, using that wicked tongue to bring me to orgasm.

She smiles widely. A real smile that reaches her green

eyes. As if she's actually happy to see me. "Good morning, love."

I'm not a nickname kind of person, but from her it feels remarkably natural. "Hey." I hesitate. Should I try to explain why I wasn't there when she woke up?

But it seems to be a moot point. Monroe loops her arm through mine and turns us toward the door. "It seems the baby Paine has drawn the short straw of delivering us today. Poor thing."

Sure enough, Gabriel is in the courtyard, standing next to one of the identical trucks we use to get around. He nods at me, though his gaze flicks to where Monroe is plastered to my side. I open the door for her and raise my brows at him. "I would think you'd be with Fallon." Like Monroe, as heir, she gets to travel to and from the Mystic's faction to work during the day.

"We needed a break." His tone discourages me from asking more questions. I still don't understand why Abel gave Fallon to Gabriel, of all his brothers. He's twenty-seven, so he's hardly a baby, but he's been sheltered to some degree in the way the other Paine brothers haven't. And, best I can tell, Fallon is fucking *feral*. She's like some wolf you'd find in the mountains, cold and predatory and all too willing to rip out your throat if you infringe on her territory.

I hate to say it, but Gabriel is outmatched.

The trip across the river into Amazon territory passes in uncomfortable silence. For once, Monroe doesn't seem interested in poking at me and flirting; she's too busy thinking. Or maybe things have changed after last night, and this is just the first indication of it.

I don't like the pang that goes through me at the thought. While I can't deny that things weren't working before, I've come to value my time with Monroe. I don't want to lose it.

I manage to keep my silence until we're in the elevator up

to Monroe's office, but once the doors close, the words spill out. "Are you mad at me?"

Her surprise doesn't appear feigned at all. "What? Why would I be mad at you?"

"Because I slept on the couch last night after…what happened. And left this morning before you woke up."

She blinks and then laughs. "Shiloh, you're not the first skittish person I've seduced." Her smile warms me right through. "To be clear, I *am* seducing you. Present tense."

I blink. "What?"

She catches my hand and flips it over to run her nails lightly over my wrist. "That is, if you want me to." She steps closer. Not quite close enough to be inappropriate, but she's certainly in my space. Monroe looks up at me. "Do you want me to seduce you, love?"

"Yes," I whisper.

She doesn't move. "Even if that means Broderick is involved?"

My body flushes hot and then cold. I was so incredibly reckless last night, but I can't quite bring myself to regret it. "He's my best friend. I don't want to ruin that." I don't mean to say it, but I don't mean to say a lot of things when it comes to Monroe. She has this way of pulling back my layers and shining the light on the parts of me I keep close to my heart. It's unnerving in the extreme.

"You won't," she answers so easily, I almost believe her.

It's tempting, so goddamned tempting, to tell her that I don't want Broderick to be involved. I can't be that selfish, though. Not only would it be a lie, but it would ultimately endanger Monroe herself. She and Broderick need to figure things out in order to preserve peace. *That* is more important than anything, even my potential heartbreak.

It's just sex.

No reason to complicate things more simply because I'm scared.

I swallow hard. "Then yes, even if it means Broderick's involved." A small part of me can't help wondering if maybe blowing up our old friendship is the only way to fix it. I *miss* him. I miss him showing up, seemingly at random, during my night shifts sometimes, and keeping me company. I miss the long meandering conversations we used to have, ones about everything and nothing, but felt so fucking *safe* because Broderick always cared about what I had to say. I miss the movie nights, and the after-shift drinks, and having him drag me to some hole in the wall pub he discovered.

I just flat out miss him.

"It's hard when a friendship jumps the tracks and you don't know how to get it back, isn't it?"

The question sounds sincere enough, so I answer honestly. "It's the worst."

"Stick with me, love. We'll figure it out."

The elevator doors open before I can summon a response, which is just as well. Falling to my knees and begging her to touch me so I can stop thinking so fucking hard about things best left alone is out of the question. I manage to hold it together as I follow Monroe out of the elevator and down the hall to her office.

We barely get a chance to settle in before her mother arrives.

It doesn't matter how many times I've seen her in the last two weeks; Aisling Rhodius is a terrifying woman. On the surface she's no different than any other posh CEO with expensive style and a ton of money invested in her appearance. But beneath? Every time she looks at me, I can practically see her categorizing all the ways she can kill me with the fountain pen in her hand. She wouldn't hesitate, wouldn't blink, and once she'd taken me down, she'd methodically ensure any evidence of my presence disappeared from the face of this city.

She would certainly kill me if she knew the truth about me.

I can definitely see this woman ordering a squad of her people to slip into Raider territory and set a strategic fire to their base, one that blocked the exits and ensured mass casualties. I've heard the story; it's a damn miracle Broderick and his brothers escaped.

She narrows icy eyes in my direction, but her words are for her daughter. "I need to speak with you."

Monroe doesn't look up from the paperwork she's paging through. "You know the rules, Mother. Shiloh has to stay, or the Paine brothers will get cranky."

Aisling gives me another long look, and I can't shake the feeling that she's mentally murdered me and shoved me out a window. She finally sighs. "Very well. I have it on good authority that Abel Paine threatened your life yesterday."

"I see." Monroe pauses, a paper still in her hand. She doesn't look at me, which is just as well. *I* didn't even know that happened until Broderick told us. How the fuck did Aisling find out? Monroe hasn't had any contact with her; if she had, there'd be no reason for Aisling to inform her now.

"Either handle the situation, or I will."

At that, Monroe shakes off her surprise. She narrows her green eyes and pushes to her feet. "Excuse me?"

"You heard me." Aisling doesn't move. She's got a few inches on Monroe, is closer to my height, and she uses it to her full advantage. "I will respect the rules of Lammas and the Bridal handfasting, but that only goes so far. You are the Amazon heir, and I will not have you threatened by Raider scum."

"Being fucked by one of them is fine, though."

The temperature in the room seems to drop ten degrees. "There is no shame in being a Bride. It's an ancient tradition, one that's kept our faction from war more than a few times. There's a reason that tradition endures and it will be respected."

"You're saying all the right words, Mother, but your tone leaves something to be desired." Monroe props her hands on her hips. "If you move against the Raiders, you know very well that you'll endanger Winry and Jasper."

"They're Amazons. They'll be fine."

I probably shouldn't find her coldness shocking. After all, one doesn't hold the position of queen of the Amazons for decades without being ruthless to a fault. But she's talking about her daughter and brother. Her *family*.

I hold perfectly still, barely daring to breathe, as Monroe stiffens. "I would happily sacrifice my life if it meant they stayed safe." She means it, too.

"You are the Amazon heir. That's not an option."

Monroe gives a bitter little laugh. "So the truth comes out. You're willing to wager Winry's life on this. She's my *sister*. She never asked for any of this, and you'll throw her to the wolves to keep me safe when I don't need it."

Aisling lifts her brows. "Your information leaves something to be desired, daughter. Cohen Paine is approaching an obsession with your sister. He won't allow anything permanent to remove her from his grasp until his feelings have run their course. I'll have the situation rectified by then."

If anything, Monroe looks more horrified. "That doesn't make your hedging your bets better. You don't know what he'll do to her."

"She's an Amazon," Aisling repeats. "She'll survive."

Not exactly a ringing endorsement. It's never been clearer

how differently the Amazons and Raiders function. Things weren't great in the Raider faction under Bauer Paine, but Abel is a different kind of leader. He's just as ruthless—when it comes to other people. *That's* the distinction. When it comes to his people, especially his brothers, he'll lie, cheat, and steal to keep them safe. I've witnessed it countless times over the years. He would never, ever pull some shit like this, purposefully endangering one of them to punish an enemy. He'd find another way.

"Ultimately, it's in your hands, daughter. Fix the situation, remove yourself from danger, and I won't have to take any steps." She glances at me and then to Monroe. "You know what I'll do otherwise. The ball is in your court."

"You're a real piece of work." Monroe's face goes red with fury, a break in control I've never seen from her. "Excuse me, I need some fresh air."

I go to follow her out of the office, but Aisling steps in my way. I glare. "Move, or I will move you."

"You will certainly try." Her lips curve, but her eyes remain icy. "You might even land a few blows, being an Amazon yourself."

The room takes a sickeningly slow spin around me. Surely she didn't say what I think she just said. "Excuse me?"

"Honestly, it was rather clever of you. I had no idea I should be looking for your past right under my nose. Shiloh Demaki, daughter of Esther and Lucas Demaki, both priests to the crown."

Holy fuck. *She knows.* I clear my throat. "I don't know what you're talking about."

"I think you do." Her gaze flicks to my legs, and there's no way to deny it further. She knows exactly who I am and exactly what happened to me. Aisling's face doesn't exactly go soft, but something almost like remorse appears, there and gone so quickly I'm half sure I imagined it. "That was a great failing of mine. I didn't realize the extent of their abuse until you were already gone and they'd moved on to other children. Children who didn't stay silent."

Rage whites out my vision for one long moment. An echo of Monroe's voice in my head layers over her mother's. *We don't blame victims.* Apparently that's only true for the next Amazon queen—not the current one.

When I finally manage to speak, my voice is hoarse. "I know you are not blaming me for my parents' actions."

"Of course not." Her tone is less than convincing. "However, it's been dealt with, and it's important to me that we move on."

Understanding comes in slow waves, spiking my fury higher, hotter. It loosens my tongue and has me spitting words best kept internal. "I see. You fucked up and let precious Amazon children be hurt by people who were close to you. An unforgivable sin in your daughter's eyes. If Monroe knew my parents were Amazons, that *you* knew—"

"I didn't know," she says it so sharply, I almost believe her.

If not for her own words. "You just said you didn't know the extent of it, which means you *did* know something."

Aisling's expression goes even colder, a confirmation in and of itself. "It's in the past."

In the past, and yet it's shaped my entire life, my future even. If not for what I experienced at my parents' hands, I wouldn't find coming to Sabine Valley so challenging. I wouldn't have started pushing Broderick away when he needed me to pull him close and have his back. I wouldn't be having this conversation right now.

"If that's true, you wouldn't be bringing it up now, trying to smooth away the sins of the past." I don't move, don't shift in any way that could be construed as a physical attack. Why bother when my words will do the trick? "Monroe cares about me, you know."

"I've been made aware." Her mouth twists. "Which is why we're having this conversation. It's in your best interest to keep your mouth shut about your childhood. I will not interfere with your relationship, but I will also not allow *you* to interfere with *my* relationship with my daughter." She turns to the door. "No matter what the cost. It will hurt her to lose you, but only in the short term." Then she's gone, closing the door softly behind her.

It takes several beats for me to reconcile the fact that she just threatened me. I have absolutely no desire to tell Monroe that her precious Amazons are responsible for the abuse I suffered as a child. No matter what else is true of her, she's got rose-tinted glasses when it comes to her faction. If I were another person, I wouldn't hesitate to rip them off her face and force her to see the truth—that monsters lurk everywhere, and Amazons aren't exempt—but it would hurt her to discover that.

I don't want to hurt her.

I...care about her.

The door opens again, and Monroe stalks back into the room. She drops into her chair. "Well, this is a giant clusterfuck."

I've never seen her look so off-center. I don't make a conscious decision to move. One moment I'm standing there, still trying to process the enormity of what Aisling dropped on me, and the next I'm moving, crossing the office in giant strides to pull Monroe into my arms. I half expect her to push me away. She's not the type to lean on someone, let alone someone like *me*. Someone who's technically an enemy.

But...she does lean on me.

Monroe hugs me tightly to her for one long moment... two...three.

It turns out I need this hug just as much as she apparently does. I close my eyes and inhale the sunny scent of her, letting her presence wash away the shadows clinging from the past. I knew my parents had a connection with the Amazon throne, that they were protected by it, but I had convinced myself that Aisling didn't really see me that day, that she had no clue what they'd done to me.

At some point, I'm going to have to process that information, but not right now. Nothing that happened to me as a child was Monroe's fault, and right now, Broderick is in more danger than I am.

When she finally loosens her hold and shifts back, she almost looks like herself. Or she would if I didn't know her well enough by now to see the fine tremor in her hands as she fixes her hair. She clears her throat. "Well, that's one way to start the day."

"She's going to kill Broderick." She didn't have to speak the threat explicitly for it to be clear. Just like she didn't have to voice the direct threat against me. If Aisling kills Broderick... No force in Sabine Valley will stop Abel from razing the Amazon faction to the ground. I can't even blame him for that; I'm feeling particularly murderous right now, too. Coming back to this city, embroiling ourselves in the power games and political bullshit... How am I supposed to see it as anything other than a mistake if *this* is the cost?

Home isn't a place, it's the people you surround yourself with. The ones you choose. Maybe the Paine brothers don't realize that, maybe they never would have chosen to return to Sabine Valley if they had. I've never asked.

It doesn't matter.

We've come too far now. After Lammas, if Abel and the others buckle, they'll bring the entire Raider faction down with them. They were hunted after they were driven out of Sabine Valley the first time, but it's nothing compared to what will happen if they run again. Now both Amazon and Mystic leaders know exactly what kind of threat Abel Paine and his brothers can bring to the fore. They'll do whatever it takes to ensure they never get another chance.

No, we have no choice.

We have to see this through.

CHAPTER 20

BRODERICK

I spend the day training with Donovan, Ezekiel, and Cohen. Or, to be more accurate, checking in on those three. I like to check in with my brothers at least once every couple of days normally, but things have gone sideways since returning to Sabine Valley. I know Abel's doing fine. Cohen, too. But the others? Impossible to say.

Tomorrow, I'll search out Gabriel and Finnegan and make sure they're holding up fine, too.

I'm quickly coming to realize that nothing is the same as it was. No one is perfectly okay, and my brothers are fighting their own battles, even if they're not overt about it. I wipe the sweat from my forehead and glance at the twins.

Donovan and Ezekiel couldn't be more opposite if they tried. Oh, they are damn near identical and favor the same dapper style, constantly overdressing for everything. But that's where the similarities end. The sweet kid Ezekiel used to be burned away over the last near-decade, leaving the monster he is now. He's *our* monster, but I'm aware enough to call a spade a spade.

Donovan reacted to our exile in a very different way.

Instead of grasping so tightly to whatever he values the way the rest of us do, he grasps on to nothing at all. He moves through life, carried by the force of his whims and sense of humor. It boggles my mind.

We're nearly done when a woman walks into the courtyard. She's tall and built like a tank, and she's wearing a muscle T-shirt and basketball shorts. It takes me a few moments to recognize her. Sonya, the self-appointed bodyguard to Donovan's Bride, Mabel. No one was happy that she tagged along that first night, but she's kept her head down and hasn't caused trouble since, so her presence is tolerated. That doesn't explain why she's *here*.

Donovan gives an easy grin when he sees her. "You're late."

"Sorry. Mabel lost track of time talking with Rae. She's not feeling well, and they had some suggestions. And then they got to talking and...you know how it goes."

Is she blushing?

I exchange a look with Ezekiel. He doesn't seem inclined to jump in, so I clear my throat. "Is she sick?" If she is, that will complicate things, especially if it's serious. Mabel is one of our Brides. Her health and safety are paramount to maintaining the Bridal peace.

Sonya opens her mouth, but it's Donovan who answers breezily. "Just menstruation stuff. She has nasty monthlies, and I thought Rae might have some suggestions to help."

"Jesus, there's more than one of them right now?" This from Cohen, low enough that I don't think he intended me to hear it.

I'll focus on *that* later. I frown at Donovan. "Since when do you know a single fucking thing about periods?"

"Since my Bride has one."

I guess technically, my Bride has one as well. I haven't seen evidence of it yet, but I've also spent most of the past three weeks avoiding her. Not that it matters one way or another. I learned enough to be helpful to Shiloh when she was feeling like garbage because of her body's cycle. But Donovan has never been particularly close to any of the menstruating people in our group. "You sent her to Rae, though?"

Rae is the doctor Harlow brought into the compound after Eli took a bullet for Abel. And then they...never left. Not that I'm complaining. It's useful having a doctor around, and best I can tell, Rae is brilliant. I think I heard Harlow say that they were a prodigy back in the day. I don't understand how someone *used* to be a prodigy, but having a doctor on the compound has already come in handy.

Even if they are a giant pain in the ass with an attitude problem.

Really, Rae fits right in.

Donovan shrugged. "Mabel said that level of pain is normal for her, but it seems kind of extreme. It's not like the Mystics have much in the way of real doctors over there. They're more likely to shove a crystal up your ass and send you on your way."

"*Donovan.*"

He grins at Sonya, completely unrepentant. "Tell me I'm wrong."

"The Mystics have plenty of healers." She tries to glare at him, but her lips curve a little.

"Healers, not doctors. Rae has a fucking medical degree. They didn't just wake up one day, check the stars, and decide they knew a single damn thing about human bodies."

This conversation has the feel of well-tread ground, which means it could go on for some time. I stride over to where we left our phones and check the time. I have to go if I'm going to make it to Amazon territory in time to pick up

Monroe and Shiloh at the end of the day. "I'll catch you all later."

Cohen walks with me into the house. He doesn't speak until we climb the stairs and approach my room. "You taking care of the Monroe problem?"

"Yeah. I've got it covered." It's even the truth. Really, I should thank Abel for being such a fucking asshole about this, because he's paved the way for me to take what I want. I *have* to, after all. For the greater good of the territory and the Raider faction.

I'm a fucking liar.

I duck into the bedroom and take a quick shower. I made a few trips this morning from the room I was essentially squatting in and this one, transferring my stuff back into the closet. Or at least a corner of the closet available. Between Monroe's stuff and Shiloh's stuff, there isn't much space.

I take slightly more care in dressing than I would normally. A navy suit with a crisp white button-down. I could blame it on being about to enter enemy territory, but the truth is that I want to look good for my women.

My women.

Calling either of them mine feels strange and not entirely accurate. But it's not *not* accurate, either. What we have is messy in the extreme, but I'm enjoying it despite myself.

Driving out of the compound feels strange. I don't leave the walled space that often. Abel runs the territory. Cohen runs our forces. Donovan, Ezekiel, Finnegan, and Gabriel all have smaller responsibilities geared in different specialties. Things are a little different now that Abel has Harlow and Eli as Brides. Harlow has become his Bride wrangler. Eli is his bridge between the past eight years of absence and our presence here now.

And me? I run the household.

I source shit we need, ensure things function as they

should, and problem-solve where there are problems needing solved. I keep track of my brothers, ensure they're all where they're supposed to be, that no one has fallen through the cracks.

I leave the compound and take my time driving north toward the bridge that connects Raider territory with Amazon. The last three weeks haven't changed much on the surface, but I can already see the difference in how people react to the truck I'm driving that marks me as being connected to my family. The first week, people watched us as if expecting violence. Now, most of the suspicion has dissipated, and I even get a few waves.

That cautious acceptance stops the second I cross the bridge. There isn't a marked difference between the Raider faction and Amazon faction at first. Not unless you count the skyscrapers clustered in the center of their territory. The people still look exactly the same. Normal. So incredibly normal. That's not the case with the Mystics and their love for dramatic clothing and flowing robes in a mishmash of colors. Amazons don't go for that kind of in-your-face style. You wouldn't know they're even Amazons until they're sinking a blade between your ribs.

I head for the building at the very center of the territory. It's a giant steel-and-glass monstrosity that stretches many floors higher than those around it. Any other city in the world, that would just be a coincidence, but not here. Here, this marks the Amazon queen's work and living space.

Thankfully, I don't have to get out of the truck or go up. Monroe is one Amazon too many. Her sister seems fine, and her uncle used to be someone who was almost a friend, but Monroe is the very essence of an Amazon. Ruthless and savvy and willing to use whatever weapon is at hand to accomplish her goal.

I'm still not sure what her goal is.

No, that's not quite true. I might not know her goal when it comes to our factions and the future, but I know her immediate goal.

Get Shiloh into bed with us.

A slow heat curls through me as I catch sight of the women standing on the sidewalk in front of the building. Monroe looks just as good in her green dress as she did this morning, and Shiloh is gorgeous in her customary black tank top and jeans. Her clothes hug her lean body, and I can't help curling my fingers and remembering how good it felt when she clamped around them.

I can't believe I agreed to this, but this moment feels almost fated. Like we've been on this path, hurtling to this juncture, from the moment we met. Or maybe that's just what I'm telling myself to excuse taking what I want.

Her.

Them.

Monroe climbs into the truck first. She practically lands in my lap, and then her mouth is on mine. The kiss is messy and a little rough. Fuck, this woman drives me wild. It's not a comfortable feeling, but I'm slowly getting used to how much I enjoy it.

She leans back and uses her thumb to wipe her lipstick from my mouth. "Missed you."

"Liar."

"Only a little." She laughs. "Are you coming, Shiloh?"

That's when I notice that Shiloh hasn't gotten into the truck. She's staring at us with a strange expression on her face, one I've never seen before. It almost appears to be a cross between jealousy and longing, but I afraid to assume. Monroe promised me that we wouldn't bully Shiloh into doing anything she doesn't want to do, but part me can't help the suspicion that she was only in our bed last night for

Monroe. Yeah, she got off on my fingers, but it was Monroe's tongue that pushed her over the edge.

Shiloh gives herself a shake. "Yeah, I'm coming." She hefts herself up into the truck and shuts the door.

Monroe slides off my lap but stays pressed to my side. "I'd like a favor, husband."

"What?"

She walks her fingers up my thigh, and it's everything I can do to keep my physical reaction to a minimum. "I'm parched. I'd like to go get a drink."

On the other side of her, Shiloh narrows her eyes. "That's the second time this week."

"What can I say? I like what I like." Monroe laughs. "Come out with us, love. It'll be fun." She sinks enough innuendo into *fun* to launch a thousand ships.

Shiloh hesitates but finally nods. "Okay. I guess I could use a drink."

"That's our girl," Monroe murmurs.

Our girl.

The shared term goes straight to my head. As hard as I get off on going head-to-head with Monroe, working together is so much more intoxicating. I keep waiting for the feeling to fade, but it only seems to grow stronger the more time we spend on the same wavelength. It's enough to make me forget myself, forget the reasons I'm here.

For Shiloh.

For my brothers.

For the faction.

I drive back over the bridge and past the compound and Old Town to a little bar a few blocks south. It's stood here for decades and used to be a place where Abel, Cohen, and I would drink before we turned twenty-one. The old owner was a friend of our father, and he never bothered to card us. He's been dead a few years now, and his daughter has run the place ever since. Jennifer is a large white woman who looks like she could crack my head with her bare hands. Her longtime girlfriend, Renée, a petite Black woman with braids, is her exact opposite, as sweet as she is tiny. She's the one who waves when we walk through the door and into the dim interior. "Go ahead and sit wherever."

The place is the same superficially as it was the last time I walked through the door. The bar still stretches across most of the wall across from the door and there are a scattering of tables and chairs, mostly empty. But it's changed. This place used to be a dump, exactly the kind of bar a person would expect to find minors drinking in because they don't bother to card. Sticky floors, smoke perpetually gathering in clouds against the ceiling, all sorts of unsavory types lingering in the shadows created by not enough light.

It's still dim in here, still welcoming in that specific way, but it smells faintly of lemon cleaner, and there are actual framed pieces of art on the wall. They're all stylized drinking glasses and bottles, nice enough to look at, but they don't try to make this place anything but what it is. A dive bar, if a cleaner and safer one than it used to be.

Even the clientele seems different, though it's still too early in the day to say for sure. But the few people already here are wearing clothes that suggest they're stopping by for a drink on their way home from work.

Things really have changed.

I try for a smile at Renée. "Is the back room open?"

She grins. "I knew you looked familiar. Broderick Paine, right?"

"Yeah."

"It's been a while. For you, it's open." Renée jerks her thumb at the doorway in the back. "You want me to come back and get your orders, or do you need privacy?"

"Privacy, please. I'll grab our drinks and take them back

myself."

Her grin widens as she takes in Monroe and Shiloh behind me. "Go on ahead, then."

The women slide past me and head toward the doorway. Shiloh looks nervous and jumpy. Monroe is all wicked smiles and a loose-limbed stride that somehow manages to scream sex without her doing anything overt. I give our drink orders to Renée, wait for her to fill them, hand her some cash, and follow the women into the back room.

Shiloh and Monroe have their heads close together when I push through the door. The room is exactly like I remember it, if a thousand times cleaner. My shoes don't stick to the floors as I cross the half-circle booth that takes up most of the space. It's been reupholstered sometime in the last decade with leather, and the tabletop has been replaced with shiny wood that isn't cut all to shit. The last time I was back here, there was a knife sticking out of the center of the table.

Monroe grins. "Right on time. I was thinking we'd have some fun and play a game."

I carefully set the glasses down and eye her. "A drinking game?" I am fully on board with seducing Shiloh, but I'm not going to touch her if she's drunk. I would assume Monroe is the same; if she hadn't also been buzzed out of her mind the other day, I don't think they would have hooked up in the bar's bathroom. In fact, I'm certain of it. Monroe is too damn protective of the people in her sphere to take advantage of someone like that.

"No, silly man. Drinking games are best done with shots and a determination to get into trouble. This is just a fun little game for *friends*."

I raise my eyebrows. "Why don't I believe you?"

"I couldn't begin to say. That sounds like a *you* problem."

She holds up a hand, her expression the very picture of innocence. "Don't you want to play with me?"

Shiloh makes a choked sound. "You're so much sometimes, Monroe."

"You aren't the first person to say it." She tucks a strand of blond hair behind her ear. "It strikes me that neither of you had a proper childhood." She pats the spot next to her. "Stop looming and sit down."

"I'm not looming." But I sit, curious on where she's headed with this. "I had a childhood."

"You had Bauer Paine as your father, a dead mother, and five younger brothers that you mostly raised." She snorts. "You had to grow up fast."

Monroe isn't exactly wrong. My mother died a long time ago, and my father was hardly the poster child for good parenting. Abel did his best, but he always had his eyes on the role of leading the faction. It inevitably fell to me to supervise my younger brothers. Considering my brothers, that was a full-time job.

It's still a full-time job, even if I've been shirking my duties since coming back to the city.

She leans against me as she turns to Shiloh on her other side. "And don't even try to tell me that *you* had anything resembling normal teenage years."

I tense, but Shiloh just shrugs. "It was normal for me."

I don't like the shadows that flicker across her face when she talks about the past. She survived horrific things at the hands of her parents. We've touched on the subject enough for me to know that, even if I don't know all the gory details. Her parents were religious and abusive, and they hurt her terribly. I clear my throat, determined to bring the conversation around. "You're the Amazon heir. You can't honestly tell me your childhood was *normal*."

"Normal enough." She tilts her head back to lean against

my shoulder. "I'm sure most children don't have weapons training and the various things my mother required of me, but Amazons take childhood very seriously. There was plenty of fun, too." She gives a sexy little wiggle. "We can work on recreating other memories later, but today I was thinking of a tried and true experience."

Even though I'm technically in on this, my stomach goes a little hollow. "What experience?"

The satisfaction in her voice is nearly overwhelming. "Truth or dare."

CHAPTER 21

MONROE

*T*his is all technically part of a plan for Broderick and me to seduce Shiloh, but there's a reason I decided to go about it in this way. Truth or dare is a silly game, and it was sort of a rite of passage within my friends when I was a teenager. I want to share that experience with these two people who are rapidly becoming...important to me.

Neither of these two had much in the way of "normal" childhood experiences. Best I can tell, Broderick was second father to his brothers. It's no wonder he's got such a stick up his ass after being responsible for so many people for so long. And I've been training to be queen long enough to be able to identify a person's fault lines. Broderick wants to protect the people he cares about, the people he feels responsible for.

We have that in common.

Truth be told, we have a *lot* in common.

And Shiloh? When I look at her, at the wariness on her face, I suddenly want to give her new memories to overshadow the old ones. The bad ones. My heart gives an uncomfortable thud, and the sensation only gets stronger when I shift my attention back to Broderick. He watches me with a contemplative expression on his handsome face. Serious. Oh, so serious. Was he born that way, or did it happen after his mother died and he was forced to share the parental load of raising his five younger brothers? I bet it was the latter.

Oh fuck, I'm in trouble.

I grab my drink and take a long pull. Another time, I'll ask Broderick how he knew I like Old Fashions. Right now, I'm hunting larger game. "Some ground rules before we begin. There are both penalties for lying and for taking a dare and then backing out."

"Of course there are," Broderick says. A small smile pulls at the edges of his lips, a true smile. "What penalty?"

"Sleeping on the couch for a week, with no Monroe-induced orgasms."

He snorts. "Who says that's a deterrent?"

"Me." I bump my head against his shoulder. "Both of you were having excellent orgasms last night because of me. Don't try to pretend you're not counting down the hours until you're inside me again." I nudge Shiloh with my knee. "And don't lie and say you want to do anything but come all over my face again."

She crosses her arms over her chest. "Okay, fine. Let's play."

It's cute how she's trying to be so cranky, as if I can't see the anticipation licking through her the same way I'm dying to. I smile at her, letting lust seep into my eyes. "You're up first, love. Truth or dare?"

She glances over my shoulder at Broderick, and her face goes pink. "Dare."

Smart girl.

The second she picks truth, I'm going to ask her if she

wants to fuck Broderick. She knows it, too, so I wager Shiloh will go dare every time. "Let's start nice and slow." I tap my fingers against my glass. "Shiloh, I dare you to kiss me."

Her sigh of relief is audible enough that it almost makes me laugh. This woman has obviously never been properly seduced before. It's important to ease a person into it, not to shove them off the cliff. It took me three weeks to work us up to a kiss. I'm not about to throw away my first dare by having her jump on Broderick's cock.

By the time he fucks her, she's going to be begging for it.

Shiloh leans forward and cups my face with one hand. She's got calluses, evidence of the weapons training she leaves me to do a few times a week. Her lips are soft as she presses them to mine. My girl might seem sweet, but she wastes no time slipping her tongue into my mouth and kissing me properly.

It lasts long enough that Broderick clears his throat. When Shiloh sits back, she's flushing, and I ache for more. *Patience.* I can be patient. I lick my lips. "Your turn."

Shiloh turns hazel eyes on Broderick. "Truth or dare?"

"Truth." There's an edge to his tone, a dare all its own.

She gives a small smile, but there's an edge of cruelty to it. "Do you enjoy how you are with Monroe?"

He goes rigid behind me. "I don't understand the question."

"I think you do." Shiloh takes a small drink of her beer. "You are so careful with everyone else around you—with me. With Monroe, you're different than I've ever seen you. Harder. Meaner. You..." She looks away. "You fucked her like you were mad at her. Did you enjoy it?"

I don't mean to hold my breath. I really don't. Obviously Broderick likes how he is with me, even if it torments him at the same time, challenges the role he's stepped into. The good man. The caretaker. There's no room in that role for cruelty, and yet he's cruel to me, especially when it comes to sex.

He finally curses. "Yes. I enjoy the way we fuck. Yeah, I enjoy the way I am with Monroe." Broderick snags his glass and takes a long drink from it. He speaks before I can process how I feel about his admission. "Truth or dare, Shiloh."

"What?" She blinks. "It's Monroe's turn."

It's an effort to keep my body relaxed. I might have started this game, but it's rapidly slipping beyond my control. Maybe that should concern me, but there's something magical brewing between the three of us. It's hot and sticky and oh so dangerous. I want to see what happens when this powder keg explodes. I wave a lazy hand through the air. "The previous person can choose whomever they like."

She narrows her eyes but finally says, "Dare."

"Take off your pants."

I cough. I can't help it. I didn't expect him to go for it so hard, to ask something that seems so simple on the surface but is anything but. "Broderick—"

"No one is coming through that door." His voice is low and ruthless. "It's just us. Either you trust us, or you don't. Either you trust *me*, or you don't."

"That's not fair."

"I'm not interested in being fair." This is the man I met on Lammas, the one I've provoked time and time again. The targeted determination curls my toes. Broderick shifts, draping his arms over the back of the booth. The new position has me tucked against his side, and once again it feels like it's us versus Shiloh.

Like we're *aligned*.

She hesitates but finally curses and fights her way out of her jeans. Broderick studies his drink instead of her newly revealed legs—newly revealed scars—but I look my fill. I have no business being so turned on by black cotton panties, but everything about Shiloh gets my engine revving.

Shiloh glares. "Monroe. Truth or dare?"

"Dare."

She worries her bottom lip for a moment, and I can practically see her mind going a hundred miles an hour as she contemplates her options. "Suck Broderick's cock." A meaningful pause. "Not enough to get him off, though."

That draws a laugh from me. "Mean."

"I don't know what you're talking about. I'm just playing the game."

"And playing it well, love." I climb over Broderick's lap to arrange myself on his other side. Yes, this should do perfectly.

Shiloh's eyes go wide. "What are you doing?"

"Sucking Broderick's cock." He doesn't move as I slowly undo his pants. I blink innocent eyes at her. "It's your dare. Surely you want to witness it." I delve a hand into his pants and can't help a sound of pleasure when I wrap my hand around his hard cock. I don't give Shiloh a chance to sputter out a response before I dip down and take Broderick's cock into my mouth. I sucked him off last night, but this feels different.

He's so fucking huge, my jaw quickly begins to ache. That's okay. I'm no quitter, and I fully intend to put on a good show for Shiloh—and torment Broderick a little. I lift my head enough to flick my tongue against his slit, and he curses.

His big hand lands on my head. I fully expect him to tighten his grip and fuck my mouth, but he simply gathers my hair away from my face.

Giving Shiloh a better view.

My pussy clenches at the realization. This man really is cruel in the sexiest way possible. Just for that move, I give him an extra few minutes of the pleasure of my mouth before I slowly lift my head. His hand tenses in my hair as if he wants to drag me back down, but he slowly releases me.

Broderick starts to tuck his cock away, but I shake my head. "No point in wedging that thing back into your pants. I think we'll be needing it again." I smile slowly. "Won't we, Shiloh?"

It's the first time I've looked at her since I started sucking Broderick's dick. She's got her legs crossed *hard*, and the flush from her cheeks has coursed down to encompass every bit of skin I can see. Shiloh has a death grip on the seat of the booth. I bet she caught herself trying to either reach for us or slip her hand down her panties.

I lick my lips. "Broderick." I say his name without looking at him. "Truth or dare?"

"Dare."

I hold Shiloh's gaze. She tenses, the barest flinch that tells me she might be worked up, but she's not ready for the next step. *Soon.* "Take my dress off." I ease out of the booth and stand before them. "Do it properly."

He stares at me for a long moment, and the hunger in his blue gaze has me shaking a little bit. No matter if the goal here is to seduce Shiloh, this man still wants me. A lot. He stands slowly and moves to stand at my back, both of us facing the table where Shiloh sits.

Broderick shifts my hair over my shoulder to bare the back of my dress. I don't think any of us draw a full breath as he slowly drags down my zipper with the same care he zipped me up this morning. He coasts his thumb up my spine and then along my shoulder to dip beneath the strap of the dress. "No bra."

"It doesn't work with this dress." My voice sounds too breathy, but there's no help for it. I can't pretend to be unaffected; not when I'm about to come out of my skin just from this simple touch, from the careful dance the three of us engage in.

Shiloh's staring at Broderick's thumb beneath the strap as if she can will him to move if she concentrates hard enough. His hand twitches a little in response, and then he's sliding the strap from my shoulder and tugging the fitted fabric down, down, down to expose my breast. Shiloh licks her lips as he repeats the slow process with the second strap. I expect that to be the end, but Broderick isn't done. He brackets my ribs with his hands and coasts them along my sides to my hips, taking the fabric with him. Over my hips and down my thighs, until I have to brace myself on his shoulder to step out of the dress. I'm wearing only a lace thong and my heels, and the look he gives me as he kneels before me...

Gods, I might alight in an inferno just from that.

Broderick stands before I can do something foolish like dig my hands into his short hair. He folds my dress with the utmost care, pauses to do the same with Shiloh's discarded jeans, and then sets the clothing on the far side of the table. "Monroe." His voice has gone deep. "Truth or dare?"

"Dare."

Broderick slides back into the booth and holds his hand out. "Get over here, and let me make you feel good."

"Broderick." I'm already moving, taking his hand and letting him guide me to sit on his lap, facing away from him. He has to adjust his cock and it ends up pressed against my ass. "That's a very open-ended dare."

He nudges my legs to drape over the outside of his and cups my breasts. "Stay here until someone dares you otherwise."

I shiver. "Still too open-ended."

"So sue me." He rolls my nipples between his fingers, drawing them to hard points. He's not even touching my pussy, depriving me of the contact I desperately need as pleasure builds inside me. I turn my head to look at Shiloh. She's staring at his hands on my breasts and shifting in her seat as if looking for the same kind of contact I am.

Not yet, baby.

I could pretend it's all part of the plan when I gasp, "Truth or dare, Shiloh."

"Dare."

Right now, I can't think of the plan, the proper steps. I'm too turned on. I just need to orgasm. "Make me come, baby."

She scoots close and, after a quick look at Broderick, hesitates. For his part, he ignores her. Smart man. He must realize how skittish she still is because he starts kissing my shoulder, my neck, all of his attention seemingly focused on my breasts.

Once she realizes he won't interfere, Shiloh huffs out a breath and cups my pussy though my panties. I can't hold back my moan at the touch; I don't even try. She drags her knuckle down the center of my panties and then back up again to press against my clit. The next descent, she moves back enough to hook her fingers inside the lace and move it away from my heated flesh. "It's a shame I can't see you," she murmurs.

Broderick doesn't hesitate. He nudges her back and moves me easily to sit facing her. Without missing a beat, he wraps a hand around one thigh, and Shiloh shoves my other leg wide. "Better." She tugs my panties to the side again.

I look down, feeling Broderick doing the same. My pussy is framed by the black lace, pink and glistening with need. Shiloh parts me with two fingers as if offering the view up for our pleasure. "I should tease you."

"Don't." I sound needy, but I can't help it. They've barely touched me and I'm so fucking close.

"Broderick." She doesn't look at him, doesn't look away from my pussy. "Hold her legs for me?"

"Sure." He hooks my other thigh on the outside of his knee, keeping me wide for them. It takes some maneuvering with the table. He can't spread me as wide as he obviously wants to, but he manages to hold me open as Shiloh continues to deliver those teasing little strokes down either side of my pussy, parting me in a teasing rhythm.

For a moment, I think she really will tease me until I beg, but Shiloh curses and shoves two fingers into me. The penetration bows my back, and I can't help crying out when she adds a third. With her other hand, she idly strokes my clit. The light contact contrasted with her fingers slowly, thoroughly fucking me has me writhing. Or at least I would writhe if Broderick weren't pinning me in place, a butterfly spread out for their ministrations.

"I…" I can't catch my breath. I can't do anything but take it. I was supposed to be in control of this situation, but I've quickly barreled past the point of no return. There's no holding out, no trying to make this last. Against their touch, I don't stand a chance.

I come with a cry that Broderick swallows down in a kiss, owning my mouth just as much as Shiloh owns my pussy. She eases me down, but not all the way. I'm still shaking when she sits back and clears her throat. "Monroe. Truth or dare?"

CHAPTER 22

SHILOH

I know what this is. I understand what they're doing. Monroe recognized my lie the moment I told it last night, and she's not one to let something like that go unanswered. She wants us both in her bed, and she's not going to stop until it happens.

I didn't expect Broderick to be on board with it.

Or for the two of them to work together so seamlessly.

But here we are, in the back room of this bar, Monroe still shaking from her orgasm, and Broderick looking at me like *I'm* the next thing on the menu. Things have changed while I wasn't looking, and now I'm adrift. If I were smart, I'd cut and run now. Nothing good comes from continuing this *game* that feels like anything but.

Except... I don't want to stop.

I stare down at Monroe's pussy, pink and swollen with pleasure and so wet, she's leaving a damp spot on Broderick's thigh. I can't see his cock from this position, but knowing it's there, hard and aching from Monroe's mouth...

I really, really don't want to stop.

I'm not fearless, though. I can't take this step on my own.

"Dare," Monroe finally gasps.

"I dare you to fuck Broderick."

She laughs a little as he lifts her to straddle him. He's got a look on his face that I've only seen once before, and only in shadows. Last night. One that almost makes him a stranger, hard and a little intimidating from the sheer intensity coming from him. I clench my thighs together and then do it harder when his gaze drops to my lower half. I don't have my normal shield of jeans, but for once, I'm not thinking about my scars or my past or anything but this moment. Maybe I'll be self-conscious later, but there's no room in this space for it. Not now.

Monroe gives me a small smile, her eyes heavy with pleasure. "Do you like this, baby?" She reaches between them to wrap a hand around his massive cock.

And it is massive.

I can't help following her movement, watching her work him slowly. I've seen Broderick in varying states of undress over the years, but he's not into casual nudity the way some in the group are. He's not naked now, for all that the important bits are on display.

"Do I like what?" I don't intend to ask the question, but it slips free all the same.

"Like commanding us as if we're your own personal Barbies?" She lifts herself up and notches his cock at her entrance. "We'll do anything you want. You just have to say so."

The moment we started playing this game, it felt like stepping onto a slippery slope that would lead up to this moment. To them fucking and me watching. Except I'm not just watching, am I? Monroe's inviting an active participation in a way that feels almost natural. They're not throwing me off the deep end and overwhelming me. They're... inviting me in. A little bit at a time.

Her legs shake a little bit, but she holds still otherwise, the challenge clear on her face. I don't have to do this. I know I don't.

But I want to.

"Take his cock, Monroe. All of it." I hardly sound like myself.

"Happily."

Broderick holds perfectly still as she works her way down his length. It strikes me that they're not using a condom, that they obviously weren't using one last night, and my body clenches with a need so strong, it takes my breath away. It feels so fucking dirty to know they're fucking bare; it feels so sexy, I want it for myself.

Monroe finally seats herself fully onto his cock and leans back to prop her elbows on the table. The position puts her breasts on display, puts her whole body on display. She's panting a little bit but manages to arch an eyebrow in my direction. "And now?"

She's really going to make me say it. I *love* that she's going to make me say it. "Ride him slow," I whisper.

She begins rolling her body, working herself slowly up and down his cock. Even though I know better, I slide a little closer. I want to *see*. It's more than worth the proximity to witness her lifting herself mostly off his thick length, to see his cock shine from her desire, to know they're fucking at *my* command.

"Shiloh." Monroe's voice as gone breathy. "Truth or dare?"

"But you're not done."

She grins at me. "No reason not to keep going."

Broderick coasts his hands up her hips. Not guiding, simply touching her in a way I ache to. Similar to how I ache to have him touch *me* in exactly that way. Rough and yet almost reverent.

"Dare." The word emerges as a whisper.

Her grin goes victorious. "I dare you to ride Broderick's hand until you come."

Broderick goes tense and then tenser yet as I clasp his wrist and tug his hand away from Monroe's skin. I shift to kneel on the bench facing them. No matter what else happens, I don't want to miss a moment of the show they're putting on. He allows me to guide him to press against my stomach, to ease his hand into my panties…

And that's when his leash snaps.

He spears me with two fingers, curling his palm until the heel of his hand presses to my clit. His blue eyes have gone dark, or maybe it's my vision going dark because we're doing this out here in the light. There is no going back after this, no plausible deniability provided by the shadows. There is just him staring at me like he wants to devour me whole and me staring right back with an invitation I'm still not sure I'm ready to follow through on.

Liar.

I rock my hips, fucking his fingers as he holds perfectly still. I don't exactly mean to match my rhythm to Monroe's, but it happens naturally. My breath hitches. "Broderick."

"Hmm." His gaze is so intense, it feels like he's stroking my entire body. He curls his fingers inside me, unerringly finding my G-spot. Combined with the heel of his palm against my clit, it's creating a delicious friction with each downward stroke. I'm about to combust.

I'm so fucking close, I'm shaking. Just…not yet. "Broderick." I gasp. "Truth or dare?"

No hesitation. "Dare."

"Kiss me." It's not even a proper dare, but it doesn't seem to matter.

Broderick hesitates, and that might be enough to have me running for the hills, but Monroe doesn't give me a chance. She leans over and digs one hand into my hair and the clasps the back of Broderick's neck with the other. It's the barest amount of pressure, but it doesn't matter. I'm too eager to stop this. I'm the one who voiced the dare, after all.

His breath ghosts against my lips, and then his mouth is on mine. All of his hesitation seems to have been used up in that first moment, because his hand between my legs tenses before he's hauling me closer so he can take my mouth properly. And he does take my mouth. Broderick's kiss is a claiming. He dominates with teeth and tongue, and it's too late for me. I'm coming all over his fingers, sobbing into his mouth with pleasure.

Broderick pulls back a little, and then Monroe is there, taking a kiss of her own. She doesn't let me sink into it the same way, though. She leans back and looks at my face. "I would like to fuck you properly, Shiloh. Will you let us?"

Us.

If I say yes, there's no going back, but the truth is there was going back the moment I agreed to play this game. I find myself nodding, my brain still fuzzy from the orgasm. "Yes."

"Perfect." She presses a kiss to Broderick's lips. "Sorry, love. You're going to have to nurse a case of blue balls for a little bit."

"Wait."

They both look at me. It's Broderick who answers, "Change your mind?"

"*No.*" The word comes out too intense, but I don't want either of them to think, for a single moment, that I'm not 100 percent ready to take this to its natural conclusion. Okay, maybe not 100 percent, but certainly ready enough to go for it. I clear my throat. "Finish this here—I want you both to come." Broderick's fingers twitch inside me, which propels me to continue. "I want you to fill her up. I want to taste you there the next time I go down on her."

Monroe gives a strangled laugh. "You're so fucking *wicked.*"

Broderick doesn't look like he wants to laugh. He stares at me like he's never seen me before. The moment stretches out between the three of us, thick and sticky and filled with things I don't know how to put in words. Luckily, they move before I have to figure out how.

He slips his hand from my panties, but I don't have a chance to mourn the loss because he hooks the back of my neck and tows me in for a kiss. This one is just as dark and full of promise as the first. There truly is no going back after this. I sink into the taste of him, the feel of him, but then his grip shifts, and he's guiding me to Monroe's lips.

It blows my mind that I can be so fucking attracted to such different people. She's just as commanding as he is when she claims my mouth, just as intense and just as filled with a promise of things to come. But where Broderick overwhelmed, Monroe tantalizes and teases, keeping the kiss light even as I try to deepen it. She rocks a little as she fucks Broderick. The reminder has me breaking the kiss so I can see them properly.

I look down and drag in a rough breath. "*Fuck.*" His cock spreads her pussy obscenely, and all I can think is that I can't wait to get my mouth on both of them. Not yet. Soon. I lift a trembling hand and press my fingers to Broderick's bottom lip.

Bless him, but he doesn't even hesitate to suck them into his mouth, playing his tongue over my skin as I ease them back out. His eyes go darker yet. "Make her come, Shiloh."

"I was planning on it." Even though I aim for irreverent, my voice is too low to pull it off. That's fine. We're so far past pretending, it's not even funny.

I reach between them and press my wet fingers to Monroe's clit. They both react instantly. She moans, and she must clench around him, because Broderick grips her hips before dragging her up and down his cock in a rough pace I can barely match. Monroe reaches behind her and grips the table, riding out the pleasure we're dealing her. She's so fucking wet, so slippery against my fingertips, and with every other stroke, I accidentally-on-purpose touch Broderick's cock.

The third time I do it, he curses. "Kiss me, you little tease."

I don't even hesitate. I simply lean forward and kiss him as we work to get Monroe off. Even though I want this moment to last forever, it's over far too quickly. She orgasms with a cry that is nearly a scream, and then Broderick sets his teeth against my bottom lip and follows her over the edge. He slumps back against the booth, looking dazed. Hell, I feel pretty dazed right now, too.

Once again, it's Monroe who saves us before regret can take hold. She leans forward and kisses Broderick and then does the same to me. "Let's go home."

Home.

Does she realize she just called the compound home? Surely not. No matter what else is true about tonight, the fact remains that we're operating under a time limit. Monroe is the Amazon *heir*. There's no way this ends in anything but us parting ways.

I don't know if Broderick and I work without her.

What am I saying?

We don't work at all beyond friends, no matter how good it felt to come on his hands. She's the bridge between us. That means he and I end on next Lammas, too.

The knowledge creates something thick and cloying in my chest. It's an important reminder; I've always preferred the harsh truth to the pretty fiction. If anything, the limited time means I don't have another hour to lose. I want both of these infuriating people. I want them as much and often and in as many ways as possible.

In a year, I'll deal with them ripping my heart in half and each taking their part of that bloody organ with them when they go.

A small price to pay for the pleasure offered now.

CHAPTER 23

BRODERICK

*T*he drive back to the compound happens in a blur. I keep waiting for Monroe or Shiloh to put a stop to this, to knock us all back to reality. They don't. If anything, they ramp up the tension between us as I drive. Monroe has one hand on my leg and the other pressed to the juncture of Shiloh's thighs through her jeans. She and Shiloh don't stop kissing the entire time. The lust is so thick, I can taste it on my tongue.

It's not the only thing I want to taste.

My cock is so fucking hard, and Monroe rhythmically dragging the heel of her hand up and down the length imprisoned in my jeans isn't doing anything for my control. I nearly crash the fucking truck into the curb trying to park. Monroe's laugh only spurs me on. I twist and shove my hand between her legs. "Is it *funny* taunting me, you witch?"

"Yes." She spreads her legs wider. "It really is."

I stroke her a few times, until she's gone pliant against me. And then I take my hand back. "Our room. Right now. Both of you."

"Sir, yes, sir." Monroe doesn't quite manage the mocking

lilt she normally accomplishes. We're too busy piling out of the truck and heading for the main building in a tangle of need and desire.

I can't stop touching them, running my hand down Shiloh's spine, digging my other hand into the mass of Monroe's hair. Our bedroom is too fucking far away, but there's nowhere else we can do this properly. "Hurry."

For once, neither of them argues with me. As we hit the top of the stairs, I catch sight of Abel and Eli down the hallway. My older brother raises his brows, but I have no time to answer the unspoken question on his face. I flip him the bird and practically shove Monroe through the door into our room. She laughs. She always seems to fucking laugh when I'm losing control. I should hate it. I used to hate it.

But…

Okay, fuck, *fine.* It turns me on, too. It doesn't matter how shaken I am by losing control, she's always there to egg me on, to take me farther into the dark. She never looks at me with horror. There's only challenge and need in those green eyes.

I slam the door shut behind us and flip the lock. The click sounds freakishly loud in the sudden quiet of the room. I speak before the silence can become awkward and filled with doubt. "Take off her dress, Shiloh. I put on a show for you. Give me the same courtesy."

She gives me a faint smile. "Turnabout is fair play?"

"You have no idea."

Monroe turns her back to Shiloh and pulls her hair over her shoulder, exactly the way she did in the bar for me. For all her victorious grin, I can see her shivering from here as Shiloh works the zipper down and slides the green dress off Monroe's body.

And what a fucking body.

It feels like I've spent so long fighting my attraction to

her, I haven't let myself appreciate how devastating Monroe is, both in and out of clothing. She's built lean and muscular, and I've seen her in the gym in the compound enough to know she works hard to keep in fighting shape—literally. Her breasts are high and round and capped with dark-pink nipples. She looks good enough to eat.

Not yet.

"Now do Shiloh."

The grin Monroe gives me is wide and without a shred of artifice. "Gladly." She turns to Shiloh and skims off her black tank top. Monroe cups her breasts through the black bra she wears, teasing all of us for a long moment before she slides the straps down and reaches behind Shiloh to unhook it.

Greedy bastard that I am, I devour the sight of each bit of her revealed. Small breasts, pale-pink nipples. What feels like miles and miles of skin I want to kiss every inch of. Monroe hooks her fingers into the waistband of Shiloh's jeans. "More?"

"More," she whispers.

I hold my breath as Monroe works the top button and drags down the zipper. She eases Shiloh's jeans off, moving to kneel as she does. Shiloh carefully steps out of her pants, and Monroe wastes no time skimming off her black panties and then she's naked and...

Fuck.

Monroe stands, and it's impossible not to compare the two women, not to notice how Shiloh is taller but built leaner, how Monroe's curves are a bit more pronounced, as if whatever creator made her decided to balance the shorter height with more everywhere else. Shiloh has scars covering her legs, but she's obviously self-conscious about them, so while I look my fill, I don't linger longer there than I do anywhere else. Hips and stomach and breasts and her heart-breakingly beautiful face.

I'm one lucky son of a bitch.

Shiloh gulps in a breath. "You're staring."

"I'm enjoying the view." My voice has gone deep and rumbling, but I can't help it. "It's like a buffet, and it's all for me."

"It's all for *us*." Monroe arches a brow and cups one of Shiloh's breasts. "This isn't some male power fantasy."

"Honestly, that makes it better." Their bond is so unexpected, but without it, we wouldn't be in this position. Shiloh has friends within our group, of course, but even after all this time, she holds part of herself back with everyone but me.

Now Monroe has joined that exception. I don't understand it, but I'm not about to question it. Especially when she obviously feels something for Shiloh; she wouldn't be so protective otherwise.

Monroe tugs Shiloh's hair tie out and sifts her fingers through her long dark hair. "Here's how this is going to go. I've been thinking about your pussy all day, so I'm going to lay you down and fuck you with my tongue." She glances at me, mischief alighting in her green eyes. "I think Broderick is famished for you, too, so I'm going to be nice and share—a little."

"Kind of you," I grind out.

"I'm a giver like that." She turns back to Shiloh. "You have a problem with that plan?"

"No…" She swallows hard. "But, I want to, ah, return the favor."

"So shy now that we've got you naked." Monroe laughs. "You were just talking about how you want Broderick to come inside me so you can taste it later." She pauses. "On that note, do we need to use protection? That ship has kind of already sailed for us, but if you'd feel more comfortable—"

Shiloh looks away, not meeting either of our gazes. "It's a

non-issue for me. I haven't been with anyone but you in…a very long time, and I can't have kids."

Monroe blinks and then narrows her eyes. "Tell me your parents didn't do that to you."

It takes me a beat longer to connect the dots. Shiloh hasn't had any procedures since she joined up with us, especially something that would lay her out for a bit like that. Which meant it happened before, but she was only on her own for a little bit between us and…

Her parents did this to her.

Cold fury hits me in a wave. I open my mouth to demand confirmation that her parents truly took that choice from her, but she gives me a pleading look, stopping me short. "They didn't do it to me. I bribed a doctor to tie my tubes when I was nineteen. I didn't want…" She hesitates. "I would rather not talk about it."

Maybe that should make me feel better, that she chose it for herself, but I can't stop thinking about a nineteen-year-old version of my best friend going through that procedure alone, without any support, because she was so scared of continuing the legacy her parents forced on her. "Shiloh—"

"We don't have to talk about it, love. You don't have to justify your choice to either of us." Monroe brushes Shiloh's hair back from her face tenderly. She kisses her, soft and sweet, and gives her a nudge toward the bed. "Now lie down and spread your legs for me."

As Shiloh moves on unsteady legs to obey, Monroe stalks to me and grabs a fistful of my shirt. "Get your head in the game," she snarls, so low, I can barely hear her. "She doesn't need either of our anger right now. Snap out of it."

"Maybe it's that easy for you, but it's not for me." I stare down at her. I have to look at Monroe, because if I look at Shiloh, I might fucking snap. "I can't just shake off the knowledge that—"

"*Shut. Up.*" She gives me a shake. "Either take off your clothes and get ready to fuck us properly, or leave right now and I'll do it alone."

I want to yell that it's not a fair choice to make, but… It is. It's more than fair. Shiloh has made her needs very clear, and stopping everything to talk about something she obviously doesn't want to talk about is the height of selfishness. Right now, all she wants is pleasure with none of the pain.

I can give her that.

I will happily work with the woman at my side to give her that. The woman who seems to see parts of Shiloh so much clearer than I do, who will happily fight to give her what she needs. In this moment, seeing the vicious look on Monroe's face, the last of my lingering anger at her drains away, leaving something both soft and fierce in its wake.

I take a slow breath and exhale the tension out of my shoulders as best I can. I carefully remove Monroe's fists from the front of my shirt and give them a squeeze. "Okay."

"Okay?"

One look at the bed, at Shiloh lying there with her legs spread, shaking a little, and I can barely get my next words out. I lift my voice a little. "We both want a taste. I think we can be polite and take turns."

"Take turns."

I shoot her a look. "Are you going to parrot everything I say back to me, or are you going to get on that bed and worship Shiloh's pussy the way she deserves?"

Monroe chokes out a laugh. "Is that a trick question?" The smile she gives me lights up her eyes, and something in my chest thumps uncomfortably. "I knew you'd see things my way," she murmurs.

"Hard not to when you draw your line in the sand so clearly. Who wouldn't want to be on the same side as you?"

"Took you long enough to figure it out." She heads for the

bed, calling softly over her shoulder. "Get naked, Broderick. Let's have some fun."

Fun.

Right.

I drag my shirt over my head as Monroe crawls onto the bed. The sight of her and Shiloh... Sweet fuck, I don't even know how to put it into words. Shiloh's always been important to me, but sometime in the last twenty-four hours, I started to see Monroe as something other than an enemy to avoid or conquer. I don't know if it's how things went last night or seeing her interact with the woman I love, seeing her start to fall for Shiloh, though I doubt she realizes it's happening.

She cares.

If she cares for her people half as well as she does for Shiloh, she's going to be one hell of a queen. A formidable enemy, yes, but an even stronger ally.

But only if we can find a path forward.

I don't know what that looks like. The concept is still too fresh to examine closely. I'll deal with it later. I have a year, after all. By next Lammas, we'll have this figured out, one way or another.

Shiloh moans and digs her hands into Monroe's hair as the Amazon settles between her thighs. They're really too beautiful for words, and the obvious way they care for each other only ramps up that beauty.

I fumble at the front of my pants, as rushed and awkward as a teenager. It takes a few deep, slow breaths before I get myself under control. My hands still shake a bit as I ease off my pants, but I manage to approach the bed at a leisurely pace, as if I'm not dying to take these women up on what we offered each other back at the bar.

Monroe shifts to the side a little as I climb onto the bed, making some space for me. Not nearly enough, though, and I take great pleasure in wedging myself down beside her, lifting one of Shiloh's thighs over my shoulder to make room. My hand slides over the smoother stripes of her scars, but I don't linger. I don't want her to feel self-conscious, and I also can't afford to get distracted by a murderous rage right now.

Monroe's mouth is glossy from Shiloh's pussy, and I kiss her. There's no artifice in it. No strategy. I kiss her because I want to, because I crave the combination of these two women on my tongue.

I only lift my head when I can taste Monroe alone. She blinks at me, her lips curving in a surprisingly sweet smile. "I see your head is back in the game."

Shiloh props herself up on her elbows. "Can we—"

"Hush." Monroe turns her head and kisses Shiloh's inner thigh.

Shiloh blinks. "Um."

"We're discussing strategy." Monroe skates a hand over her lower stomach and parts Shiloh's pussy. "Isn't she pretty?"

My throat goes dry. "Yeah." Pretty and pink and already wet from what Monroe was doing with her tongue. I've felt Shiloh, had her coming around my fingers, but something about seeing her in the fading light of the day makes this a thousand times realer. "She's fucking perfect."

"Look at that, we *can* agree on something." Monroe shifts, nuzzling Shiloh's thigh a little higher. "Why don't you have a taste, husband? You've been so patient. I'd say you earned it."

I glance at Shiloh's face, trying to gauge if she's still on board with this. She worries her bottom lip, her eyes seemingly huge on her face. Maybe this really is a mistake. Maybe I'm damning all three of us for indulging my selfish desires. Maybe—

"Oh, for fuck's sake." Monroe says it almost fondly. She

drags her fingers through Shiloh's folds and presses them to my lip. "Taste."

I suck her fingers into my mouth. I could pretend it's a reflexive move, but the truth is that I'm dying for a taste, no matter what method is available to me. A guttural groan slips free as I play my tongue over Monroe's fingers.

"That's right," she whispers. "She's so sweet, I could eat her for hours. Tastes even better from the source." She slips her fingers from my mouth and traces them along my jaw to the nape of my neck.

I don't fight her as she guides me closer to Shiloh, as she positions my mouth right over Shiloh's clit. I don't even think to resist, not when this is what I've wanted for so fucking long.

At the first slow swipe of my tongue, Shiloh lets out a keening noise that goes straight to my cock. It's agony and perfection, and when I settle between her thighs and kiss her pussy properly, I nearly lose my fucking mind. Monroe's right; she's sweet and soft and everything I've ever wanted.

If I don't come all over the bed just from the taste of her, it's going to be a fucking miracle.

CHAPTER 24

MONROE

I enjoy watching, but I've never really gotten off on being a voyeur. I much prefer to be an active participant in any given sexual encounter, rather than simply watching. At least until this moment. Broderick looks almost *pained* as he tastes Shiloh's pussy. A man dying of thirst with his first taste of water in years. And Shiloh barely seems to breathe, for all that she's letting out little helpless noises as he explores her clit and tests out motions to see what she likes.

Of course he'd go about it like this. Methodical and intent on her pleasure. He's not some fumbling, horny fool who just wants to thrust his tongue inside her for a few minutes so he can get her turned on enough to shove his cock into her.

He wants her to enjoy this just as much as he is.

I don't want tenderness from Broderick. I like how rough he is with me, how ruthless he becomes when he forces pleasure on my body, as if I want anything but what he's giving me.

That doesn't stop a little pang of jealousy at how soft and slow he's going with her.

I jolt a little at the feeling of his hand closing around the back of my thigh. He doesn't stop what he's doing to Shiloh, doesn't so much as miss a beat, as he nudges my legs wider and coasts his hand up to cup my pussy from behind. I lift my hips a little, giving him easier access. Broderick doesn't disappoint. He shoves two fingers into me, just as rough as I need, drawing a little cry from my lips.

Shiloh's panting, but she lifts her head and looks down her body at us. She licks her lips. "He's got his fingers in your pussy, doesn't he?"

"*Yes.*" I shift my hips, nearly mindless, seeking friction against my clit. I turn my head and bite Shiloh's thigh. Not hard, just enough to make her jump a little.

I start to slide my hand down my stomach, but Broderick lifts his head from Shiloh's pussy long enough to give me a look. "Let me, Bride." He sucks Shiloh's clit into his mouth, making her back bow off the bed, and then he reluctantly lifts his head. "Make her come, Monroe. Show me how she likes it."

"I think you're doing a damn good job of figuring that out," I murmur.

"Mmm." He urges my hips up a little and then his fingers are there, in me, withdrawing to spread my wetness up and around my clit, penetrating and withdrawing. Enough to give me pleasure, but not enough to get me where I need. *Teasing* me. "Show me," Broderick repeats.

"Do I get a say?" Shiloh asks.

I laugh a little, though it morphs into a moan at the end when Broderick wedges a third finger inside me. "Are you enjoying yourself, love?"

Shiloh shudders out a laugh. "Yes."

"Then no, you don't get a say. Now lie back and let us play with this pretty pussy for a little bit. You've teased us, Shiloh. Giving some, but nowhere near enough. Neither of us is about to miss this opportunity. Right, husband?"

"Right," Broderick rasps.

I move my hair out of the way and dip down to flick the tip of my tongue lightly against Shiloh's clit. It's hard to focus with Broderick using his fingers to claim every inch of my pussy, but I'm highly motivated to make Shiloh come all over my face before he can.

Except he doesn't give me the chance. He nuzzles me out of the way enough to lick her, but I'm having none of it. I give him the same treatment. It's a strange sort of dance. His mouth to her clit. My tongue in her pussy. Meeting Broderick in the middle for messy kiss that tastes of both him and Shiloh. She's propped herself up so she can watch us, and from the way she shakes and whimpers, she's enjoying the sight of us battling over her pussy as much as she's enjoying the oral sex itself.

For all the fun and games, I want Broderick to have this orgasm. He's wanted her for so long, and has been through so much bullshit, some of it at my own hand. It costs me nothing to give him this, and it will mean everything to him.

I back off as Shiloh's moans get louder and let him kiss her properly. It doesn't take long before she cries out and tries to clamp her legs shut. Broderick and I move as one, each grabbing one thigh and pressing her up and out, baring her completely as he keeps fucking her with his tongue even as he winds me tighter and tighter with his fingers. Shiloh orgasms with a sob that yanks at my heart. I'm so fucking close and—

"Your turn, Bride." He sits up on his knees. That's the only warning I get before he flips me onto my back. He's ruthless in delivering my pleasure, and for once I don't try to fight it. I'm enjoying myself too much.

My orgasm takes my breath away. I writhe around Broderick's fingers as he uses his other hand to stroke my clit the way I like it best. Wave after wave hits me and, without thinking, I start to reach to shove him away. Shiloh catches my wrists and presses them down to the mattress before I can. It only makes me come harder.

By the time Broderick lets me drift down, I'm nearly sobbing. He presses a kiss to my lips and then leans up to claim Shiloh's mouth. Every time they kiss, it's like they'll never get another chance. It hurts my heart more than I expected. I want them to believe this is real, to sink into it until they can't see another path forward but with each other.

The temptation to try to seduce Shiloh into returning with me to the Amazons is there. Of course it's there. I like her so damn much. I don't make a habit of lying to myself, though; there's no way she'll leave Broderick. He's been her best friend and her rock for a third of her life. She's not so fickle as to throw him away, no matter how much she enjoys me.

Fool that I am, I can't stand the thought of her unhappy.

I'm going to ensure she and Broderick are solid as hell by the end of this year together. And then I'm going to fight tooth and nail to preserve the peace with the Raider faction.

Sweet gods, I'm in love with her.

The thought barely has time to sink its roots into me, burying deep, when Shiloh pushes Broderick onto his back and straddles him. They really do look good together, all needy and desperate and flushed with pleasure. I manage to stir myself to sit up and run my hands down his chest to wrap a fist around his cock. Left to their own devices, there's a good chance one of them will balk or let their impressive brains go into overdrive. "Up, love."

Shiloh lifts herself up onto her knees and whimpers as I notch his cock at her entrance. Maybe I should leave it at that, but I've never been all that good at denying myself things I want. I part her pussy and lean to the side, giving both me and Broderick a perfect view as she works herself down his impressive length. The look on her face is pure agonized pleasure. "Gods, you're huge."

Broderick gives a choked laugh. "Maybe you're just too tight."

"Hush, both of you. You're both perfect." I smooth my free hand over his stomach but keep most of my focus on her. "Keep going. You're doing great, love."

Another few sexy writhing motions and she's seated fully on his cock. I watch pleasure dawn on her face as she tentatively rocks on him, adjusting to his size, and wait for the slightest bit of jealousy to spark. I'm self-aware enough to know that I prefer to be in the center of things and, right now, when Shiloh looks down at him with something akin to wonder in her expression, when Broderick is giving her heart eyes right back, I feel almost immaterial. Yes, I got them to this place, but this will be permanent for them in a way it won't be for me.

But there's no jealousy. Just a deep contentment in the knowledge that I will forever hold space as the inciting incident in their story together. I'm not normally unselfish, but I guess love does that to a person. It's a very strange thought.

"You're thinking too hard over there, Bride."

I barely have a chance to register Broderick's words before he catches me by the hips and lifts me to straddle his head, facing Shiloh. I tense, but then his mouth is there, working my pussy with an expertise that might irritate me if I didn't derive so much pleasure from it. Broderick's a fast learner, and it only took him these few times with me to figure out what gets me off. Overachiever.

Shiloh plants a hand on Broderick's chest and leans forward, closing the distance between us to kiss me with a desperation bordering on frenzy. Caught between their two mouths, my thoughts of the future lose their purchase and slip away. Worries for another day. Right now, I have more important things to concentrate.

Like riding Broderick's face to orgasm.

Shiloh shifts slowly, chasing her own pleasure even as she kisses me like I'll disappear the moment we stop. Like she needs me more than her next breath, the next beat of her heart. Gods, this woman is a gift, and it's going to hurt so fucking *bad* to lose her.

Broderick sucks on my clit—hard—and it's too much. I come again, grinding down against his tongue until a distant part of my brain is worried I'm going to suffocate the man. He's made of sterner stuff than that, and he lifts me easily to move to his chest, going slow so it doesn't break my kiss with Shiloh.

Now that I'm closer—gods, the man has a long torso—I slide down his stomach to press my fingers to Shiloh's clit. The reaction is instantaneous. She moans against my tongue and starts fucking him in earnest, riding him in rough strokes as she chases her orgasm.

Broderick barely lets her finish. He topples us to the bed, somehow shifting things so Shiloh lands on top of me, chest to chest. He jerks up her hips, and they both moan as he penetrates her again. This time, he's intent on his own pleasure, and he fucks her just shy of brutally. From the way she moans against my throat and clings to me, she's loving it just as much as I do when he loses control.

Good girl.

Broderick's strokes go jerky, and he meets my gaze over the long line of Shiloh's back. I grin, feeling light and strange. "Come inside her, husband. Fill her up the way you want to."

He curses and then obeys, grabbing Shiloh's hips and grinding into her. He looks almost pained as he orgasms, but he never breaks eye contact with me. It's horribly, unforgivably intimate, and I should put a stop to it immediately.

But I…like it.

The more we work together, the more some part of me understands that Broderick and I aren't that different at all. In fact, we're terrifyingly similar and single-minded when we set our minds on something. On someone.

A thought for another time.

Broderick slumps down next to us. "Holy fuck."

Shiloh relaxes against my body, her head on my breasts. She stretches, and the little wench immediately starts rocking her pussy on my leg. "Are we done?"

"You're obviously not." I run my hands down her back and grip her ass, hitching her a little higher on my thigh. "Wicked thing."

"I can't help it," she whispers. "It's like I've been bottled up for so long and…"

"I'm not complaining." I manage to turn my gaze to Broderick. "Are you?"

His laugh is strained, his blue eyes so hot, it's a wonder all three of us don't burst into flames. "No. I'm not complaining." He shakes his head. "Though I need more recovery time than you two do."

"The perks of three." I drag in a rough breath as Shiloh presses my breasts together and lavishes them with kisses. "Take your time recovering, husband." I grin. "We'll be ready for you when you are."

We don't stop for a long, long time. Shiloh's stamina puts both Broderick and I to shame. Just when I'm about to collapse, he steps in and fucks her, and then they take turns eating me out until I'm damn near begging for mercy. By the time we exhaust ourselves, the sky outside the window has lightened in that gorgeous pre-dawn color that I've always loved.

Seeing it means a night well spent in my opinion.

I run a hand down my sweaty chest. "Shower?"

"Shower," Shiloh agrees from where her face is pressed to Broderick's thigh.

I should leave it at that, but I lost my head at some point during this process. I sift my fingers through her damp hair. "Stay in bed after. Sleep here. Both of you."

Which is how we end up in a messy pile thirty minutes later, Shiloh between me and Broderick. She snuggles, because of course she does. She's so fucking perfect, it makes my chest ache. All three of us in this bed is fucking perfect. I might be coming to terms with my feelings for Shiloh, but I'm more than self-aware enough to realize how seamlessly Broderick fits.

How well balanced we are as a trio.

I close my eyes and almost laugh when I realize she's been using my shampoo. A little stamp of me in her hair, and I love it entirely too much. I let her closeness wash over me. No matter what happens next, we have this time. It will be enough.

It has to be.

I'm nearly asleep when a large arm drapes over our waists. I fight my eyes open to find Broderick pressed to Shiloh's back and propped up on one arm, watching us. I'm too tired to define the strange look on his face, so I give him a soft smile and let sleep take me.

CHAPTER 25

J wake up so sore, I could almost convince myself I was tricked into joining one of Maddox's workouts instead of having hours of intense sex. Then again, Maddox's workouts never have me aching between my thighs. I'm smiling even as I open my eyes.

To a very, very bright room.

Too bright.

I shoot up. "We're late."

Next to me, Monroe throws an arm over her eyes. Even in my panicked state, I can't help the pulse of heat that goes through me at the sight of her naked body. She's so damn sexy, and I might have gotten close and personal with nearly every inch of her last night, but I can't wait to do it again. Lust is a heady drug, which is the only explanation for how we both managed to sleep in.

"Monroe."

"We're not late. I had my assistant reschedule the one meeting I had." She lifts her arm enough to open one eye. "I don't know about you, but I'm not going to be able to concentrate today. Let's stay in bed and have some fun."

The pulse of heat inside me gets stronger. It's oh so tempting to do exactly that, but there are things we really need to discuss. Like the fact that Monroe's mother wants Broderick dead. As if the thought of him draws my attention, I can't ignore his presence in this bed any longer. I twist to look at him.

He's... Gods, he's something else.

Broderick is on his stomach facing away from us. The position gives me an excellent view of his broad back and the reddened scratches marking it. Scratches originating with both me and Monroe. I shiver. The sheet is gathered low on his hips, revealing the upper curve of his ass, and I have the strangest desire to bend down and bite him.

If last night is anything to go by, doing so will ensure we don't talk about anything at all for hours. While that's an attractive solution to avoid uncomfortable topics, I can't shake the feeling that the moment this stops and we're forced to separate, Broderick to his duties and Monroe to hers, this fragile truce between them—between us—will end.

We need to talk some things out before then.

Still, I can't help running my hand down Broderick's spine. There's a scar beneath his left shoulder blade, a slashing line that must have come from a knife. It's faded with age, an injury he had long before we met. There are a lot of those to go around.

He shifts beneath my touch, but the only move he makes is to turn his face to us. "Morning."

Monroe sighs and drops her arm. "The fact that Shiloh hasn't leaped up to sit on my face means we're talking."

He nods against the pillow. "Coffee?"

"Please."

Broderick hefts himself out of bed, and I'm struck speechless all over again at the sight of him naked. His body isn't perfect. He's broad and muscular, but the man will never have a six-pack because he just doesn't give a shit about stuff like that. He pads into the closet, and Monroe nudges me with her knee. "Stop staring at him like that, or he's going to have an uncomfortable walk down to the kitchen with a giant hard-on. I need my coffee, Shiloh. You know what I'm like before caffeine."

Broderick reappears wearing a pair of low-slung lounge pants and nothing else. He shouldn't look even better with pants on than he did naked, but logic has no reason when it comes to Broderick apparently. Especially now that I've had his hands and mouth all over me, his cock deep inside me. He eyes us. "Stay out of trouble until I get back."

Monroe stretches, arching her back, and both of us follow the way her breasts bounce just a little with the movement. She grins. "No promises."

"Thought not." He shakes his head, a small smile pulling at the edges of his lips as he leaves the room.

Dear gods, everything he does it overwhelmingly attractive. I'm in huge trouble. I knew there was no going back last night, but there's something about having to live with the consequences of my actions that I don't know how to, well, live with. Broderick is my best friend, and now I know my best friend fucks like a fiend. Now I know that he's both fierce and playful in turns and absolutely ruthless when it comes to giving pleasure.

How am I supposed to go back? I laugh a little, though the sound feels forced. "Should we get dressed?"

Monroe eyes me. "That depends. How likely do you think one of us is going to be to storm out of here before the end of this necessary conversation?"

That's a good question. Pretty damn likely, judging from past experiences. I sigh. "At least if everyone is mostly naked, it will take longer to do a dramatic exit."

"My thoughts exactly." She grasps my wrist and tugs. "Come cuddle me until he gets back."

I let her pull me down to spoon me, her chest to my back. She wraps her arms around me and hugs me close, burying her face in the back of my neck. "My shampoo smells good on you."

"Thanks," I murmur. Monroe's been casually touching me since we met, but this feels different. There's a heaviness to this moment, a weight I'm not sure I'm imagining. "You okay?"

"Sure." Her laugh even sounds off. "Just having a small crisis of faith. Hold still, and it will pass."

Yeah, no. I twist, and after the slightest hesitation, she allows me to turn in her arms. "What's wrong?" She tries to lock down her expression, and I'm startled to realize I know her well enough to recognize that. I cup her jaw. "Talk to me."

"You're killing me, love." She closes her eyes. "It's nothing for you to be concerned about and nothing you can help with."

I should let it go. If Monroe doesn't need my help, it's selfish in the extreme to push it on her, but I can't shake the feeling that she's lying to me. "Are you sure?"

"Yes."

I feather my fingers along her temple. So much has changed for me in the past twelve hours, I'm tempted to project those changing feelings onto Monroe. That would be a mistake. She's not one to let her emotions get the best of her, and whatever her motivations for seeing Broderick and I finally fuck, I don't think they're malicious. Not even she's that cruel. I don't think. "Are we friends, Monroe?"

"Friends?" She opens her eyes, and there's something almost like pain there. "Yes, love, we're friends."

Then she definitely wasn't motivated by revenge or any

darker things last night. I knew that in my gut, and this just confirms it. No matter what else is true of Monroe, she's fiercely loyal when she decides she cares about someone.

When she cares about someone. "Monroe—" I don't have to find the courage to finish that sentence because the bedroom door opens and Broderick comes through. He's found a little serving tray somewhere, and there are three mugs on it and two little cups.

Monroe sits ups too fast, almost as if she's running, and yanks the blankets into some semblance of order so Broderick can set down the tray without spilling. Once he does, I realize the two containers have cream and sugar in them, respectively. He catches me looking and shrugs. "Easier this way." Without another word, he doses one mug heavily with both cream and sugar and passes it to me. I take a sip and, no surprise, it's perfect.

Broderick glances at Monroe. "Cream? Sugar?"

"I can make my own coffee." She's got that same strange look on her face, and the sentence comes out almost like a question.

"No one is arguing that you're not capable of doing it. Now answer the damn question."

"Sugar," she murmurs.

We both watch Broderick dose her coffee with sugar and pass it to her. Monroe stares into her cup for a long moment. "Did you poison it?"

"No, Monroe, I didn't poison it." He's got that fond little smile curving his lips again. This is the Broderick I know, the steady friend who cares about everyone around him. I've never seen him look at Monroe like that, though.

The warmth in my chest gets stronger. There's nowhere for it to go, though. I sip my coffee and try to pretend my heart isn't beating too hard with things unsaid. There are no words I can utter to change our situation and, more importantly, right now, in this moment, things are *working*.

These two people are more than tolerating each other. It might be the sex, it might be me, it might be a million other reasons, but I'm not about to question it or do something to cause them to go for each other's throats again. Especially if it's just to prove the point that they seem to actually *like* each other right now.

They're both stubborn enough to start a fight for the pure principle of it. I refuse to be the one to light that match.

Still, this peace won't hold if outside forces get their way. I stare hard at Monroe until she sighs and lowers her coffee mug. "My mother somehow learned that Abel intends to kill me if I don't stop embarrassing you publicly."

"That's not what he said." Broderick's voice is mild, but tension bleeds into his body. "How did she find out?"

"That's the question, isn't it? Because I didn't tell her." She catches his disbelieving look and snorts. "We both know I was handling the situation. Informing my mother of a threat against me is like keying in the codes for a nuclear launch in response to a knife fight. It's poor planning, and I wouldn't have done it unless I had no other option."

I wait to see if Broderick will argue that, but he nods. "Makes sense. So someone else did it."

There it is again, that sensation of pieces clicking into place, of Broderick and Monroe aligning themselves in the same direction. I clear my throat. "Broderick—"

"Hold on. I'm thinking." I can practically see his mind whirling. Finally, he nods. "So we have a mole."

"I expect we have several between the two factions." They both look at me, and I have to fight not to roll my eyes. "Come on. Give me a little credit. *We* have informants in both the Mystics and the Amazons. Of course they've already set up the same."

Monroe perks up at that. "Who are you informants in the Amazons?"

"Nice try," Broderick says drily. "That still doesn't explain how they found out about Abel threatening Monroe. It's not exactly something he did publicly. We were in the hallway, and the only other person present was Eli." He catches my look and shrugs. "He has no reason to run telling tales to the Amazon queen. He's wearing Abel's leash and happily."

"In the hallway," I repeat.

"There are dozens of people in this house, Broderick." Monroe scoots back to lean against the headboard, her expression contemplative. "Fallon is running off to her father every day. She might have heard and passed it on. That's probably the simplest answer."

That's not impossible, but it's missing quite a large step from where I'm sitting. "But why would he convey that information to your mother? They're enemies."

"Precisely because they're enemies. If she follows through on her threat—which was to kill *you*, Broderick—that would create a nasty conflict between Raiders and Amazons. In a situation like that, that Mystics emerge on top. War is bad for business and bad for power cumulation, though everyone believes otherwise." She sips her coffee. "There's a reason the faction territory lines haven't changed since the inception of Sabine Valley. The river creates too good a natural barrier. In the past, even when factions have taken pieces, they never hold them. You'd have to take the entire faction, and that's impossible."

The people living there wouldn't go for it, for one. The only reason Abel managed a mostly bloodless coup was because he operated within the rules of Lammas and the Paine family was here long before Eli's father took over. Not to mention Abel smoothed things over and promised not to rock the boat beyond the compound. That wouldn't work in any other territory.

There's just one thing that doesn't make sense. "How would Fallon even find out? Were one of the Mystics around when you spoke with Abel?"

"No." Broderick narrows his eyes. "But I talked to Ezekiel not long after. Maybe Beatrix heard something."

This is all getting very convoluted. "Ultimately it doesn't matter how Monroe's mother found out. We still have to deal with it."

"There's nothing to deal with." Broderick sips his coffee. "We figured things out."

"Cute, but that won't stop my mother." Monroe closes her eyes. For the first time since I've met her, she looks exhausted and stressed. "If she thinks there's the slightest danger to me, she'll act."

I stare. "Even at the expense of the faction?"

"It won't be at the expense of the faction." Her smile is mirthless. "We're better prepared than you are. That's not me being an asshole; that's facts. The Raider faction is three weeks and a few days into a regime change. No matter how easily Abel managed it, that still destabilizes things. You brought your own force into Sabine Valley, and they haven't had a chance to integrate with the locals properly. You're outgunned and outmanned."

Broderick doesn't move. "There will still be a high cost on the Amazon side of things."

"Yes, there will. Which is why I can't allow it to happen."

"But…"

Monroe's voice goes soft. "Who do you think will be the first person harmed if things go sideways? It won't be me, Broderick. It will be Winry or Jasper. My mother might be willing to gamble with their safety, but I'm not. We can't conclusively figure out how my mother got her information, but in the end it changes nothing about our plan."

It certainly seems like the only person Aisling will move heaven and earth to protect is *Monroe*. She wouldn't threaten me otherwise. The truth coming out about my parents won't change anything on the grand scale in Sabine Valley. They only had the faintest bit of power in the Amazons, let alone in the entire city.

No, the only person who will care is Monroe. It will potentially damage her relationship with her mother, and that's something Aisling is willing to kill to prevent.

It's sweet in a really fucked up sort of way.

This is better, though. If I keep Monroe and Broderick focused on putting on a show that will protect both of them, they will stop worrying so much about my past. "What do we do? I'm assuming you have something resembling a plan."

Monroe flips her hair over her shoulder. "The same thing we've been doing, love. We fuck and we play, and we let everyone know we're getting along swimmingly. We give the faction leaders no reason to get involved."

CHAPTER 26

BRODERICK

I thought taking the time to go get coffee would be the break I needed to get my head on straight. It didn't work. Sitting here on this bed with two of the most beautiful women I've ever encountered, having a conversation that doesn't involve arguing for once...

It's enough to make me want things I'm not sure are meant for me.

Monroe stretches. The sheet is bunched at her waist, leaving her breasts bare, and combined with the cute way Shiloh has the covers nearly tucked to her chin, my heart gives an uncomfortable lurch.

I care about Shiloh. Fuck, I love her. I have for a very long time.

I didn't expect to care about Monroe, too.

It's not love. That would be ludicrous. Not simply because she's the enemy, but because just a few days ago, we were at each other's throats. I can admire her strength and cunning and beauty without being in love with her. I can enjoy how seamlessly we work together when we're focused on accomplishing the same thing without my emotions getting involved. No matter how much I enjoy her in my bed, ultimately sex changes nothing.

At least in theory.

I clear my throat. "I don't know if it will be enough to fuck and frolic or whatever the hell you just said."

"As long as we're moving in the right direction, neither your brother nor my mother will jump the gun." Monroe shrugs. "War is bad for everyone, and they're not going to dive headfirst into it if there's another option. We need to be convincing enough to prove there's another option."

Shiloh pulls her knees to her chest and wraps her arms around them. "What if you're wrong?"

"I'm not."

"You say that so confidently, I almost believe you."

"You should." I clear my throat. "She's not wrong." I know Abel. He might give the impression of being a barbarian brute, but there's a reason we'd all follow him to hell and back without complaint. He's too savvy to do something he can't take back just for the sake of doing it. "Depending on how we play things, it should negate the current danger."

Shiloh curses. "Fine. What's the plan, then?"

Monroe drains the last of her coffee and slides out of the bed. "Since we have an off day, let's have some fun."

Shiloh shakes her head. "*Fun* isn't going to get both of you out of the crosshairs."

"Silly girl, I'm not talking about fucking." Monroe grins suddenly. "Though we can do more of that later, if you like. I want to visit Old Town."

Now it's my turn to narrow my eyes. "There's a reason we haven't let you run rampant all over the faction, Monroe." Though if there's a mole—or several moles—in the compound itself, it removes some of those reasons. And with her going to Amazon territory every weekday, it's not as if she can't slip information to her people whenever she feels like it. Still... "It's not safe."

No matter how formidable she is, she's still an Amazon in Raider territory. A single woman. There are plenty of people in our faction—especially in Old Town—who hate both Amazons and Mystics and won't hesitate to take that hate out on Monroe, deserved or not.

"Are you worried about me?" For once, the question doesn't have a mocking lilt to it. Monroe stares at me like she's never seen me before. Before I can come up with a response, her expression clears. "Oh, of course not. If I die, it puts you right back into the fire with war."

I honestly hadn't considered the war when I objected. "The world would be a dimmer place without you in it." I'm kicking myself before I finish the sentence, but there's no taking it back now.

She blinks those big green eyes at me. "Um, okay."

Shiloh takes pity on me and cuts in. "Broderick's not wrong. With how crowded it can get in Old Town during peak hours, it would be simple to slip a knife between your ribs and be gone before we had a chance to react. It's what I would do in their position."

"How murderous of you." Monroe waves that away. "I'll be with you and Broderick. Between the three of us, I'm safe enough."

Shiloh and I exchange a look. She smiles a little. "I'll ask Cohen for a few people to tag along. I'm sure Iris could use some shopping after dealing with that Mystic so much lately."

That Mystic being Matteo, the son of the ruler of the Mystics. I haven't interacted with him much, but Finnegan seems to like him just fine as a Bride. Or at least the sounds coming from their room the other night seem to indicate he does. I wonder what Iris thinks about that. She's always been something of a closed book. She and Shiloh are close enough, but if she's bothered by her boyfriend fucking his Bride, she hasn't shown any indication of it. She's been sleeping in Finnegan's room, after all.

"Good. Since we're on the same page for the time being, we might as well prove to the public that I'm a docile little Bride."

I snort. "No one would ever use the word *docile* to describe you."

"You're right." She snaps her fingers. "Guess we'll have to convince them you gave me such a good dicking down that I've temporarily lost my mind."

Heat flashes through my body, and I have to concentrate not to respond physically at the memories that surge forth. "No one is going to believe that, either."

"Give me a little credit." She grins. "They'll believe it enough to get our respective leaders off our backs. That's all that matters—negating the current threat."

Shiloh gets a strange look on her face but nods. "That's the wisest course of action."

"It is." Monroe gives a little wiggle, and I lose my battle to keep my attention on her eyes. She's not even flaunting her nakedness right now; she's just that comfortable in her own skin. She laughs. "Also, we're going to have some fun."

"Fun." I raise my brows. "I don't know how much more *fun* I can take from you two."

"Lies." She turns and starts for the bathroom. "I'm sure you'll rise to the occasion should we find the opportunity." She disappears through the door and, a few moments later, the shower starts.

I look at Shiloh. "Are you okay?"

"Of course. I'm always okay." She shoves the coffee mug onto the nightstand and stands.

I don't mean to react. My body just does it on its own, my

hand snapping out and closing around her wrist as she goes to move past me. "Shiloh." I tow her closer slowly, keeping my grip light enough that she could break free easily. Since I'm sitting on the bed, our positions put her breasts right at eye level, but I hold her gaze intentionally. "Talk to me. Is this about what happened last night?"

For a moment, I think she'll push me away, both physically and emotionally, but she sighs. "I know the overprotective thing is part of who you are, and I am making my peace with the fact that it's Monroe as well, but I could really do without you egging each other on to go to battle over something that happened a very long time ago." Her gaze goes shuttered.

It takes me a beat to understand. She's not upset about the sex. She's feeling off because her past was brought up and how we reacted. Relief makes me a little light-headed. I don't know what the fuck I would do if she regretted things.

I tug on her wrist again, and she slides down to straddle me as if we've been this comfortable with each other for years instead of a single night. My cock gives a twinge, but I ignore it. "I thought you wanted us to get along."

"I do, but I didn't intend have you gang up on *me*."

I carefully coast my hands up her arms and across her shoulders, stopping just short of cupping her jaw the way I want to. She might be focusing on one part of things, but I have to know the truth. "Do you regret what happened last night?"

Shiloh hesitates but finally sighs. "No. I wouldn't be sitting here naked in your lap if I regretted it."

"I could do without the reminder." I give her a look when she laughs. Some of the heaviness she seemed to be carrying dissipates with that happy sound. "This conversation is too important to get distracted in the middle."

"Every conversation is important with you."

I don't know if I can look into that comment even a little, so I ignore it. "You have been my friend since we met. You are important to me. I don't regret anything that's happened between us, but you are my friend first, and I don't want to do anything to endanger that. I can't stand the thought of losing you." Now it's my turn to hesitate. "But last night was pretty damn perfect. If you're on the same page, if you're willing to try for more, I would really like to."

"Oh, Broderick." She feathers her fingers through my hair. "What about Monroe?"

"What about Monroe?" The question feels wrong, as if I'm doing her a disservice. Monroe and I have been working together beautifully since we decided to seduce Shiloh together, but that's only a small percentage of the time she's been my Bride. We haven't talked about the future, haven't talked about *anything* but Shiloh, and plans to keep Monroe alive.

"I don't know if we work without her."

I open my mouth to argue but have to stop. I don't want to lie to Shiloh, and I'm not certain it would be the truth to say we definitely *do* work without Monroe in the picture, egging us on. "There's only one way to find out."

"I suppose." She shifts against me a little, but her expression is contemplative, not seductive. "What if Monroe stayed?"

"Shiloh." I take her face in my hands. "She's an Amazon. She's not for either of us. Not permanently."

She wraps her hands around my wrists and lowers my hands from her face. "Her being an Amazon makes her not for you."

I don't miss the way she puts distance between us with both words and actions. "Not just an Amazon, Shiloh. She's the Amazon heir. She's going to be queen. Even if this were some fairy tale where we all fall happily in love, she won't stay."

"And you won't go."

Again, she's excluding herself from this theoretical future. I don't want to ask the question, but I need to know the answer. "Would you? If she asked you to, would you go with her?"

"I don't know."

It's not the clear rejection of the idea that I want, and fuck, that hurts. "You really care about her that much?" *More than me?*

"I don't know," she repeats. Shiloh eases off my lap and turns for the bathroom. "Being in Sabine Valley has been more challenging than I expected. I just... I don't know, Broderick. I'm sorry, but that's the truth."

"I won't ask you for anything but the truth," I manage.

She gives me a bittersweet smile. "Liar. You want everything."

"Of course I want everything. I love you." The words are out before I can call them back, but suddenly I don't *want* to call them back. We've danced around each other for so fucking long. Maybe it's time to just clear the air properly. It's not like we can do more damage to our friendship after having sex last night. "I've loved you for years, Shiloh. I respected our friendship too much to endanger it, and you never indicated that you were interested in more than friendship, so I kept my feelings to myself."

"Maybe I'm not interested in more than friendship."

I snort. "You were coming all over my cock, my mouth, my hands. That's not what friends do."

"You're right." Shiloh picks up her mug and finishes off her coffee. "But I'm still not sure where that leaves us. Just... give me some time to process."

A lot has changed in a very short time. As much as I want

concrete answers—concrete assurances—now, this is something I can't rush. It has to happen naturally, or I run the risk of fucking things up permanently. "Okay."

She heads into the bathroom, leaving me staring after her and wondering what the hell we're doing. I want a future with Shiloh. But what if she's right? What if we don't work without Monroe in the mix?

And Monroe...

I sigh. I like the little asshole. I didn't expect to, but the past week has changed everything. She's infuriating, but I like how protective of her people she is. I like how she can be playful and fierce by turns. I even like that cunning mind behind her pretty face, though she turns it against me more often than we're aligned.

But what if we found something to be aligned over? I feel fucking unstoppable when she and I are striving for the same goal. If we could find a common ground beyond Shiloh, is this really a partnership I'm willing to throw away just because it's not quite comfortable?

Especially if Shiloh and Monroe are a package deal?

CHAPTER 27

MONROE

*S*omething's wrong with Shiloh.

It's subtle, but I've been watching this woman too closely for too long not to notice. It's there in the tightness of her shoulders as we walk down the main street that compromises Old Town. This part of Raider territory is a large reason why no enemy has successfully taken the faction. Removing the Paines, for example, took a whole hell of a lot of effort and both Mystics and Amazons working with Eli Walsh's traitorous father. But nothing short of a bomb would dig out Old Town and the people who live there.

This open-air market is three city blocks by seven city blocks and has three families who own most of the businesses in the space. Those families have been here since the inception of Sabine Valley. That's why the first thing Abel Paine did when he staged his coup was to come here and declare his intentions to the Phan, Rodriguez, and Smith families.

A smart move on his part. No one holds power in the Raider faction without Old Town's blessing.

I lace my fingers through Broderick's as we stroll down the street. Shiloh catches a glimpse of that and starts to move away, but I grab her hand, too. "Where are you going?"

"You're sending a message," she says softly.

Broderick has slowed. He's not looking at us, but he shifts a little closer to me as if he doesn't want to miss a single word of this. I drag my thumb over Shiloh's knuckles. Now isn't the time or place to tell her what I realized last night, but I've always been a little too impulsive for my own good. "I care about you, Shiloh." A nice, generic statement that won't send her rabbiting away. "I have no intention of publicly claiming Broderick without you being involved." When she still hesitates, I can't help pressing. "Do you care about me?"

"Yes." The word is almost lost in the sound of people walking and talking and shopping around us.

"Then what's wrong with letting everyone know?" I speak just as softly as she is, and for once I can't inject my voice with any bravado. As much as I don't want to pressure her, a part of me can't help wanting her to claim this.

To claim *me*.

For a moment, I think Shiloh is going to keep arguing, but she sighs and slips her hand into mine.

Maybe it should be awkward to walk down the street with the three of us, but it just feels horrifyingly *right*. I knew I was in over my head after last night, but this just confirms it. I'm entirely gone for Shiloh and half gone for Broderick, stubborn fool that he is. I...like him. Even when he has me climbing the walls—maybe *especially* when he has me climbing the walls.

We take our time, pausing to explore a few of the trinket shops before we end up in the center space with the handful of food trucks and restaurants. The intersection has picnic tables situated under carefully constructed awnings that keep out the worst of the weather and offer plenty of relief from the late-summer heat.

Shiloh extracts her hand from mine and gives us a sweet smile. "I'll go grab some food." She's gone before I can offer to go with.

It's just as well. Broderick and I have something to discuss. I sink onto the bench at the nearest table and pat the spot next to me. "Sit, husband."

"I'm not—" He cuts himself off and sighs. "You know what? Forget it." He sits next to me, thigh to thigh, and drapes his arm over the table behind me. "This for show, or you have something to say?"

I watch Shiloh weave through the late lunch crowd to the nearest food truck. "Both." I take a deep breath. "Last night was a lot of fun."

Broderick's arm goes tense behind me. "I had fun, too."

"I'd like to keep it up." My words try to stick in my throat, something like self-consciousness making my skin heat. "The three of us, I mean. There's no reason not to keep enjoying ourselves, and I don't think it's a stretch to say we both care a lot about Shiloh."

"Right. About Shiloh."

I try to look at him, but the sun is in my eyes, and I can't read his expression properly. There's absolutely no reason to look into it. Just because he's sitting so close, smelling so damn good, and also doesn't want me dead... None of that means he actually gives a damn about me. After working so hard to get under his skin and torment him for three weeks, I'm lucky he's not trying to throw me in front of a bus.

He wouldn't succeed, of course, but it's the thought that counts.

That uncomfortable feeling beneath my skin gets worse. "Look—"

"Monroe." He twists his body toward me and catches my

chin in a light grip. I still can't see him with the glare in my eyes, but his voice deepens. "We make one hell of a team. Do you agree?"

"Yes," I say cautiously.

"We're in agreement that we both want Shiloh, and we're both willing to share."

"Yes," I say again. It never even occurred to me to keep Shiloh to myself, not once I realized that she returned Broderick's attraction. We fit well, but I'll admit that I have a whole lot of fun when Broderick is involved, too. The power dynamics become so fluid, and our interactions just hit me in all the right spots. I'm not one to put labels on things; I've enjoyed monogamous relationships and polyamorous ones. Whatever fits everyone's needs and ensures we're having a good time is what I'm into.

Shiloh and I have a good time together.

But we have an even better time with Broderick in the mix.

Broderick strokes my bottom lip with his thumb. "That's not the only thing we're in alignment with, though. Is it, Monroe?"

"No. I guess not." I try for a witty comeback, but his tongue shorts out my thoughts. "I enjoy provoking you when we're fucking, but it's kind of nice having actual conversations sometimes."

"Yeah, it is kind of nice, isn't it?" He strokes my lip again. "I don't like the thought of you dead."

I swallow hard. It doesn't mean anything. No matter how I push and provoke him, at his core, Broderick is a good man. Of course he wouldn't want me dead. But I can't leave this tiniest of olive branches unanswered. "I don't want you dead, either."

"Thought so." He slowly drops his hand, but he doesn't lean back. "Look at that. Two things we're in agreement on. I think that's more than enough to ensure some peace between us. Don't you think so?"

I feel like he's hypnotized me. I sway toward him before I can stop myself. "Yes."

"Three things." He leans down and brushes a light kiss to my lips. "We're off to one hell of a start, Bride."

My whole body is zinging by the time Shiloh makes it back to us. She got us all tacos, and it's just as delicious as the smells promised. Or I assume it is. I'm so distracted, I can't properly enjoy it.

It's only reasonable for Broderick and me to officially call a ceasefire. I don't want him dead, and apparently he doesn't want that fate for me, either. Even as my rational side tries to convince me that it's to avoid war, a small part of me can't help replaying his soft words.

I don't want you dead.

Maybe this really could be the start of…something.

* * *

THE NEXT TWO weeks pass in a strange, happy blur. My days are filled with reassuring my mother that she doesn't need to take extreme measures against the Paine brothers, and all the millions of tasks that come with helping run a very successful corporation.

My nights are filled with Shiloh and Broderick.

It's just so fucking *easy*. Broderick and Shiloh seem to have gotten over that bump from friendship to fucking, and if part of me was a little worried they'd move on without me, it hasn't happened.

Every single morning, Broderick gets up before us and brings coffee back to the room before we go our separate ways, Shiloh and I to the office, Broderick to oversee most of the day-to-day stuff in the compound. Every single evening, he picks us up and we spend a little time exploring the Raider faction, revisiting places from his childhood, planting new memories of our own.

We make Shiloh come so hard she cries in the park where he and his brothers used to hang out and get up to mischief. He and Shiloh take turns fingering me at the old movie theater that used to be one of his teenage haunts. The three of us nearly get caught fucking in the truck at his old make-out spot near the train tracks that cut through the south part of the faction.

It's *fun*.

The only blip is Shiloh.

Sometimes I catch her with a strange look on her face, something almost like fear. It's usually in the office or on our way back to Raider territory after work. No matter how many ways I approach the topic, she won't let me in.

I should let it go. Surely there are people in relationships that don't know every little thing about each other, that don't dig and dig and dig until they find out what's wrong with their partners. It's probably normal to let little things like this go.

I don't have it in me, though.

Something's wrong with her, something she's obviously actively worried about, and I'm about climbing the wall trying to resist shaking her until the truth pops out.

"Stop staring at me like that," she says as we walk into the compound.

Today ran long, and she's been practically vibrating the entire drive back. For once, Broderick had a meeting and couldn't act the part of chauffeur, and I catch myself wishing he was here to back me up. Sometimes his softer touch gets through to Shiloh where my brash nature doesn't. I should wait for him to have this conversation, but I've never been one for patience.

I follow her up the stairs, biting my tongue, but the second we get into the room, I can't hold the words back any longer. "What the hell is going on with you?"

"Nothing."

Hurt lances me, made all the more potent by the sheer shock at her audacity. "You're not even going to hesitate before you lie to me?"

"It's nothing," Shiloh repeats. She yanks her tank top over her head.

I watch her strip in methodical movements that I normally enjoy. "You're sexy as fuck, love, but not even your perfect tits are going to get you out of this conversation."

"Mind your own business." She veers past me and heads for the bathroom.

Maybe I should let it go. Shiloh is so damn even-keeled most of the time, I've never seen her like this. But that knowledge drives me even more than the terrifying feeling that she's slipping through my fingers. The feeling that if I don't do something and do it now, she'll be gone.

A good leader knows when to push forward and when to retreat, but my instincts are all fucked up when it comes to Shiloh. I don't know whether I'm coming or going.

I follow her into the bathroom and lean against the counter as she turns on the shower. "Are you not happy with the current arrangements? Are you tired of me? Of Broderick?" The question clogs my throat, but it has to be asked. No matter how much fun I'm having with these two, I don't want to stay in this situation if everyone isn't on the same page. At least when it comes to enjoying themselves.

I don't expect Shiloh to love me.

I sure as fuck didn't expect to slide right into the possibility of loving Broderick.

She stops short and finally looks at me. I don't think she's feigning the shock in her eyes. "Why would I be tired of you? Of either of you?"

Whatever is going on, at least it's not that.

I can't breathe a sigh of relief, though, because we haven't solved anything. "How would I know? You're not talking to me."

"Leave it alone."

A laugh slips free, bitter and heavy. "You know better by now, don't you?" I should try a softer tactic, shouldn't back her into a corner, but there's something frantic beating in my chest, a desperation to fix this so I don't lose her. "If it's not about me, and it's not about Broderick, then what?"

"Back off, Monroe."

"It's not Iris," I muse. I saw her and Shiloh joking just yesterday. Their friendship isn't experiencing any strife. "It's not Cohen or Maddox, either." I refuse to think too hard about *either* of them. Winry claims she's content enough, and even though the older sister in me wants to wade in and get some fucking answers, I am *trying* to respect the fact that Winry is an adult and not in any active danger, so she can handle the situation herself.

"Monroe." Something creeps into Shiloh's voice, something almost like begging. "Please leave it alone."

There's only one subject this woman avoids on that level. The pieces click together in my head, but the picture still isn't clear. "This is about your past. About your parents."

She jerks like I've struck her. "God*damn* it. You're like a fucking terrier with a rat."

The reaction says it all, but I still don't understand. "Has Broderick been pushing you about it when I wasn't around?"

"No."

Well, I know *I* haven't. As much as I haven't given up my desire to rain fiery fury down on her parents if they're still alive, I'm trying to show some restraint and not push her. A novel concept for me, but I'm fucking trying.

I narrow my eyes. "Did something happen? Have your parents tried to contact you or something?" I don't see how, but I've only known Shiloh a little over a month. It's not like she's shared every bit of herself with me; I never expected her to. If she's maintained contact with her parents, it's not like she'd shout it from the rooftop, especially considering how verbal I've been about wanting them six feet in the ground.

"My parents are dead."

I blink. "Recently?"

"No." Shiloh steps into the shower and ducks her head beneath the spray. She washes systematically while I consider everything she has and hasn't said.

It doesn't make sense.

I'm missing something, something important.

I bite my tongue and strive for something resembling patience as Shiloh finishes her shower and turns off the water. She steps out and grabs a towel, very pointedly not looking at me.

"Shiloh."

"Monroe, I swear to the gods—"

"I love you." I don't exactly mean to say it, but the words pop into existence between us all the same.

"What?" She stares at me like I've sprouted a second head. Not exactly the reaction I was hoping for.

"I love you," I repeat, stronger this time. "I want you to be happy and healthy and safe, and right now something is wrong, and it's worrying me because you won't tell me what it is. Even if I can't fix it..." I drag in a breath. Fuck, but being vulnerable is *hard*. "Even if I can't fix it, I don't want you to be going through shit alone. I'm here. Broderick is here." The next part is harder. "If you're not comfortable talking to me, then at least talk to him."

"Monroe," Shiloh breathes. She pads to me and cups my face with one hand. "Say it again."

No misunderstanding the command. I lick my lips. "I love you."

"Do you mean it?"

"Of course I mean it. I'm a bitch, but I don't throw around words like that without meaning them."

Her smile is almost sad. "I love you, too."

"Why are you saying it like you're apologizing to me?"

She pulls me into a hug that steals my breath. Her next words finish the job. "Would you like to see the house where I grew up?"

CHAPTER 28

SHILOH

*T*he past two weeks have been agony. The closer I get to Monroe—the more comfortable I get with this new relationship with Broderick—the worse I feel about keeping something so important from them. It's not just that I'm an Amazon; or, rather, I was. It's that the current queen has painted a target on my chest.

She hasn't said a single word to me since the last time, but the threat is there every time she's in the room. The only thing that's stayed her hand is Monroe's obvious affection for me and the fact I've kept the truth about my past to myself.

But it feels like lying.

More, I can barely contain my flinch every time Monroe talks about her mother or mentions something about children. It's not that I want to be pregnant; I stand by the choice I made at nineteen and have no regrets about making it. It's more that Monroe's beliefs about the Amazons are just flat-out false.

Maybe they really do revere children. Maybe they really do protect them.

Or maybe it's all bullshit, a lie fed to her by her mother.

Of course *she* was protected as heir. Monroe has never been expendable a day in her life. She doesn't know what it's like to have the truth of her helplessness drilled into her going back as far as she can remember.

It's not that I want her to feel that pain.

I just…

Maybe I really am selfish. As soon as I offer to show her my childhood home, I want to take it back. Why am I so willing to hurt her just to take this strange load of guilt off my shoulders?

She loves me.

I love her.

Gods, when did that happen?

Movement draws my gaze as Broderick leans against the doorframe. His blue eyes flick over us. "Everything okay?"

"Shiloh's going to take us to her childhood home in the morning," Monroe says, cutting off any chance I have of changing my mind. For better or worse, I'm committed now. The truth will come out tomorrow.

He doesn't move, though he tenses the slightest bit. "I'll clear my schedule."

There's no point in telling him he doesn't have to come. Broderick has been very, very careful not to push me for more details about my past, has been so fucking respectful when it comes to how self-conscious I am about my scars. He takes every single opportunity he can to reassure me without words that he wants me, that he cares.

I love Broderick.

This realization has a softer touch than the one about Monroe. That felt like being hit with a tidal wave. This is freshly falling snow. I've been falling in love with Broderick from the moment I met him. Two weeks of sharing a bed, of having each other over and over again, has only solidified it into a truth. This man holds half my heart.

Monroe holds the other half.

I don't know what to do with that knowledge, so I set it aside. Tomorrow, things will fall out where they may. I don't know if the truth will change things between the three of us, but we don't have a shot at a real future as long as I'm lying to them, even by omission.

Broderick crosses to us and wraps his arms around both of us. "Thank you for trusting us with this."

Against all reason, tears prick my eyes. I close them, but it doesn't help. A single tear slides free. "Things have been so damn good the past two weeks. I'm afraid of that ending."

Monroe nuzzles my neck. "There isn't a single thing you could do to ruin us, Shiloh. Trust that."

If we're going to have this conversation, we might as well have it. I take a deep breath and open my eyes. "What about you two?"

Monroe leans back, expression carefully blank. "What about us?"

"Don't play coy. You know exactly what I'm talking about. You and Broderick have gotten along great the past two weeks."

"So?" She doesn't draw back, but she's also not looking at him.

Broderick's arms have gone tense around us, but he doesn't pull away. "That's complicated."

"Now who's lying?" I push slowly away from them. "You two like each other. More than like."

Monroe shakes her head. "Let's not get hasty. He doesn't want me dead, but that's hardly putting us in the realm of *like* or more."

Or more.

I stare at her, my chest aching. She's so fucking tough, so brazen and brash and in everyone's face. Does she do it so they won't realize what a tender heart she has beneath all that armor? A heart Broderick has obviously touched, even if he's not aware of it.

I turn to him. "We work as a throuple."

For once, Broderick doesn't bother giving me the runaround. "Yeah, we do."

"We'll continue to work as a throuple."

Monroe wraps her arms around herself and looks away. "Only for this year. I'm the Amazon heir. Next Lammas, I go back to my faction and stay there. Even if there were someone else for the role, it's mine by right, and I won't shy away from that responsibility. No matter what I feel."

Broderick shifts away from her, just a bit. "I'm Abel's second-in-command. The Raider faction is where I'm needed." He glances almost guiltily at Monroe. "I realize that's making a lot of assumptions about what you'd want, but ultimately it doesn't matter. You're needed there, and I'm needed here."

Horror takes root inside me as they both turn in my direction. "You're going to make me choose."

"We'd never ask that of you," Monroe says.

"But the fact remains that one of you will stay and one of you will go, and I lose no matter where I end up." My stomach dips alarmingly, and my head goes a little fuzzy. "What kind of choice is that?"

Broderick shifts. "Look, it's ten months and change away. A lot can happen in that amount of time, and this thing might very well run its course. There's no point in borrowing trouble. It's working right now, with the added bonus of it getting both our respective leaders off our backs and removing us from danger."

If I already love both of them at this point, how much more is it going to hurt in another month, two, ten? When this thing reaches its inevitable conclusion, one of them will rip out half of my still-beating heart and take it with them.

I have been at Broderick's side for nearly ten years. I can't imagine not being in his proximity. It'd be like losing a vital piece of myself.

But… Monroe has become so fucking important to me. She has no preconceived notions when it comes to who I am. I feel like she sees me in a way no other person does, brings out parts of me that I didn't even know I had.

I skirt around Broderick and walk out of the bathroom and into the closet. It's become a mishmash of the three of ours clothing and items, Monroe's spilling over mine and Broderick's the same way she spills over us in real life, touching every part of my life and making it hers.

My throat is so tight, I can barely breathe.

Maybe it will all be for nothing. All this worrying about the future and things will end tomorrow when they learn the truth. Broderick might be getting along fine enough with Monroe right now, but he has such strong opinions about the other factions. They're his enemies.

Will he see me as an enemy once he knows I grew up as an Amazon?

And Monroe?

No matter how she feels about me, she's not going to thank me for shining the light on the seedy underbelly of the Amazon faction that she doesn't seem to realize exists. For such a savvy woman, she has an intense lack of perception when it comes to certain elements. I don't know if her mother intentionally keeps these things from her, but Aisling's two interactions with me seem to indicate that's the case.

I yank on a pair of sweats and a T-shirt that I only realize is Broderick's when it hits me at mid-thigh. I turn and jump to find him behind me. "You've got to stop lurking in door-ways. It's creepy." The joke comes out flat.

Broderick doesn't hesitate. He steps forward and pulls me

into his arms, hugging me tightly. "I know this isn't an ideal situation, but I'm really fucking grateful to be in it all the same." He presses a kiss to my temple. "I don't think we would have ever become more than friends without Monroe involved."

That's the other thing I'm worried about, the one I can barely give voice. I wrap my arms around him and hug him back. "What if we don't work without her?" Broderick tenses, but I keep going. "What if she and I don't work without you? Have either of you thought of that?"

He hugs me tighter. "Yeah. I've thought about that."

I wait, but he doesn't provide anything more. It almost makes me laugh, but not like anything is funny. I finally lean back and look at up him, taking in his troubled expression. "What happens then?"

"I don't know." He smooths my hair back from my face. Amazing how quickly I've gotten used to touching and being touched by Broderick like this. It feels so natural, it makes my heart ache.

"Do you…" I should leave it alone, but too much hurts right now. There's nothing to stop me. "Will you miss her when she's gone?"

For a long moment, I don't think he'll answer me. But he finally sighs. "Yeah. I'll miss the little witch."

This is so ridiculous. Why did we do this to ourselves, knowing this couldn't last? I start to ask, but apparently there is a limit to my need to poke this thing until we're all in agony. I want to kiss him, to provide the way for us to spend a few hours distracted and happy, but it feels dishonest considering what I'm revealing tomorrow.

Instead, I hug Broderick tighter and press my face to his shoulder. "Can we have a low-key night? Maybe co-opt the movie room and watch something mindless and distracting?"

He cups the back of my head. "Sure. Whatever you want."

I want forever.

A child's cry. I learned a long time ago that childish fantasies have no place in the real world. The real world is rough and horrible and all too cruel. Even in love. Maybe especially in love.

Monroe comes into the closet a few minutes later, her blond hair wrapped in a towel and a second one around her body. She eyes us. "What's the verdict?"

"Movie night."

Her slow smile has me reconsidering my choice to keep things tame. "Let's watch *DOA: Dead or Alive.*"

Broderick releases me with a laugh. "You *would* want to watch that movie. It's all tits and ass and half-naked women."

"Exactly." She drops the towel and pulls on a pair of Broderick's gym shorts and a tank top that I'm nearly certain is mine. "It's also about the power of lady friendship and also the dad is super supportive of his daughter's sexuality. You can't tell me that's not progressive, especially for its time."

I blink. "That movie is entirely fan service. Just like the video game."

"It can be both. Goodness, you two, expand your horizons." She pulls the towel off her head and gives her hair a shake. "Though I'm willing to take other suggestions if you have them."

"After that argument? No way." I find myself smiling, some of my stress abating. I can do this. I can focus on the here and now and leave the future to the future. If it means I have to squirrel away every little memory I can to hold against the moment when we inevitably fall apart, then that's what I'll do.

It takes us a little time to get dinner squared away, but then we head into the movie room, carting along a wide array of what Monroe insists are vital movie-watching snacks. She was incredibly put out that we didn't have Milk

Duds stashed in the kitchen, but we made do with popcorn, hot tea, cookies, and some licorice.

Monroe and I end up on either side of Broderick, the best position to reach the food we have placed in front of him, and it's so...easy. So fucking easy. She and Broderick exchange good-natured barbs, and I can't shake the feeling that they're putting in a little extra effort to comfort me.

The movie is hot garbage, but it's incredibly enjoyable, especially with Monroe's ongoing commentary and Broderick's commentary about *her* commentary.

I want this forever.

It's really a shame that I'm about to drop a bomb on our happy time in the morning.

CHAPTER 29

BRODERICK

*T*he next morning, Monroe pulls me aside while Shiloh is in the shower. She's got a pinched look on her face that I've never seen before. She seems almost...worried.

Fucking fitting, because I'm worried, too.

She squeezes my arm. "I think we're on the same page about Shiloh, but I want to make sure."

It's the most natural thing in the world to cover her hand with mine and give her a squeeze. "There isn't a damn thing she can show us that will change how we feel about her."

"Yes." Monroe exhales. "Yes, that's exactly it. I don't know why she's acting like a cat in a room full of rocking chairs, but I think it's going to take both of us to anchor her through this. Has she gone home since she joined with you guys?"

"No." She shared the broad strokes of her story with me, but never the details and never the location. I can admit that Monroe brought out a strange sort of safety net for Shiloh that I never could have managed on my own. When I get overprotective, it pisses her off. When Monroe does it, Shiloh finds her amusing and reacts indulgently. Maybe I should resent that, but I'm not one to ignore tools just because they aren't in my toolbox.

Monroe still looks uncertain, so I pull her into a hug. "It will be okay, Bride. We make a good team, especially when it comes to giving Shiloh what she needs." We make a good team when it comes to other things, too. For the last two weeks, things have been damn near seamless between us, even when we're bickering.

"We do, don't we?" Monroe lays her head against my chest. I can't see her face from this position, but her voice goes almost wistful. "It's almost a shame that this was destined to be temporary. I don't like wasting time on what-ifs, but it's kind of hard not to wonder what we'd accomplish if we had longer than a year."

It feels downright traitorous to agree with her, but fuck, I can't argue. We still bump up against each other's razor-sharp edges sometimes, but now that we're not actively at odds, it's impossible to ignore how much I enjoy her company. How much I just flat out enjoy *her*. "I know."

She gives me a squeeze and slips out of my arms. "Oh well. Let's be there for our girl today and enjoy the rest of this time together." She hesitates. "I don't like the thought of asking Shiloh to choose after next Lammas, though."

It's like she's pulled the thoughts right out of my head. I clear my throat. "I was thinking we could share."

"Joint custody?" Monroe's smile is on the bitter side of bittersweet. "It won't last before that blows up in our faces."

"Nothing lasts forever, Bride."

Monroe gives herself a shake and grins at me, though her bravado doesn't reach her eyes. "Miss me a little when I'm gone, yeah?" She strides to the closet before I can come up with a response.

I will.

It's the fucking truth. Gods, how did this get so messed

up? Life wasn't easy when I hated Monroe, but it was certainly less complicated. I head into the bathroom to finish getting ready. One look at Shiloh's face heavily discourages trying to make conversation. She's spooked, too pale, the circles beneath her eyes confirming what I experienced last night with her tossing and turning—she's exhausted and stressed out.

"You don't have to do this."

She dries her hair with perfunctory motions. "Yes, I really do."

Which is how we end up in one of the compound trucks an hour later. I should probably have talked to Abel or scheduled some backup, but Shiloh's already so edgy, I don't want to pave the way for more witnesses to this moment of vulnerability. There's a reason she hasn't told most of the people in our group about her history, and I respect that enough not to bring them into it unnecessarily. I didn't tell my older brother for that very reason; he would have insisted on backup, Shiloh's feelings be damned.

Monroe sits in the middle of the bench seat, and I'm grateful for that as Shiloh guides the vehicle out of the compound. For all her spikes, Monroe is far better at navigating Shiloh's emotions without pissing her off. I'm not sure how she manages it, especially when she gets under *my* skin so intensely, but that comfort is what we need today.

I'm so busy running scenarios on how to provide that comfort, to support Shiloh, that I don't realize what direction we're headed in until Monroe tenses next to me. She speaks softly, but there's an edge to her tone. "This isn't the way out of Sabine Valley, love."

I look around. She's right. Instead of heading south and then east toward the highway, she's gone north toward the river. Toward Amazon territory.

Shiloh's got the steering wheel in a white-knuckled grip. "No. It's not the way out of Sabine Valley."

Monroe sucks in a breath as we cross the bridge. For once, she doesn't seem able to ask the hard question, so I drop my hand to her thigh, squeeze, and do it for her. "Shiloh, where did you grow up?"

She still won't look at me—at us. Several city blocks pass before she finally answers, so softly, I strain to hear her over the faint hum of the engine. "Sabine Valley."

"No." Monroe starts to lean forward, but I use my arm to keep her pressed back to the seat. It's a token of how distracted she is that she allows it. "No," she repeats. "I would have known if you were one of us."

"How?" Shiloh still sounds too distant, too empty. "How would you have known, up in that expensive penthouse, living in the shadow of the throne? How could you possibly have known, Monroe? You were fifteen when I left the city. Still a child."

For the first time, I feel actual sympathy toward Monroe. I shift my arm to tuck it around her shoulders. I almost pull Shiloh in, but she's holding herself so tightly, I'm worried she might strike out or just drive us into the nearest building. Still, I can't help brushing her shoulder with my fingers and saying the thing Monroe obviously can't quite bring herself to. "Amazons value their children. They don't do shit like what was done to you." Her parents made my father look like a saint.

Shiloh laughs, a broken sound. "Everyone says that. Do you think if they repeat it enough, they'll change the truth?"

We drive north and north and north, until we near the edge of the city limits. This far from the center of Amazon territory, the buildings are all one and two stories, and a good portion of them are residential. People who can't afford the higher cost of living nearer to the river. It should set them up for raids from the perimeter, but Aisling has several blocks along the edge of the city converted to what is essentially a kill box. Anyone attempting to invade will be met with force and eliminated.

Both the Mystic faction and ours have something similar, though Ezekiel has been overseeing the revamping of ours. Those blocks in all three territories are part of the reason we chose to return the way we did—using Lammas to force a ceasefire.

Not that any of that shit matters right now, but I'm still trying to wrap my head around the fact that Shiloh is a fucking *Amazon* and has been this entire time. Monroe is shaking against me, but I can't see her face to tell if she's upset or furious, so I just hug her tighter against me. "Shiloh—"

"We're almost there." She turns, too sharply, and slams to a stop in front of an empty lot between two buildings. Judging from the charred remains and a few concrete half walls, it wasn't always empty. She throws the truck into park and climbs out before I can dredge up some kind of verbal response.

What the fuck am I supposed to say?

"An Amazon," Monroe murmurs. "Her parents were fucking *Amazons*." She twists to look up at me, her green eyes shining. "I know this place, Broderick. The people here hurt a child when I was twenty-one, and I killed them and burnt their home to the ground." Her lower lip quivers before she seems to make an effort to still it. "I killed Shiloh's parents. I didn't even know they had a child."

"How could you have known?" As Shiloh said, Monroe was only fifteen when Shiloh left the city.

"I should have known." She reaches past me for the door. "They were fucking *priests* for my mother. *She* should have known."

Ah.

That's the crux of it.

I open the door, and we slowly climb out and join Shiloh where she stands at the curb, staring at the charred remains of her childhood home. Monroe is still moving strangely, but she waves me off when I lean in her direction. She's right. Shiloh is our priority. I move to stand behind her and carefully wrap my arms around her, moving slow so she can shrug me off if she wants.

She doesn't.

Shiloh tucks my arms around her like a security blanket and leans back against me, hard. This close, I can feel the fine tremors shuddering through her body. "I'm sorry," I murmur.

"Why are you sorry, Broderick?" She's speaking too fast, her words tumbling over each other to escape her lips. "Is it a problem that you've been fucking not one but two Amazons this whole time?"

I turn her in my arms until I can see her face. Her eyes are red, but there are no tear tracks on her face. Somehow, that makes it worse. I carefully take her shoulders. "I love you."

Shiloh flinches. "But—"

"I. Love. You," I repeat. "You are more than the faction you were born into, more than the abuse you survived, more than everything that came after. Why the fuck would something that happened before we met have any relevance on how I feel about you, Shiloh?"

Her tremors get stronger. "You hate Amazons."

Next to us, Monroe gives a wild laugh. "Not all Amazons, love. Not..." She drags in a rough breath. "I killed your parents. Did you know that?"

Against all reason, that seems to steady Shiloh. Her lips curve in a sad smile. "Guess you got your wish, after all."

"Don't do that," Monroe whispers. "Don't make light of this catastrophic failure on my part."

"Monroe." Shiloh shakes her head, her hair brushing across my arm. "I said it before and I'll say it again—you're three years younger than I am. What could you have possibly done?"

"I could have killed them sooner." Monroe reaches out but hesitates before she touches either of us. "I'm sorry. I'm so fucking sorry, love. I didn't..." She makes a pained sound. "I can't believe the shit I said to you. Why didn't you punch me in the face when I was talking about how that would never happen in my faction?"

"The thought did cross my mind." Shiloh's still shaking, but she feels a little steadier, less likely to shatter. "What happened to them?"

I open my mouth to ask if she's sure she wants to know, but Monroe beats me to speaking. She always did have more faith in Shiloh's strength, more willingness to let our woman stand on her own two feet without a protective cocoon around her. "They hurt someone about six years after you left."

"A child."

"A child," she confirms. "I was the one sent to handle the situation and to make examples of them."

Shiloh draws in a full breath and releases it in a shuddering exhale. "I'm glad. I... I should have done it myself, but I couldn't."

"No. No, Shiloh, you shouldn't have done it yourself. No part of this is on you." Again, Monroe reaches out. Again, she drops her hand before it makes contact. "*We* failed *you.*"

Shiloh catches her wrist and pulls her into our hug. It's the easiest thing in the world to lift my arm to encompass Monroe. It feels so fucking right, something gets lodged in my throat. We'll figure this out and find a way through. I don't have any doubts about that, not right now. I hug my women tightly to me, offering them comfort the best way I know how. "This changes nothing for me, Shiloh."

"It changes nothing for me, either."

Shiloh looks between us as best she can with our positions. "Seriously? I'm an Amazon, and you're just going to accept that?"

"Yes."

Monroe nods. "Yes." She narrows her eyes. "Though my mother and I are going to have a discussion very soon about this."

"Monroe—" Shiloh makes a choked sound. I'm still trying to figure out what's going on when her eyes roll back in her head and she goes limp. It's only my arm around her waist that keeps her off the ground.

"What the fuck?"

"Mystic." Monroe curses, and then she's gone, sprinting toward the building to the right of us.

"Monroe!" She ignores me yelling her name, and I can't chase her down without abandoning Shiloh, and I still don't know what the fuck is *wrong* with Shiloh.

I see it as I ease her limp body to the ground. A tiny dart sticking out of her neck. There's already a black ring around it, which is confirmation of Monroe's claim. The Mystics love their fucking poison. "God*damn* it." Monroe is out there going after a fucking Mystic, and if the fact they made it this far behind Amazon territory is any indication, it's one of the leader's elite squad.

Monroe might die.

Shiloh might die.

Panic grips me, and I fumble for my phone. It takes three tries to dial Abel and as the phone rings, I watch the black spread from the dart in creeping lines. This poison is a Mystic specialty. No one has ever figured out what exactly it is, and even with all our research, we've never found anything similar out in the world. It has to be something they cooked up in their greenhouses and labs at some point, which means only a Mystic will know the antidote.

"What?"

I have to set my phone on the pavement because I'm shaking so badly, I'm afraid I'll drop it. "I need help."

"Where are you?"

"Amazon faction, northern border. Shiloh's been attacked, and we need an antidote to Mystic poison, and we need it now."

Abel's silent for a beat, two. When he speaks, his voice has gone soft with menace. "What the fuck are you doing there, Broderick? We have a treaty with them, but that doesn't mean you can come and go as you please. You're going to send us to war, and we're not ready."

I can't think clearly enough to lie. "Shiloh brought us to her childhood home."

Another pause. "Are you saying that Shiloh is an Amazon? Has been an Amazon *this entire fucking time?*"

"Yes. No. I don't fucking know, Abel. She left the city years before we met her. What the hell does it matter?"

"It matters," he bites out. My brother curses. "We can't do a damn thing for her."

"The fuck you can't. Talk to Fallon. She'll have—"

"I cannot do a damn thing for her," he repeats, harder this time. "If we come in there to pick you up, guns blazing, Aisling will use it as ammunition to prove we broke treaty first. She and Ciar will join forces to crush the Raider faction."

"If we don't get the antidote, Shiloh will die!"

"I'm sorry." He actually sounds like he means it. "But I have to weigh the lives of everyone in the faction against hers and, fuck. Broderick, I'm sorry but I can't help her. If you can get her across the river to us…"

"Monroe went after the Mystic. I can't leave her." A decision I wouldn't have hesitated to make a few weeks ago in this same situation. But Monroe went after the assassin on her own. She has no backup. I can't leave Shiloh unattended, but I also can't leave Monroe hanging here.

It's not because she's the Amazon heir and if she's harmed, it will go just as badly for us as if Abel brought a squad to rescue us. I can't leave her because... Fuck, I care about my Bride. More than care.

Gods, this is so fucked up.

"What am I supposed to do?"

"Do you trust Monroe?"

"Yes." It's the truth.

"The Mystics carry the antidote on them. If she can get it, it will help Shiloh faster than anything I can do." He pauses. "We'll be waiting at the western bridge. Get back to us safely, brother. That's an order."

I hang up. A quick look around shows the street is still deserted, but I don't know how long it will stay that way. As much as I don't want to move Shiloh, we can't stay here. I hold my breath as I ease her into my arms and stagger my feet, heading for the truck. "Hang on. Just hang the fuck on. Monroe will get the fucker and bring us the antidote."

I hope like hell I'm not lying.

CHAPTER 30

MONROE

*R*age gives me wings. I fly over the ground in pursuit of the Mystic. I can just see their robes, a deep purple and blue that would blend perfectly into a twilight skyline. They're moving fast, having obviously already scouted out a quick exit, but I know this faction better than anyone.

I follow for another half a block before I feel like I have a good read on their direction. Then I veer right, cutting down two blocks and scrambling up a porch column to the roof of the building. I pick up speed, easily jumping the gaps between the buildings as I head for the street they should be coming down any moment.

Sure enough, the fucker is pelting in my direction. Their face and hair is hidden beneath a hood, but they don't bother to look behind them. Fool.

I throw myself off the building as they approach. They look up as my shadow passes over them, but by then it's too late. I hit them hard enough to drive the breath from my lungs, but who needs to breathe when fury is propelling them? I straddle them, easily dodging a punch, and grab their throat, slamming their head back into the pavement. Once. Twice. On the third time, their arms fall back to the street and lie still.

Not dead. Unconscious.

I keep one hand on their throat and fumble through their robes with the other, searching for… Ah, there it is.

I yank back the hood to find a man with light-brown skin and black hair. He shudders and opens his eyes. Good. I hold up a dart, careful to keep my fingers away from the sharp end. "Is this what you shot my girlfriend with?"

"Fuck off, Amazon."

"Hmm. Thought you might say that." I release his throat and grab his arm. It's a better location, because it will give him time to react instead of knocking him out cold the way he did Shiloh.

Hang on, love.

I jab the dart into his forearm and jump back. Predictably, he doesn't hesitate. He scrambles at the pack at his waist, pulling out a tiny vial of green liquid and downing it. The man shudders with relief. "You *bitch.*"

I shift a little farther away, eyeing him. A beat passes, two, three. When he doesn't keel over and die, I decide he's actually given himself the antidote instead of taking some other poison. More, the dart should have taken him out by now if it wasn't counteracted. Good. While he's still finding his feet, I punch him in the face, knocking him to the ground.

Then I make sure he won't ever get up again.

The squeal of tires against the street brings my head up. I dig through the assassin's pouch as Broderick screeches to a halt next to me. It takes a few seconds to find another vial filled with green liquid identical to the first one and then I run to the truck and yank open the door. "I have the antidote."

He's too pale, the lines bracketing his mouth looking

deeper than I've ever seen them. "Are you sure it's the right one?"

"As sure as I can be." I wait a beat, but he doesn't try to stop me as I reach for Shiloh's limp form and carefully tilt her head back. "Hang in there, Shiloh. This won't be comfortable." I drag in a breath. "She's still breathing, but I don't want to take any chances. Pour it in while I help her swallow."

"Okay." He takes the vial from me, and I hold her mouth open as Broderick dumps it down her throat. Then I do my best to ensure all the antidote actually makes it to her stomach.

"Please don't be too late. Come on, love. Come back to us."

Time ceases to have meaning as we watch her, waiting to see if the antidote works. A million things flash through my mind in those short minutes. The possibility that the assassin faked me out. The implications of a Mystic this far inside Amazon territory. How desperately I don't want to make Shiloh choose between me and Broderick.

Because she *will* wake up, damn it.

"Shiloh..." My voice breaks. "Gods, this is so fucked up."

Broderick takes my hand. He's obviously just as terrified as I am, but he's still so fucking steady, still offering support even when he needs it just as badly as I do. I can't stop shaking. "What if—"

"She'll wake up." He says it quietly. Firmly. "Give it time."

"Okay," I whisper.

"You did good, Monroe. That was quick thinking to get the antidote." His thumb ghosts over my knuckles. Only a fine tremor in his hand lets me know he's just as fucked up over this as I am. "How the hell did you catch up to them so fast?"

"I'm a bad bitch." I try to smile, but I can't quite pull it off.

"They don't get to come here on *my* territory and fuck with my people." I look down at Shiloh, measuring her slow inhales and exhales. "I don't care if she's an Amazon or not, Broderick. She's mine." I meet his gaze. "She's ours."

"Yeah. She is." He gives my hand a squeeze. "We—"

Shiloh drags in a ragged breath and whimpers. "Fuck, that hurts."

"Shiloh!" Broderick and I say her name as one, and nearly smack our heads into each other in our effort to help her sit up. We ease her against the seat between us. She's pale, and the black marks on her throat are still fading, but her eyes are open, and she's breathing deeper now.

She lifts a hand and touches a trembling finger to my cheek. It comes away wet, which is when I realize I'm crying. "That close?" she murmurs.

"Yes." I won't lie to her. Not even about this.

She leans back and closes her eyes. "Damn."

Broderick clears his throat. "We need to get back across the river to Raider territory."

It's the smart thing to do, and it makes sense why he'd want to get Shiloh back to safety. I even agree with the plan…with one caveat. "Drop me off at the main tower."

He shakes his head. "You know I can't do that."

"You don't have a choice." I don't want to speak the next bit, but we've come too far and if I trust them. "There is absolutely no way a Mystic assassin would make it to this point without getting tagged by one of our patrols." I hold up a hand before Broderick can argue. "We have precautions against exactly this sort of thing, the same way you do. We know how they work, and we guard against it."

"What are you saying?"

I don't want to say it. I truly don't. But with both of them looking at me, I can do nothing but tell the truth. "Someone gave him permission."

Shiloh closes her eyes, but not before I see the truth there in their hazel depths. The very thing I was beginning to suspect but didn't want to face. I take a slow breath. "I thought you were irritated because of the longer days in the office guarding me, but that's not it, is it?"

She doesn't say anything, but she doesn't need to. Not with all the puzzle pieces clicking into place, faster and faster. "I know who your parents were to my mother. Not close, exactly, but close enough that she preferred me to be the one to deliver their punishment. I thought it was the first offense, but she also neglected to mention they had a child at one point." An intentional omission in hindsight. Revealing that knowledge after their abuse became public would open my mother up to uncomfortable questions.

Questions I now want answers to.

I might be able to write it all off as coincidence if not for the assassin's target. Not me. Not Broderick. Either of us would make more sense. If Broderick dies on Amazon territory, it will mean war between Raider and Amazon. If I do, it means the same thing. It wouldn't matter that the surviving members claimed a Mystic was behind the death. They would be called a liar because of the nature of our relationship.

But Shiloh?

No one is going to war for our girl. No one is hurt by her loss except me and Broderick. No one gains from her death...

Unless her existence is a secret someone doesn't want shared.

Someone like my mother.

The thought makes me sick, but my mother is more than capable of it. She's willing to leave Winry hanging in the wind; how much more so would she do the same to some child unrelated to her by blood? A small price to pay, a cost weighed against a thousand things she has moving in her head.

I know about making hard choices. I've been doing it for years now, and when I'm queen, it will only get that much more challenging. It's what I'm trained for.

It doesn't make it right.

Finally, Broderick releases a breath. "We'll come with you. Back you up."

"You really don't have to—"

"Monroe." Shiloh puts her hand on my arm. "We're coming with you."

I start to argue but... I don't want to. I want them with me. Having these two at my back is comforting in a way I can hardly put into words. Finally, I nod. "We need the body."

"On it." Broderick climbs down from the driver's seat and strides to where I left the body in the middle of the street.

Shiloh squeezes my arm. "How close?"

"Do you want the comforting lie or the scary truth?" When she gives me a look, I sigh. "Another few minutes and we wouldn't be having this conversation. I'm not certain whether or not the poison has long-term effects, either. Usually when the assassins get close enough to use their darts, it's too late."

I almost lost her.

The reality of that sets in, sending shakes through my body. I want to cling to Shiloh, to run my hands over her until I'm satisfied that she's really here, really safe. I settle for leaning in and kissing her lightly. "I love you."

"I love you, too," she says faintly.

The truck dips as Broderick dumps the body in the bed of it. He wastes no time reclaiming the driver's seat and putting it into gear. "You sure about this?"

No. There's only one path forward, and it terrifies me. There *must* be consequences for putting a child in danger, even if it was decades ago. It's not the same penalty as actually doing the harm, but even my mother isn't exempt from it.

Pushing forward with justice means I'm going to lose everything.

I look at Broderick, at Shiloh. We always knew this was temporary, but I thought I had more time. I *needed* the next ten months. Now, our time together numbers in the hours instead of months. It doesn't matter if I'm a Bride. Brides don't *have* to reside in the same location as their partners do. It's unspoken tradition, but it's not a law the same way as consummating the handfasting or keeping the Bridal peace. We'll figure it out. The peace will hold, but this is happening one way or another. "Yes. I'm sure."

"Okay." He takes me at my word.

The drive to the main tower takes no time at all. I direct Broderick to park against the curb, and then we grab the body and head into the building through the front door. I don't normally bring bloody business in this way, but don't want to give my mother the chance to shove this mess under the rug and pretend it never happened. The Amazons in the lobby stare, but they make no move to interfere as we stride to the elevator and step inside.

I'm heir, after all.

Soon enough, I'll be their queen.

The receptionist, Gladys, sees me coming and jumps to her feet. "Monroe—"

"Is my mother in her office?"

Gladys attention snags on the body over Broderick's shoulder, and she pales. "Yes."

"Thank you." I lead the way back to the corner office where my mother spends most of her time. It's decorated similarly to mine, classic and chic with an emphasis on the windows and the view they offer. I couldn't give a shit about the view right now.

I step aside, letting Broderick and Shiloh into the room, and then shut the door behind me. "It's time to talk, Mother."

If my mother is surprised to see Shiloh alive and walking, she doesn't show it. Then again, she's always had one hell of a poker face. She folds her hands and raises her brows. "Is there a reason you have a dead Mystic in my office? We've worked rather hard to avoid inter-faction conflict."

"Mmm." I cross my arms over my chest. If I let her get control of this conversation, it won't end well for anyone. "I'm more worried about conflict within the faction. The Amazon queen contracting a Mystic assassin to kill one of her own people isn't a good look, especially when it's to cover up the fact that she facilitated the horrific abuse of a minor for *years*." I glare, refusing to be the one to drop my gaze first. "You've fucked up, Mother. And now I have to clean up your mess."

"You're overreaching." Steel enters her tone. "I'm the queen here."

"A queen who allowed two priests to torture and abuse their daughter. A queen who then tried to murder that daughter to cover up her neglect of her duties. Not much of a queen from where I'm standing."

She considers me for a long moment. "I do what I do for the good of the faction."

"Don't lie to me!" I pause and concentrate on keeping my voice modulated. "You chose the easy path. I don't know why *this* was the time you decided to be anything less than a queen, but you made your choice, and now I have to make mine." I drag in a breath. "You will step down and allow me to take the throne."

She raises a brow. "If I don't step down?"

"Then I will allow this story to circulate, which will weaken the faction as a whole."

"You don't think a queen who is Bride to a Raider and a Paine brother would weaken our faction?" Her gaze flicks over my shoulder to Broderick.

My earlier fury returns full force. I love my mother. I have no doubt that she loves me. But that does not mean that she's infallible, and she facilitated harm on a scale that leaves me breathless. "She was a *child*. We protect our children. You have fed me that line over and over again, have bolstered my belief that the way we value our children sets us apart from the rest of the city—the country, even. All this time, you have been the biggest fucking hypocrite."

My voice breaks, but I power through. "So, yes, I will commit a little harm to our faction in order to set the tone for my reign. It's a small price to pay to reassure our people that their children are safe under my rule. *That* is my priority. I will deal with both Raider and Mystic factions as required."

My mother's mouth goes tight, but she finally rises. "I suppose you're set on this route."

"I am."

"Very well." Her lips curve, the first indication that I've played right into her hands. "I'll step down immediately. Long live the queen."

Behind me, I don't think Shiloh or Broderick draw breath. Neither of them expected this, and I allow myself a beat of sorrow to mourn the loss of them. It's going to hurt so fucking much when they walk away, but if I'm going to avoid being the hypocrite my mother is, I can't let my own personal feelings get in the way of my people's safety.

Even if it breaks my heart in the process.

CHAPTER 31

SHILOH

*T*hings happen quickly after that. Monroe is swept away. The dead Mystic is taken from us. Broderick and I are politely but resolutely guided out of the building and back to the truck. Neither of us speaks as we drive back over the river, not even when a convoy of other Raider vehicles surrounds us and escort us back to the compound.

Broderick parks and looks at me. "I'm sorry." He makes no move to get out of the car despite Abel and the others who provided our escort through Raider territory waiting.

"You have nothing to be sorry for." My throat feels like it's on fire, and I can't tell if that's an aftereffect of the poison or the fact that we just drove away from the woman I love. I can already feel the dynamic shifting between Broderick and I, both of us too tentative without Monroe here to urge us forward.

Well, I'll have to be the one to be assertive this time.

I clear my throat and wince. "We made the wrong call."

"What?" He catches Abel's gaze through the windshield and waves his brother off. After the barest hesitation, Abel leads his group toward the main building, though he lingers outside after the rest of them have dispersed.

"We shouldn't have left her there."

"Shiloh, we didn't have much choice."

I twist to face him. "Yes, we did. We could have fought for her. She's fighting for me right now, and we just turned around and let them shove us out."

"You heard her. She's going to be queen."

"I heard." I press a shaking hand to my chest. "Broderick, I love her. And I love you. I know it's not the same for you, but—"

He curses. "I'm falling for her, too. Have already fallen, if I'm going to be honest. It's not convenient, and I want to shove her out a window half the time, but I'm self-aware enough to recognize the feeling." He drags his hand over his face. "What do you want from me, Shiloh? I don't know how to make this work. It's all happening too fast. I thought we'd have more time."

My brain still feels fuzzy, but I try to focus. There's a way through this. There has to be. "Do you want us? To be a throuple in a permanent way?"

He hesitates, his hands flexing on the steering wheel. "Yeah. I do."

"Me, too." I shift on the seat. This next part is more difficult. "She's still your Bride. They can't deny access to you."

"She won't come back here as queen. There's no fucking way. It would never work."

"You're right. She won't."

It doesn't take him long to connect the dots. He curses. "You're really willing to live among the Amazons again after everything? I can't ask that of you. Monroe sure as fuck won't."

The idea isn't exactly comfortable, but the alternative is a thousand times worse. I take a slow breath. "It wasn't the entire Amazon faction responsible for what happened to me. The people who hurt me have been punished. Gods, Broderick, she went after her own mother on my behalf. If the other Amazons are like Monroe, I think we'll do just fine."

"If the other Amazons are like Monroe, I don't know if I'll survive it," he mutters. But his grip has loosened on the steering wheel. "Are you sure? I don't know if this is a decision we can change our minds about after the fact. If we go to her with the intent of staying, we'll be under suspicion every time we interact with the Raiders."

I think about Iris, about Maddox and Cohen and the others I've become friends with over the years. They've been a family of sorts, and if that means there's a new distance between us, I don't think it will break those relationships entirely. How novel. "What about you? You're Abel's second-in-command. That's not exactly an easy position to fill."

"You'd be surprised." He stares out the windshield for a long moment. "Be sure, Shiloh. If we do this, there's no going back."

"I'm sure if you are."

Another, longer stream of curses. "Well, shit, guess I better go talk to my brother."

Abel must have seen that our conversation was finished, because he ambles over. Broderick rolls down the window. "You're not going to like this."

"Strangest thing." Abel looks at him and then at me. "I just got word that Monroe Rhodius is stepping up as queen of the Amazons. This have anything to do with what went down this morning?" He focuses on me. "Glad you're okay, Shiloh."

"Me, too."

Broderick nods slowly. "Yeah, it has to do with that. I'll fill you in later, but the bottom line is that she's my Bride, and I'm not willing to give that up, queen or no. Donovan can take over my duties. It will even be good for him—he's spent too fucking long floating through life. It's time he took on some responsibility."

Abel studies him. "So you're really going."

"Yeah, I'm really going."

Another glance at me. "You, too?"

"Yes."

He sighs and drags his hand through his hair. "Well, fuck. This isn't ideal, but the fact is that it positions you better than I could have dreamed to—"

"No."

"What?"

Broderick shakes his head. "No. I won't give Monroe and her people information about our family and the Raiders, but if we're going there for her, I also won't ferry back information about the Amazons."

Abel narrows his eyes. "That's one fucked up tightrope you're going to be walking."

"We'll figure it out."

"I could stop you, you know."

Broderick snorts. "Maybe for a little bit, but then you appear weak when you finally fail to hold us. Better to look like we're following my Bride. Hell, it actually makes you and the Raiders look even better."

"Hmmm." Abel leans back and crosses his arms over his chest. "That Amazon of yours feel the same way?"

"Only one way to find out."

She does. I know she does. But I keep my mouth shut because ultimately, I am just another solider in Abel Paine's small army, while Broderick is his second-in-command, at least until Donovan officially steps in for him. They have to hash this out properly now in order to minimize potential issues in the future.

Finally, Abel nods. "I'm not going to pretend I understand, but I've chased my own love in unexpected places. Good luck. To both of you."

"Thanks."

Broderick is already rolling up the window and putting the truck in gear. "I'll touch base later to get our shit."

"Sure." Abel stands there and watches us drive away, an unreadable expression on his face.

Broderick reaches over and takes my hand, and I let him tug me across the seat to tuck under his arm. He presses a kiss to my temple. "Let's go get our woman."

It's easier than I could have dreamed. We even park in the same spot. A few of the Amazons look like they want to stop us, but no one gets in our way as we take the elevator up to Monroe's floor. Gladys is even in her normal spot.

Broderick manages to sound almost polite. "I'm here to see my Bride."

Gladys makes a face like she doesn't want to tell him—to tell us—where Monroe is but also can't think of a reason to keep her from us. "She's in the room at the end of the hallway."

Broderick takes my hand as we move quickly in that direction. A little touch to anchor me in the midst of so much change. *Everything* is changing.

He opens the door without hesitation. We find Monroe standing in front of a full-length mirror. Alone. She looks beautiful in a silver dress with her hair pinned up and her customary red lipstick. The shock on her face has me wondering if we made a mistake. Broderick doesn't hesitate, though. He all but drags me after him as we step into the room.

Monroe looks from him to me. "What are you doing here?"

"You're my Bride."

She goes still. "I can't leave the Amazon faction now,

Broderick. Bride or no, my people need me. I'll hold to the agreement and I'll work with you and Abel to ensure peace as well as I can, but I have to be *here*."

I step around him but keep my hold on his hand. "We're going to be here, too. If you'll have us."

"What are you saying?"

"I love you." Now it's my turn to tug on Broderick's hand, pulling him closer. "We both care so much about you. Ten months was never going to be enough for us. The three of us work. *Together*. As a throuple. We don't work as well in pairs."

"But..."

"She's right," Broderick cuts in. "About all of it. I won't inform on the Raiders to you, but the Amazon's secrets are safe with me, too. I give you my word. I don't want any of that shit, Bride. I just want you." He smiles at me. "Both of you."

"Are you sure?" she whispers. "You have to be sure. If you do this while I'm queen, there's no going back. We can't be on-again, off-again. It has to be all or nothing."

"Then we choose all."

"We choose you," I say.

He holds out his empty hand. "Will you choose us, too?"

She doesn't hesitate. She practically throws herself into our arms. "Of course I choose you. How could I not? I love you." She hugs us so tightly, she steals my breath. Fitting, that.

Monroe has been stealing my breath since the moment we met.

She grins at us, her expression relaxing into something truly happy. "If you're absolutely sure, then now would be an excellent time to name both of you Consort."

"Just like that?" Broderick looks almost shocked. "Won't we have access to quite a bit of information under those titles?"

"Yes." She presses her lips together. "But you've given your word that you won't use it against me. I...love you. I trust you. Both of you."

I cup her jaw and kiss her, careful of the lipstick. "In that case, Consort sounds like it would look good on both of us."

* * *

THANK you so much for reading Broderick! I hope you enjoyed my version of a slow burn with Broderick, Monroe, and Shiloh! If you did, please consider leaving a review.

Need more of these three in your life? Sign up for my newsletter to receive a bonus short!

The Paine brothers' story continues with COHEN. For years, Cohen has done whatever it takes to keep his brothers alive, no matter the cost to himself. Now he's got a fragile, innocent Bride in Winry and no idea what to do with her. Good thing Maddox is there to lend a hand...

JOIN my Patreon if you'd like to get early copies of my indie titles, as well as a unique short story every month featuring a couple that YOU get to nominate and vote on!

ABOUT THE AUTHOR

Katee Robert is a *New York Times* and USA Today bestselling author of contemporary romance and romantic suspense. *Entertainment Weekly* calls her writing "unspeakably hot." Her books have sold over a million copies. She lives in the Pacific Northwest with her husband, children, a cat who thinks he's a dog, and two Great Danes who think they're lap dogs.

www.kateerobert.com

Keep up to date on all new release and sale info by joining Katee's NEWSLETTER!

Printed in Great Britain
by Amazon